LIGHTS CAMERA, Passion

BESTSELLING AUTHOR
ISABEL LUCERO

PROLOGUE

THIS JUST IN, RYAN. IT LOOKS LIKE WE CAN ANNOUNCE THE TWO actors who will be portraying everyone's favorite book couple, Andrew and William. You, of course, know them from the number one New York Times Bestselling book, Another Life. *Playing Andrew is the hot new actor on the block, Roman Black. You've probably seen Roman in* Broken *where he played a troubled teen wanting to get his mom out of an abusive household. There was also* In School Suspension *where he acted alongside Faye Crespo in the high school rom-com.*

"Oh, yeah. Didn't they date?"

"That was the rumor."

"And everyone's going to love this, Jules. Playing William is none other than Hollywood sweetheart and heartthrob, Jacoby Hart."

"It's in the name, Ryan."

"Indeed it is. Jacoby is known for his roles in* Never Forget Me *and* The Artist. *Both of these emotional films showcase his acting chops and versatility."

"Don't forget* The Voyeur *where he showed the world a

1

lot more. The erotic thriller was the number one movie in the world for several weeks."

"Oh, I don't think anybody is going to forget that one. Wasn't Faye Crespo in that too?"

"She was. I believe there was a bit of contention between the actors when it came to Faye."

"Well, let's see if they can bury the hatchet and bring the chemistry we know William and Andrew have in the book."

"I hope so, Ryan. This is one of my favorite stories, and I definitely don't want to be let down."

"You and the rest of the world."

"All right, let's move on."

I turn off the TV and throw the remote at the couch. "See? They like him more. He gets compliments on his acting skills and looks while I get questioned about who I was dating."

"They said you were a hot new actor," my sister offers, gesturing to the black TV screen.

I roll my eyes. "I'm not that new. Also, did you hear the way they said his announcement? 'Everyone's gonna love this' with an emphasis on *love*. They made it seem like his casting was more important."

"They're gonna love you," Chelsea says, reaching for her phone. "He's just been around a bit longer. I mean…he's Jacoby Hart."

I drop onto the couch with a scoff. "I can't believe I got this incredible role but I have to act opposite him."

"Why do you hate him so much?"

I snap my head at my sister, who's now focused on her phone. "Do you not remember what he said about me in that interview with CNT?"

Her brows furrow and she finally meets my gaze. "No."

"Right, because when asked about the rumors that we might be playing brothers in that movie I didn't get picked for, he acted like he had no idea who I was. When told again, he laughed that smug fucking laugh and said, 'Oh, I hope not.' Who fucking does that? Entitled little shits, that's who. I bet he's the reason I didn't get that role."

"He doesn't have that much pull," Chelsey says. "Otherwise you'd probably not be in this movie." Before I can open my mouth to argue, she shoves her phone in my face. "Look. They love you."

I scroll through the comments under the announcement from the studio.

Oh my godddddd. This is gonna be so good!

Jacoby and Roman in the same movie?? Take my money!

Roman is so hot.

Jacoby. The love of my life.

They are going to be so good together. Oh my god, I'm so excited.

They better not mess this up for me.

Screaming, crying, throwing up.

Need the trailer ASAP.

My ovaries.

My gay heart is so happy.

Roman is my man, so y'all better back off.

I give her back the phone and she grins. "Hope you can play nice. You know how readers are when it comes to book-to-screen adaptations. They're gonna have high hopes, and you can't hate the man you're supposed to love with every fiber of your being."

"Hey, I'm an actor," I say with a shrug. "I will out-act that douche, Jacoby, at every opportunity. The world will believe what I want them to believe."

Chelsey shakes her head. "You started this whole beef. You know that, right?"

"I did not."

"You dated Faye when he was dating her."

"I didn't know they were dating!"

She purses her lips. "Everyone knew."

I scoff. "He slighted me at an event first. He looked me up and down like I was a peasant and he was the king of England. I was trying to be nice, but that's when he showed me how snobbish he is."

"And that's why you dated his girl?"

"Yea—no!"

Chelsey laughs. "Anyway, filming starts soon, right?"

"We meet next month for rehearsals and table reads, then we start filming."

"How long?"

"Three months or so."

She lets out a low whistle. "That's a good amount of time with your BFF. Not to mention all the promo you'll have to do. Cute little videos and pictures. Interviews. Especially since the movie doesn't come out till when? Next year?"

"Why do you like to make me mad?"

She leans over and kisses my cheek. "It's so fun. I love you. I gotta run, though."

"Will I see you before I leave for Montana?"

"Of course." She gets to the door and turns around. "I'm proud of you, kid."

I smile at her. "Love you."

CHAPTER ONE

"ALL RIGHT, GUYS. SO, I MIGHT DO THINGS A LITTLE unorthodox, but I swear by my methods, and you just gotta trust me on this," the director, Mike Campo, says to me and Jacoby.

"I trust you, Mike," I say with a charming smile.

"Good. Now, since part of the story takes place in a remote cabin, forcing William and Andrew to get reacquainted under unusual circumstances, I'm putting you two in a cabin for three days. I believe I mentioned this to you at the audition, but it's been a while since then. You will be supplied food and everything you need, but I'm getting you into the headspace of the characters before we start filming. My understanding is that you two don't know each other real well, right?"

Jacoby and I glance at each other, jaws tense.

"No, we do not," Jacoby answers.

"Perfect," Mike says, clapping his hands together once. "My assistant, Sheera, will take you to the cabin, and your belongings will be delivered to you. The rest of the cast will start rehearsing and doing table reads, and you two can jump in when you're done here. Thanks, guys. I'll be in touch."

He's gone before we can say anything else, quickly replaced by a woman with beautiful umber skin and jet-black hair. "A truck is coming now. Your luggage is in the back. Do you have any questions?" she asks.

"Are we allowed to have our phones?" Jacoby asks.

"Mike would rather you not have your cells. William and Andrew didn't have service, but since we're in the real world and something can come up, we do have the cabin outfitted with a landline that will be at your disposal. I will get you the number, and you can pass it on to your family if they need to get in touch with you."

A black truck pulls up in front of us, and Sheera goes to the back door, opening it up.

Jacoby and I glance at each other again before marching to the vehicle and climbing into the backseat.

A Black man with a bald head drives us in silence through the snow-covered land where massive pine trees surround us. Jacoby sits to my left, typing out a million text messages, probably attempting to stop this forced proximity thing from happening. I send one message to Chelsey to let her know about the cabin plan and then put my phone down.

Jacoby frantically types like he'll die if he doesn't get these messages out before we get to the cabin. I peek at the screen as covertly as I can and see an email.

RE: Douchebag.

My brows furrow as I attempt to scan the actual message but I only catch glimpses of words here and there.

He
I told you
will not be good
kill

rather die.

"What the hell?" I say aloud, not meaning to.

Jacoby's head jerks toward me while his hands angle his phone away. "Are you reading my fucking emails?"

"Are you being a fucking baby?"

He turns his phone off, scoffing. "You're so full of your-self, you know that?"

"Not as much as you are. Are you really crying to your agent about doing this with me? And I thought you were a serious actor."

"You have no idea what I'm talking about or who I'm discussing it with."

"Oh yeah? So, who's the douchebag?"

"Funny that you see the word douchebag and automati-cally assume I'm talking about you."

"Oh please. I know you hate me."

The driver clears his throat, stealing my attention. When I look forward, I catch his brown eyes in the rearview mirror.

"We're here," he says. "You guys can head inside, and I'll bring your luggage to you."

"Thanks," Jacoby and I grumble at the same time.

I slam my door harder than necessary and round the back, picking up speed so I can get inside before Jacoby does.

He scoffs when I shoulder check him on my way up the stairs. In my defense, it was an accident, but I'm not about to apologize. If he thinks I'm a douchebag, then I guess I'll act like one.

When I open the door, I'm startled to see Sheera standing in front of it, a phone in her hand and a pad of paper in the other.

"Here's the number to the cabin," she says, handing me the paper. "Send it to whoever needs it."

I take out my phone and send the number to Chelsey

before I try to hand her the pad. She points behind me where Jacoby walks in, brushing snow off his shoulders.

"Here," I say, thrusting it at his chest.

"Let me give you a quick tour," Sheera says, strutting through the living room in knee-high black boots and a matching trench coat. "There's a fireplace in here and in the master bedroom. The wood is stored in a mudroom near the back door."

"I claim the master," I state.

"Uh, I don't think so. I think since I—"

"Boys," Sheera says, turning around. "There's only one bedroom. That's the master."

My eyes find Jacoby's, both of us as frozen as the ground outside.

"One room?" I question.

"Don't worry. Two beds. Here's the kitchen. We've stocked it up, but if you have any dietary restrictions or specific requests, we can try to adjust before the end of the day."

"I'm not picky," I say, turning to face Jacoby. "You only drink almond milk or something? You seem the type."

"The type to be lactose intolerant?" he snaps back. "Yeah, make fun of me for something I have no control over."

I choke out a laugh. "Oh, you really do drink almond milk?"

He rolls his eyes and focuses on Sheera. "Almond or oat milk would be great, Sheera. If not, it's not a big deal."

"He may send a strongly worded email later, but yeah."

"Stop being a child," he mutters in my ear before passing me up and following Sheera to the back.

"Bathroom's outfitted with everything you'll need," she says, pointing it out as we pass. "Here's the room. The beds are queens and there's two dressers."

"No TV?" I ask.

"Nope."

"Great."

She starts typing into her phone as she walks back to the living room and doesn't look up for at least sixty seconds.

"Okay, the milk will be delivered in the next few hours. If you don't mind handing over your phones, that would be great," she says, putting out her hand, palm up. "On the second page of that pad I gave you is my number. Use it if you need anything. Otherwise, take this time to get to know each other, go over your lines, whatever you need to do."

I hand over my phone first. "Okay. Thanks, Sheera. I really appreciate it."

She smiles at me and I'm pretty sure I hear Jacoby make a noise in the back of his throat. "Yeah. Thanks."

"Have fun, boys," she says before turning around and marching through the front door.

The two of us stand in place, staring out the rectangular window that shows her getting into a car and leaving.

I spot our luggage near the door and go over and grab mine, eyeing Jacoby's three bags.

"Wow. We're only here for three days. You need one bag for each day or what?"

"Don't talk to me," he says, heading for his fancy suitcases.

"I wish I didn't have to but that's the whole reason we're here, so get used to this voice, sweetheart."

I roll my bag down the hall and into the bedroom, claiming the bed nearest the window. Jacoby enters as I'm opening my suitcase.

"I was going to sleep there."

"You still can. I'll just be here too."

"You're the worst," he says, lifting one suitcase and dropping it onto the bed.

"By the end of filming, I'm going to prove to you that I'm the best."

He snorts, lifting his other bag onto the bed. "Sure."

CHAPTER TWO

AFTER I UNPACKED, I LAID ON THE BED WITH MY SCRIPT while Jacoby busied himself in the living room.

We haven't spoken words to each other in three hours, so I'd say this little plan for us to get to know each other is really going well.

When we auditioned, it was done separately. He probably just walked in and they gave him the part, meanwhile I had two call backs before I was notified that I got it. Where sometimes there's chemistry checks and the leads have to read lines together to make sure their connection works, we didn't get that. He was busy shooting another movie, so I guess they booked us with the hope that we'd be good together. Now here we are, unable to talk to each other.

When the aroma of food makes its way down the hall and into the room, my stomach growls, reminding me it's been hours since I've last eaten. With a sigh, I get out of bed and make a stop in the bathroom. After washing my hands, I look in the mirror and push my long strands out of my face, slicking them back. My beard needs a bit of a trim, but I'm not worried about it right now. I'll have to change my appearance for filming, so I'll wait until then.

With a deep breath, I step into the hall. "What's cookin', good lookin'?"

When I enter the living room area, Jacoby is already facing the hall, his brows raised. "What?"

I laugh. "You've never heard that saying?"

He turns back to the stove. "I'm making chili."

"Ooh, that sounds good," I say, making my way closer so I can peek over his shoulder.

He angles his head to level me with a stare. "Do you mind?"

I step back, holding up my hands. "Need help?"

"No."

"Is it...for both of us, or do I need to make my own dinner?"

He sighs. "Well, there's a lot, so I suppose you can help yourself once it's done."

"Cool." I stand awkwardly in the kitchen, looking around.

Jacoby turns to glance at me. "I can let you know when it's done." It's a dismissive comment, but I'm not leaving.

I jump onto the counter and sit. "Why don't you like me?"

He lets out an exhale before continuing to cook the meat. "Excuse me?"

"I can tell you why I don't like you, if that helps."

He turns around with an incredulous look on his face. "Is it because I'm lactose intolerant? Because you know nothing about me to give you reason to hate me."

"I could say the same."

"Oh, I think you're wrong," he replies, turning his back on me.

"I think you're pompous."

"Pompous?" he exclaims, spinning back around with wide eyes.

"Don't know that word? How about egotistical?"

"Oh wow," he says with a humorless laugh. "*I'm* egotistical."

"As long as you admit it."

"Uh. No. That was said with sarcasm, because it's ironic that *you* would call *me* egotistical."

"Are you saying I am?" I ask.

"You are. Always wearing those flashy outfits, just screaming for attention. You might as well just strip naked and walk the red carpet."

"Maybe I will. And what do you mean *flashy*? Or are you jealous that you can't pull off colors and patterns and can only wear black or gray?"

"Please. I wouldn't be caught dead in the shit you wear."

"This sounds like jealousy. Do you hate me because, dare I say, you ain't me?"

He laughs, but stops himself quickly. "Definitely not. And why am I egotistical?"

"You tell me. Why didn't you want me to work with you on *In the Dark*?"

"I never said I didn't want to work with you."

"Okay, so I guess you're just a liar now," I say, hopping off the counter. "You're lucky I don't have my cell, because I'd bring up that video right fucking now."

"What video?"

"The one where you told the reporter you hoped I wouldn't be playing your brother in that movie."

He stops moving for a while before shaking his head. "I don't remember that at all."

"Yeah, well." I go to the fridge to see what there is to

13

drink and end up grabbing an apple juice. While I uncap it, I ask, "So, is it because of the whole Faye thing?"

Jacoby's weird blue-green eyes find mine. "The what?"

"You know. Faye Crespo."

"What about her?"

"I dated her for a while."

"Did you?" he questions, taking the skillet of meat to the colander in the sink.

"You know we did, and you also know it overlapped with when you two were dating."

His lips quirk just slightly, but he doesn't say anything until he's pouring the meat into the mixture of beans, tomatoes, and chili peppers.

"So, you did know."

"Know what?"

"That I was dating her."

"I mean, not until after the fact."

"Sure."

"So, that's it? That's why you don't like me?"

The sigh he releases is full of exasperation. "Grab some bowls, will you?"

I open a few cabinets before I find the one with the bowls and then place them on the counter.

"Well, regardless of our issues, we have to make sure we turn it off when the cameras are on. I know you've done bigger movies than I have, but this is my first starring role, and I'm not about to let anything, especially you, mess it up."

He pins me with a look as he snatches one of the bowls. "I'm a professional, Roman, therefore I don't need any instruction from you. As you said, I'm by far more accomplished."

I cock my head. "Uh, not sure I said that."

"That's what I heard."

He piles food into his bowl before moving to a small table.

"Well, your hearing sucks."

I take my food to the table and sit across from him.

He stares at me like I'm lost, but when I only continue to stare back, he sighs and takes a bite.

We eat in silence for ten minutes before I can't take it any longer. "We're supposed to be getting to know each other, and all I know about you is that you're even more boring and annoying than I thought."

He lets go of his spoon and pushes his bowl forward, crossing his arms on the table. "What do you want to know, Roman?"

"You can call me Rome." He raises his brows. "Fine. Favorite food, movie, snack to eat at a theater, and favorite hobby."

"Steak, the 1968 version of *Romeo and Juliet*, plain Hershey bar, reading and playing basketball."

I swallow down my food and absorb the rapid-fire answers. "*Romeo and Juliet*?"

He gives a slight shake of his head and brings his bowl closer so he can continue to eat. "And your answers?"

"Hmm. Probably pizza. You can't go wrong with pizza. Well, unless you're lactose intolerant, I guess. Favorite movie is hard, because are we talking about favorites in a specific genre or just in general?"

"You came up with the questions."

"I prefer Skittles when I watch a movie. And popcorn, of course." When he doesn't react, I change the subject. "Have you read the book?"

"Of course," he answers quickly, taking another bite.

"Thoughts?"

"It's good."

"That's it?"

"Oh my god," he says, standing up to take his bowl to the kitchen. "I think the director made a mistake, because coming out of this weekend, I don't think I'm going to like you more."

I follow him. "More? So you like me a little?" I tease.

"No."

"I don't know why asking about the book we're bringing to life is too much for you. I simply wanted to know your thoughts about the story. Scenes you were glad they included or upset they didn't. You're such a fucking baby. I don't know how any of your co-stars like you."

The dishes clatter in the sink before he spins around with fury in his eyes. His chest heaves with shallow breaths, and his lips part like he's about to say something, but instead, he swallows them down along with his frustration and turns back to the sink.

"Roman, you are the only one of my co-stars who doesn't like me. That's fine, but maybe my reaction to you is based on how you feel about me. Ever think about that?"

"I haven't done anything to you. I tried being friends with you years ago and you blew me off."

"I believe you're thinking of someone else. I was never rude to you."

He finishes washing his dishes and goes to the fridge for a bottle of juice. I stew in my anger as I clean out my bowl, debating on what to say to him. He clearly doesn't have the best memory. It doesn't seem like we're going to get anywhere with this, so maybe I should leave it alone. We have two more days here, so maybe I can *act* like he doesn't annoy the shit out of me.

I turn around to say something, but he's gone.

CHAPTER THREE

When I wake up, I rush to take a shower before Jacoby gets in there and uses all the hot water.

After dinner last night, we didn't speak to each other, and the tension is really starting to get to me. I want to take this seriously. I don't have huge films to fall back on if this one tanks. This is my big break. Sure, a cute teen rom-com TV show is fun and has a fanbase, but I was one of eight main characters and hardly given strong material. My last movie, *Broken*, was a good breakthrough, but again, the woman who played my mom was Luna Miller—a four-time Academy Award winner and one of the most popular actresses this century. I was a supporting actor under a woman who steals every scene she's in, even if she hardly speaks.

This movie has to be perfect, and even though Jacoby is a snobby little shit, I want to make this work, so I will attempt to put my issues on the back burner.

"I have to use the bathroom!" Jacoby's voice booms from the other side of the door after a few loud knocks.

"So go outside!"

Okay, I guess putting it on the back burner is going to be

harder than I thought. It's just so fun to get him angry. It really doesn't take much.

"So it can freeze before it hits the ground?"

"It's not that cold."

"Roman," he growls.

"Just come in. I'm still rinsing out the conditioner."

Silence. Finally the door opens.

"I hope when I flush this the water turns ice cold."

"Maybe don't flush it until I'm done."

I turn my back to the showerhead and let the water rinse my hair out. The toilet flushes and a few seconds later the temperature of the water drops.

"You asshole."

"I'm about to brush my teeth too. Maybe I'll use hot water."

"That's fucking weird."

The sink comes on, but luckily I'm done, so I shut the shower off and pull back the curtain just enough to get my towel.

Jacoby's eyes flicker over to me before he turns to stare at the drain while brushing his teeth.

With the towel around my waist, I step out and do my best to crowd his space. Everything I need is on the other side of him, next to the wall, so I keep stretching my arm out to grab each thing individually, my chest and shoulder bumping into him. First, I get my comb and place it on my side of the sink, then I get my deodorant and put it on, and my elbow almost hits him in the face as I apply it. When I reach for my lotion, I really push my body into him, my wet torso pressing against his shirt.

"Could you not?" he bellows, taking a step back and yanking the toothbrush from his mouth.

"You're in the fucking way."

"I'd say the same thing. I'm using the sink."

"I was in here first."

He makes a rumbly noise in his throat before quickly finishing up and storming out. I let out a light chuckle, and then remember I was supposed to play nice.

When I go into our room to get dressed, he quickly leaves and closes himself in the bathroom to take his own shower.

I don't know why there's certain people in the world who really bring out the worst and most childish in others, but Jacoby is that person for me. I'm not usually this way, so it has to be his fault.

Since he made dinner last night, I go to the kitchen and start breakfast. I'm not much of a cook, but you can't mess up scrambled eggs.

I crack eight of them into the skillet and pop some bread into the toaster. By the time the eggs are done, I push down on the lever of the toaster and start scooping the food onto a plate.

Jacoby comes in, causing a woodsy-vanilla scent to fill the air.

"I made eggs and toast," I tell him, staring at the toaster and waiting for it to pop up.

"Thanks," he says begrudgingly.

Even the way he says that makes me want to have a snide remark, but I bite it back. I take my toast, get the butter and smear it on, then head to the table.

Jacoby sits down a few minutes later, and we eat in silence. I chance quick glances at him, wondering who will be the first to talk. I'm generally pretty talkative, but he gets upset each time I open my mouth, and we end up in a verbal sparring match. Would he really ignore me for two whole days if I didn't push him?

His dark hair is a little curly on top, and his jawline and

cheekbones really work in his favor. With perfectly proportionate lips and eyes that seem to constantly change between hazel and blue, or maybe it's just a mix of both, he definitely earns the heartthrob title. It's too bad he's a dick.

"Do you want to go over some lines today?" I ask, breaking the silence.

His eyes finally move up from his plate and land on mine. "Are you worried you don't have them down?"

I let out an exasperated sigh and get up to wash my dishes. "Never mind."

His chair scrapes across the wooden floor, and then he's next to me at the sink. "Which scene?"

I shrug. "I don't care. I just think we should get an idea on how we'll work together since their relationship is so much different from ours."

"Clearly," he mutters.

"You know, I'm trying," I say, moving to the side as I place my clean plate on the counter.

"Fine. I'll meet you in the living room."

I move down the hallway and grab my script before sitting on the couch and flipping through it. *Another Life* is a new adult, queer romance between two guys at different places in their lives.

I play Andrew, who travels to Ennis, Montana in the winter with plans to meet up with some friends for New Year's Eve. He arrives a day before everyone is set to show up, but William, Jacoby's character, has the same plan. Andrew and William knew each other in high school but haven't seen each other in three years. While Andrew always had a crush on William, Andrew was never out of the closet and William was straight. The last time they were together, they almost kissed.

While waiting for their friends to show up and ease the

tension, a blizzard hits and traps them inside while preventing anyone else from traveling the roads. In forced proximity, with outages that prevented them from using their phones for the first two days, their friendship reignites and sexual tension emerges once more. New Year's rolls in, and they share a drunken kiss at the stroke of midnight. When they wake up in the morning, their friends are there and so begins the secret moments, longing gazes, lingering touches, and things left unsaid. They depart from their trip to homes separated by thousands of miles and connect through flirty messages before they plan to meet up again.

It's a story that spans two years and includes lots of angst, pining, heartache, and finally, a hard-earned happily ever after. They each visit the other—William able to be himself when he's with Andrew, but both of them having to be secretive when Andrew visits William; he comes from a Mormon family and attends a Mormon college.

Their sex scenes range from passionate and fiery to romantic and sweet. The author, RG Blake, didn't hold back on the explicitness nor the emotions. It gives both of us range to fight, cry, laugh, and express ourselves with our bodies.

"Ready?" Jacoby asks.

"Yeah. I was thinking maybe the scene on New Year's."

He dips his chin and sits next to me on the couch. I shift to face him and put my script down.

I watch Jacoby's face as he sifts through the lines in his head and becomes William.

"Do you remember when we last saw each other?" he asks, doing a good job of speaking like he's been drinking.

I nod, swallowing. "Vividly."

"I've thought about that night a lot since then." He looks to the side, rubbing his palm over his knee.

"Oh yeah? About what exactly?"

His eyes land on my face and briefly drop to my mouth. "Would haves and should haves."

I lick my lips. "Should haves," I repeat.

"Hmm." His lips curve up into a carefree smile before he looks at his watch. "It's almost midnight."

I watch as he moves to the kitchen and grabs a couple of glasses, jogging back with a wide smile.

With a laugh, I take a glass and stand up. "We've already been drinking for three hours. Do we really need fancy glasses now?"

"Come on, it's New Year's. We need champagne glasses to toast to a new year. And these are plastic anyway. Not too fancy."

"Okay, sure."

With another glance at his watch, he says, "Fifteen seconds."

I nod and swallow. For the next fourteen seconds, we stare into each other's eyes. It's amazing what can be said without words, but in those moments, I spot pain and desire in the depth of his gaze.

"Happy New Year, Andrew," he says, lifting his glass to mine. There's something vulnerable in the way he's looking at me.

"Happy New Year, Will."

We clink our glasses together and take pretend sips, our eyes still stuck on each other.

He slowly lowers his glass, full-on lust in his expression before he tosses it onto the couch and moves forward. Toe-to-toe and chest-to-chest, our breaths come in soft pants as our eyes inspect each other's mouths.

My heart thumps rapidly behind my ribs as his hand lands on my hip and slides around to my lower back, pulling me toward his body.

"Andrew," he whispers, his mouth heading toward mine.

I close my eyes briefly, touching my forehead to his. "Please," I say in a voice just above a whisper.

"I…I—" he stutters.

"Shut up and kiss me," I say, dropping my glass and wrapping my arms around him, making sure there's no space between us.

His lips barely ghost over mine before he's stepping back, clearing his throat.

"I think we'll do just fine," he says with a tight-lipped smile and curt nod.

His absence takes a second to get used to. I lick my lips once more. "Yeah."

Jacoby flees down the hall, and I'm left in awe over how well he can switch between his character and the real him…

Because I don't feel much like myself at all.

CHAPTER FOUR

ON OUR FINAL DAY IN THE CABIN, I VENTURE OUTSIDE TO GET some air, leaving Jacoby on the couch reading a book.

It's cold, but I bundle up in a sweater, jacket, and sweatpants that I shove inside a pair of boots. The snow is only five or six inches, but it's due to pick up some more while we're filming. I walk for about thirty minutes, getting lost in nature instead of my own head. When I get back to the cabin, I decide to head in through the back so I can leave my wet boots in the mudroom.

As soon as I open the door, I hear Jacoby talking.

"No, I mean it. I can't do this."

I creep in quietly, wondering if he's talking about me again.

"That's fine. I know. You don't understand. He's...he's —" Jacoby lets out a frustrated noise. "This will not be good. I shouldn't have agreed, honestly."

My jacket gets caught on a hook on the wall and pulls it down, letting Jacoby know I'm in the house.

"I gotta go. Yeah. As soon as I get my cell back I'll call you."

I heard enough to deduce what he's talking about. Seems really similar to the email he was sending before we got here. He doesn't want me in this movie. Or at least doesn't want to do it if I'm attached. After our scene yesterday, I thought we both proved we work well together. Our regular bullshit didn't affect the scene, and I honestly can't believe how unprofessional he's being. Fuck it, if he wants to act like this, I'll let him, but I'm not quitting. I'm gonna prove to everyone that I deserve to be here and want it more than he does.

When I walk through the hall, Jacoby's heading toward me.

"How was it?" he asks.

I stare at him, annoyed that he's only trying to talk to me now because he's afraid I overhead him.

"Fine. I'm gonna shower."

His brows dip in the middle slightly, but he doesn't say anything. We fall into our usual silence for the rest of the day, and I make a sandwich for dinner before taking it to my bed and eating it there.

Once I'm done, I take my plate to the kitchen and come back to start packing. I can't wait to get out of here. I hope they show up at six in the morning.

At seven-thirty, Sheera's at the door. "How was it?"

"Good. Fine, yeah. What's next?"

Her eyes move past me to find Jacoby dragging his bags in. "Well, we're gonna get you set up in your actual lodgings, then we'll need you to do a quick little video we can post on social media to get the fans excited. Just something saying you're ready to start filming. After that, you'll meet with the director and the rest of the cast. We'll do some read-throughs and start filming in about five days."

"Okay, cool."

"Put your stuff in the truck and we'll leave soon."

She presses a button on her phone and brings it to her ear before strutting past us.

"If we're about to announce the start of filming, you better be fucking sure you're gonna do it," I tell Jacoby as we're loading our luggage in the bed of the truck.

"What are you talking about?"

I glare at him. "Don't play dumb. It's not cute."

"Your attitude isn't cute. Neither is your constant hostility."

"Okay, Pot."

"Who?"

"Pot," I state. "Pot calling the kettle black? Just forget it. I don't need you to think I'm cute, but I do need you to be all in or just quit. I want an acting partner I can count on."

"Are you kidding me?" he questions, lifting the second of his three bags to the bed.

I march around the truck and get in the backseat. Jacoby climbs in soon after. "Okay, fine. I might've had some reservations."

"I don't care. This is important to me. It should be to you, too. This is the kind of movie that's going to have a rabid fanbase. It's got a fandom. I'm over the weird tension between us. We don't have to be friends, but I need to know you're committed and won't leave me high and dry because you can't get over the fact that I wear *flashy* clothes."

"It's not—" He bites his lip. "Fine. I'm in. I'm doing it, okay? Don't worry about that."

"Good."

Sheera slides into the driver's seat and takes us to the hotel we're staying at, and of course, Jacoby and I are neighbors.

We meet some more of the cast who's also put up in the same hotel, then we're taken to the set where Sheera corrals us next to a trailer and gives us a serious look.

"The rumors are already all over the internet."

"What rumors?" Jacoby asks, his voice thick with concern over his Hollywood sweetheart title.

"That there's contention between you two." We're both quiet, unwilling to lie or deny, but Sheera reads it instantly. "So, you're going to put all that talk to rest by acting like the best of friends. You can write hate notes to each other or pull each other's hair behind closed doors, but out in public, during promo, on set, or wherever there is another person in close proximity, you will laugh and smile and joke and make everyone believe there's never been a problem between you two. You got it?"

"Maybe if everyone thinks we hate each other they'll be more inclined to see the movie to see how we work," I offer.

She stares at me for several seconds, her gaze a little frightening. "No. You can't be out there staring him down like you want to kill him and sell a movie. If you put that narrative out there, people will see it in the movie even if it isn't there. Then all we'll hear is how you two clearly didn't have chemistry because you hated each other. No. Not happening."

I hold up my hands. "Okay. Got it."

She produces a phone from her black slacks and shoves it at my chest. "Take this, film a quick clip, and make it good. We have somewhere to be in fifteen."

"What do we say?"

"That you're on set, you're about to start filming, how

excited you are to be working together. That you're gonna have a sleepover and make friendship bracelets. I don't care."

She looks at her personal phone and walks away, leaving me and Jacoby standing side-by-side.

I take a breath and push my shoulders back, tilting my head from left to right. "Okay. I can like William, so you are now William to me, and that's how I'm getting through this."

Jacoby rolls his eyes. "Whatever works."

I open up the camera and face it toward us, ready to hold it out.

"Are you talking first? Maybe I should hold the camera."

"Why?" I question, taking a step to the side to stare at him.

"I'm taller."

"By two inches? So what?"

"You'll cut my head off on the screen."

"Oh, god forbid the world doesn't see your perfect curls. Just stop being a Jacoby and turn William on, please. I can't take this anymore."

"If you would just—"

I start recording. "Hey, guys! I'm Roman Black, but you might know me as Rome, or as my friend, Jacoby, refers to me, the most well-dressed guy on every red carpet." I flash a smile and angle the phone to Jacoby.

He grins, putting a hand on my shoulder. "I'm Jacoby Hart, or as Roman refers to me, the man with the best head of hair in showbiz."

I put the phone down and face him. "Okay, stop. This is just coming off snarky and ridiculous."

"You started it."

"I guess we're in first grade again."

Jacoby steals the phone from me and starts recording. "Hey guys, Jacoby Hart here with Roman Black."

He angles the phone, and I creep into the shot with my arm around his shoulder. "We're so excited to start filming *Another Life*, and will do our very best to bring these beloved characters to life in the most authentic way.

"We're getting started today after having spent an incredible few days together. Did you know Roman makes five-star worthy scrambled eggs? Anyway, we hope you're ready for Andrew and William," Jacoby says with his heartthrob smile.

"We'll bring you as many updates as we can," I say, grabbing the phone. "In the meantime, follow us on social media so you can see what we're up to. I may be able to convince Jacoby to make me another delicious dinner, and I'll let you all know how it measures up to my scrambled eggs."

Jacoby pops his head back into the screen with a smile. "Bye, guys!"

"Bye!"

I stop the video and release a breath. "Well, hopefully that's fine."

"Just take it to Sheera. I'll be over there in a minute."

He pulls out his phone and turns his back on me, and I do my very best to bite my tongue.

"Yes, your majesty," I mutter before finding Sheera. "Hope this works," I say, handing it over.

She pockets it without watching. "I'll send it to both of you later, and you need to share it on your social sites. In the meantime, grab Jacoby and find Ashlyn. She's got a lot of red hair. Can't miss her. She's a PA, and she's going to show you where to find wardrobe and makeup."

"Okay."

I turn around and look for Jacoby, catching glimpses of him as he paces between trailers with the phone pressed against his ear.

With a sigh, I start heading over, hoping like hell I don't

overhear him talking about me again or we may end up in a fight in front of everyone—and that's the exact opposite of what Sheera's requested.

"Hey," I say as I approach. He lifts his head. "Sheera wants us to find someone named Ashlyn so she can take us to wardrobe."

"Okay." He turns his back. "Gotta go. Yeah, talk to you later. Love you."

Jacoby falls in step with me as we make our way to set. "New girlfriend?"

"What?" His head snaps in my direction, brows furrowed in confusion.

"You said, 'love you' so I was asking if you had a new girlfriend."

"What does it matter?"

"Don't worry. I'm not gonna steal her."

"Right. Because you're so trustworthy."

"I'm telling you, I didn't know you were with Faye."

"Whatever. I don't even care about that."

"I think if we're to sell our amazing friendship, we should know a little about each other in case we're asked questions."

He sighs. "I'm not dating anyone, Roman. Happy?"

"Me either."

"Great. We have something in common," he deadpans.

I shake my head. He's so rude. To think I admired him at one point in time is crazy. Well, they do say *never meet your idols*. Not that he was my *idol*. But he was just a few years older than me and doing amazing things in movies, and I wanted that for myself. I really longed for a friendship with him until that very first meeting.

Now I just long to wrap my hands around his throat.

CHAPTER FIVE

JACOBY STANDS IN FRONT OF ME, A COCKTAIL OF EMOTIONS warring behind his eyes. He clenches and unclenches his hands at his sides, fighting off an action that tries to work itself out of him.

"I don't know what to say," he says quietly. "You don't understand my life or where I come from. I know I come off carefree and happy-go-lucky, but I'm not. I'm riddled with self-doubt and overflowing with fear. It's been years. I don't know how much longer I can pretend."

I shake my head, taking the tiniest step forward and almost reaching for him. "Elaborate for me."

He throws his hands in the air before running them through his hair. "I'm gay! I've always been gay. My parents, they…" He stops, turning his head like he's searching for the right words. "They love me. I know they do. But I also know they're entrenched in a religion that preaches about the wrongness of homosexuality. They say we can be gay but can't act on it. They don't think we can get married. How do I live my life knowing I'll never be able to be myself? That I'll never find happiness?"

His tears roll down his cheeks as his back bows with soft sobs. I wrap my arms around him and bring him into my chest. Jacoby snakes his arms around my waist and squeezes.

"And cut!" the director calls out. "Great job, guys. We're gonna break for lunch and be back here at one."

Jacoby and I pull away from each other, and I keep an eye on him as he wipes the tears from his face. He's such an incredible actor.

When he finds me watching him, he does a double-take, so I turn and walk away.

Jessica, an actress who plays one of our friends, walks alongside me. "I'm starving."

"I had a couple tiny sandwiches from craft services earlier, but I'm dying for a whole pizza."

"I'll order one and we can eat in my trailer."

"Okay, cool."

She pulls her phone out, and I turn my head and find Jacoby walking to his trailer alone. I think about inviting him, but we'd probably end up arguing in front of Jessica, and then Sheera would kill us both.

"Oh, go get Jacoby," Jessica says, pointing at him as he opens the door.

"Why?"

She gives me a funny look. "Y'all are friends, right?"

Silence stretches for a few seconds. "Maybe I just wanted time alone with you," I say with a wink.

She rolls her eyes with a smile on her lips. "I do not date people I work with."

"Who said anything about dating?" I wiggle my brows.

Jessica smacks me in the arm. "I've heard quite enough about you, Rome. Mr. Seen-with-a-new-girl-every-week."

"Ooh, jealousy. I like it."

"Go get Jacoby and leave me alone," she says with a laugh, climbing the steps to her trailer.

I groan. "Fine. Oh!" She turns around. "Jacoby is lactose intolerant. Grab him a salad or some breadsticks or something. Whatever doesn't have dairy."

She nods and disappears inside while I drag my feet to Jacoby's trailer.

After a couple knocks, he opens the door. "What're you doing here?"

"Nice to see you, too, sweetheart."

He looks out past me before directing his eyes on mine. "You need something?"

"I'm here to invite you to Jessica's trailer for lunch," I say, jerking my thumb over my shoulder.

Jacoby looks over and then back at me. "Why?"

"So we'll be graced with your positive nature and sense of humor, obviously."

He flattens his lips. "I'll eat here."

With a sigh, I slide my hands into my pocket. "Look, I questioned her too, and she threw our pretend friendship in my face. If I go back without you, she's gonna wonder why, and I can't tell her that being around you is literally the most exhausting thing in the world, so would you just come on?"

"Hey guys!"

We turn our heads and find a young woman with a camera looking at us.

"Hey," I greet with a smile, even though I'm not sure who she is.

"I'm Keisha. Sheera has me taking behind the scenes footage for social media since this movie is geared toward a younger audience."

"Oh. Cool," I reply, glancing up at Jacoby.

"Can I get a shot of you two?"

Jacoby finally steps out of the doorway and down the two steps until he's next to me. He's so stiff and awkward, and there's no way people won't notice.

"Of course," I say good-naturedly, wrapping my arm around Jacoby's shoulders. "We were just about to head over to Jessica's for lunch. Swing by there in a little bit for more photos."

"Perfect!" she says, lifting her camera as I tilt my head and rest it against his. "Thanks, guys."

I nod, my smile stretched across my face until she's gone.

"You're unbearable," Jacoby grumbles, shrugging my arm off his shoulder before going inside his trailer.

I stand there staring at his door, sort of in shock, but a few seconds later he returns, slipping his phone into his pocket.

"You're coming?" I ask with a little smile.

"Do I really have a choice?"

"Good point." We start heading toward Jessica's trailer. "Remember, we're friends. We're cool. We don't hate each other."

He shakes his head and rolls his eyes but doesn't say anything. When I pull open Jessica's door, she greets us with a smile.

"Hey! So there was a place not too far away that had some other options besides pizza. I ordered you a salad and some chicken strips and fries since Rome said you're lactose intolerant. Hope that's fine."

"Oh," he says, his eyes briefly finding mine before focusing on her again. "That's good. Yeah. Thank you."

She nods and looks back at her phone and his gaze lingers on mine as we sit on a tiny little couch together.

"Cam, one of the assistants, is gonna bring it over in a bit." She exhales. "So, are you guys excited or what? This movie is going to be huge, especially for you two."

I smile at her. "Very excited. I know this guy over here"—
I playfully nudge Jacoby in the side with my elbow—"has
had some popular films, but this one is my biggest as a lead.
And it's my first book-to-movie adaptation, so with an established fanbase, it's exciting but also scary."

Jacoby nods. "It's my first book-to-screen adaptation, too,
and the pressure is a little higher. People already have expec-
tations."

"Ah, you'll be fine. The people love you. Mr. Heartthrob
over here," I say, winking at Jessica.

She smiles and a tinge of red colors her cheeks as her
eyes flicker to Jacoby. Well, looks like someone might have a
crush.

"Is your last name actually Hart or is that a stage name?"
I ask, turning a little to face him and knocking my knee
against his.

"That's my actual name."

"Damn, guess you just got lucky that you ended up being
so attractive too."

His brows dip slightly, and I look away.

"You didn't know if that was his real last name?" Jessica
questions. "Hell, I knew that."

I clear my throat, trying to figure out where to go from
here. Deflecting is always the answer. "Ohhh, well, I'm not
an internet stalker like some people. You know his govern-
ment name, you know who I'm seen with every week," I
tease.

She rolls her eyes. "Please. Who doesn't? You're always
photographed. Jacoby, do you know the girl he was making
headlines with right before coming out here?"

"He's not gonna—"

"Chrissy Blough."

I snap my head in his direction. "Oh my god. I have two stalkers."

"It's not stalking if it's on every social media site and shoved in our faces," Jessica says.

"But you're not in a relationship with her," Jacoby says with a slight grin. "Since you don't do that."

"Ooh, insider secrets," Jessica says, leaning forward. "Why doesn't he do relationships?"

I roll my eyes and slouch back into the couch. "Yes, Jacoby, why don't I do relationships?"

"Hmm," he says, shifting in his seat. "Because you're young, your star is rising, and you're not going to lock yourself down to one person when you have the pick of the litter."

My eyebrows reach for my hairline. "The pick of the litter? Huh. I can just be with whoever I want?"

His chin dips slightly and Jessica giggles. "With their consent, but who's not consenting to you? You know you're hot."

I smile at her, my brows still high on my face. "If you didn't tell me you don't date co-stars, I'd think you were interested in me."

She scoffs. "You wish."

"Maybe."

"You're a habitual flirt," she says with a grin as she stands up. "Watch yourself around him, Jacoby. I'm gonna go look for Cam. I'm starving."

Once she's gone, the tension settles over us and we both try to scoot as close to the edges of the couch as we can. When our bodies still touch, I stand up and walk to the other side.

"So, you know about Chrissy Blough."

He gives me his signature eye roll. "What happened there? Too blonde? Too blue-eyed?"

"What're you trying to say?" I ask.

"Nothing, but you clearly have a type."

"No, I don't."

"Okay, Roman."

"What's wrong with blue-eyed blondes? Are you prejudiced against them?"

He shakes his head. "They clearly aren't working out for you. First it was Amelia and then it was Beverly. Are you going through the alphabet or something?"

I let out a genuine laugh, because it's something I hadn't even realized. "No, but I've also been with an Emerson and Dakota, so just a few more before I get to J."

His eyes find mine through thick lashes. "Funny."

"I bet you don't know what Emerson looks like."

"I can assume some variation of the same."

I smirk at him. "Well, to be fair, Emmy is a bleach blonde, so not really natural."

He snorts. "Okay then."

"What about you? What's your type?"

"I don't date."

"You dated Faye."

"And look how that turned out."

"Okay, pizza's here," Jessica says, bursting through the door.

I grab the boxes and put them down on the countertop. I take the paper bag and hand it to Jacoby.

"This has to be yours."

"Thanks," he replies.

I take my pizza box back to the couch where I squish in next to Jacoby, pop open the lid and start digging in. Jessica puts two slices from her box on a plate and sits in the chair across from us.

"Oh my god, this is so good," I say with a mouthful.

"Doesn't look good all chewed up in your mouth," Jacoby says, eyeing me with disgust.

"Eat your bunny food and shush."

He rips open the salad dressing packet and squirts it onto the lettuce. "You still have that young metabolism."

"Why are you acting like you're old," I say after swallowing.

"I'm older than you. That's obvious in many ways." He says it like he's teasing, giving Jessica a smile so she thinks we're just two friends giving each other shit.

"You're twenty-nine. I'm twenty-four. Plus, a study says that your metabolism doesn't really start to slow down until you're sixty, so…there."

Everybody gets quiet and then Jacoby laughs. "You read a study on metabolism?"

"I'm pretty smart, contrary to what *some* people might think."

"Salad is better for you," Jacoby says before crunching into his lettuce.

"Pfft. Not better than this pizza." I pull up a slice and watch the cheese stretch. "Look at all that yummy cheese. So good."

Jessica laughs. "You two are too much."

After a while, I put the box down on the ground, having eaten three quarters of it. Jacoby's done with his salad and chicken and is now on his phone while Jessica reaches for another slice.

There's a knock on the door. "I'm here to take pictures."

Jessica looks confused.

"Oh, the behind the scenes photos. I told her she could come over here," I tell her.

"Ah," Jessica says, getting up to open the door. "Hey."

"Sorry. I'm just gonna grab a couple shots and be on my way."

"You're fine," Jessica tells her, going back to her seat. "Get any good stuff yet?"

"A couple of the guys were out there having a pushup contest," Keisha says, "so I documented that."

Jessica shakes her head. "I bet it was Steve and Marco."

"Yep," Keisha replies with a laugh.

I swivel around and rest my feet across Jacoby's lap, my shoes on the arm of the couch.

"What—" He starts to question me but I widen my eyes at him.

He smiles and rests his arm on my leg as he faces the camera. Jessica holds up her slice of pizza and I hold up a peace sign.

"Thanks guys. See y'all around."

"Guess we should get ready to head back to set," Jessica says.

I don't move my legs as I continue to lounge on the couch. "Yeah, it's when all you guys show up after our night together," I say, gesturing between me and Jacoby.

"Oh, have you filmed the first intimate scene yet?"

I shake my head.

"It'll be a closed set. Less people around to see," Jacoby adds, gently smacking my leg to get me to move.

"Unfortunately for them, because I have a pretty nice ass," I joke.

Jacoby stands and clears his throat. "I'll take this to the dumpster," he says, gathering the trash left behind from lunch. "See you guys over there."

CHAPTER SIX

WE GET THROUGH A COUPLE SCENES WITH THE GROUP OF friends, and then we reset for one of William and Andrew's secret moments while their friends play drinking games in the living room. In this scene, William disappears into the bathroom, and I follow him a minute later, telling everyone I'm going to see if I can get in touch with my parents.

"Action!"

I look to my right, making sure nobody can see me, and as soon as he opens the bathroom door, I push inside.

"What—"

"Shh," I murmur, pressing my lips against his.

He releases a soft moan, his tense body melting in my arms almost immediately.

Pulling away, he says, "We shouldn't do this."

"I can't help it. They're always around, and I'm always thinking about you."

His lips quirk up and he pulls me closer, his hand sliding through my hair at the back of my head before he kisses me.

"I love your lips," I whisper against them.

His eyes find mine, staring deeply. "I've wanted this for

43

so long. Since I walked away from you at that party all those years ago."

"I wanted you before then."

We clash together again, arms wrapping around each other, hands squeezing muscles before drifting lower. Our lips are like magnets, unable to keep apart.

I move forward, backing him into the sink before lifting him up and placing him on the counter.

"I want more," he whispers desperately into my neck. "You've unleashed a beast inside me and only you can tame it."

"Fuck."

I lean my forehead on his, but I do it too hard and Jacoby's ass falls into the sink.

"Oh!"

I laugh first and then he joins, both of us facing the director. "Sorry!" I call out.

We chuckle and I help pull him off the counter. "Sorry about that, man," I say, my hand on his upper back.

"It's okay."

"It's all good, guys. Let's start right before you put him on the sink. Just shift over to the right a little. After this, we'll break and clear the set and have you two back for New Year's night."

I swallow and glance at Jacoby before giving the director a nod. Jacoby and I find our places and he stares at me in the way William was staring at Andrew.

"What?" I ask.

"Nothing," he says with a shake of his head. "You good?"

"Of course," I say, a little defensively.

He sighs. "Okay."

I can't tell him I'm nervous about the sex scene. He'll just hold it over my head or judge me for not being as good as him or as professional. But he's acted in an erotic movie before. I have not. I've done cutesy kissing scenes, but that's it.

The intimacy coordinator comes over with a gentle smile. "You guys did very well. Everything's still okay?" We nod and he continues with instructions before the director signals us to start again.

We finish up with our scene, and we're told we have a small break before we're due back. It's a little after nine by the time we walk off the set and head to our trailers. We have to be back in thirty to meet with the intimacy coordinator again so we can go over the choreography of the scene. Andrew and William don't have penetrative sex in this scene, but they get naked and kiss quite a lot. We'll also simulate mutual hand jobs, though that won't be seen.

"Are you okay?" Jacoby's voice pulls me out of my thoughts.

"What? Why? Why do you keep asking me that?"

"You've been chewing on your thumbnail the whole walk over, and you haven't stopped scowling since we stepped off set."

"I'm fine. I know you're more experienced than I am, but I'm still perfectly capable."

He exhales. "Why do you do that?"

"Do what?" I stop and face him.

"Project. I've never said I was better than you. I've never acted as if I thought I was better than anyone. You keep saying it, and it's obviously something that bothers you."

I snort. "Only except when I first met you. I was excited to meet you then, Jacoby. I had been a fan of yours and wanted nothing but to say hello and introduce myself. You looked me up and down with the most pretentious look I've ever seen on anyone's face, and then you turned and walked away. It was clear then, and even more clear later, when you kept me from getting the role as your brother, that you don't respect me. Maybe you're threatened by my *rising star*, but guess what? There's room for both of us."

"You want to talk about respect?" he says, stepping closer to me. "How about not stealing someone's girlfriend? You've always been disrespectful. I heard enough about you before knowing you to understand who you are. You put on this act like you're just this happy-go-lucky, fun to be around kind of guy, but you're a fucking asshole. Don't think I don't know the truth about you."

I'm so taken aback by some of what he said, and I don't quite understand, but I'm also so furious to be called an asshole and disrespectful. "I don't know what you're fucking talking about, and for the last time, I didn't know you were dating Faye!"

He scoffs and turns around to head to his trailer. "Whatever. It doesn't matter."

"Do you want her back, is that it?" I ask, following him. "I can call her up and—"

He spins around, his jaw clenched and eyes fiery. "No! It's not about her. It's…" Jacoby trails off and takes a breath, attempting to stifle his anger. "Never mind. You don't get it, and you never will."

His eyes look vulnerable as he stares at me, but before I can say anything else, he spins around and walks away.

I shake my head, confusion and frustration swirling inside me, then I go to my trailer and flop onto the couch with a sigh.

CHAPTER SEVEN

WHEN WE BOTH GET BACK ON SET, THE TENSION IS OBVIOUS. He doesn't want to look at me, and when I look at him, I can feel my face contorting into a scowl. Good thing Sheera isn't here to see us, or that Keisha isn't here for the behind the scenes shot. Right now it's us, the director, a camera operator, sound guy, and the intimacy coordinator, Sean.

Sean spoke with me first, and now he's talking to Jacoby. I clear my head of all the crap going on with my co-star and remember that I'm a professional, and I can put everything to the side to deliver this scene.

"Okay," Sean says, coming to a stop in front of me with Jacoby behind him. "You two have your modesty pouches on. If at any time you feel uncomfortable or need an extra barrier, don't be afraid to let me know. I have my kit with me, and we can adjust."

"Thank you," I tell him.

"Of course. I'll be over there if you need me," he says, pointing to the corner.

We both met with Sean before filming started and went over the basics of protecting ourselves during intimate scenes, and he also warned us we'd probably want to shave, considering we'll be using lots of tape and adhesive with these garments. I'm still afraid of how it'll feel coming off, but I'll worry about that later.

"Look, I don't want things to be weird with us. Not right now. So, can we move past what happened earlier?" Jacoby asks, taking the high road, and it kind of annoys me because he looks like the better person. I was going to offer the same statement, but he beat me to it.

"Yeah." I loosen my shoulders and spot the director talking to the cameraman. "Um. I've never done this, so, do you have any tips?"

"Oh." His head tilts to the left a little as he watches me. "You're nervous." He doesn't say it like he's teasing me; he's saying it like it's a revelation.

I blow out a breath. "That's normal, right?" I ask with a bit of a bite.

"No, of course," he offers. "Sorry. I just…well, you don't seem like the type to ever be nervous. Is it because…" He doesn't finish, leaving me hanging.

"I'm a person, too. I experience all the same emotions you do. And is it because what?"

"Well, you know, because I'm a guy."

My eyes widen as my brows stretch upward. "No. I mean, I'd be nervous with anyone."

"Oh. Okay, well, yeah. The movie I did before was with a woman, so this is my first time simulating and acting out intimate scenes with a guy, but it'll be fine. We know the lines and actions. Sean walked us through each movement. The barriers we're wearing in the garments will protect us from, you know, feeling anything. I think we just have to trust each other."

I nearly scoff, my eyes finding the ceiling. "Well."

"Hey," Jacoby says in a soft voice. "You're gonna be fine. You're a great actor."

My gaze slowly drops until I'm staring into his light eyes. Something weird happens to my heart at his compliment. I've admired him for his acting ability for years, and *he* just complimented *me.*

"It's just us, okay?"

It's not, and we both know it, but I understand what he's doing.

I nod. "Okay. Thanks."

"Quiet on the set!" Mike calls out, letting us know it's go time.

We get to our markers beside the bed, facing each other, and wait to start.

"Action!"

"Are you sure about this?" I ask.

"Yes," he says quietly, his voice shaky. "This is the only thing I've ever been sure about."

Since this scene is supposed to be our first time doing more than the kiss at the stroke of midnight, everything is slower and more gentle than the scene we had in the bathroom, considering that takes place later in the movie. Right now, we're both cautious and gentle.

I remove my shirt and drop it to the floor. His eyes slowly roam down my torso before meeting my gaze again.

"Your turn," I tell him.

Jacoby starts unbuttoning the buttons on his shirt, giving a torturously slow strip tease as he reveals a tank top underneath. Once that's been discarded, I study his body and fight to keep from touching him.

My character, Andrew, is now out and comfortable with his sexuality and attraction to men, but this is William's first experience, and my character is afraid of making him uncom-

49

fortable. Plus, they've been drinking to celebrate New Year's, and he's afraid William will blame the alcohol for this experience.

"You're not drunk, right?" I ask, stepping forward and dragging a finger between his abs. "I don't want you to have any regrets."

He grabs my wrist and yanks me into him, his other hand trailing down my back. "I won't regret knowing how your skin feels against mine. It's all I've ever wanted."

Jacoby walks me backward until my knees hit the bed and I fall back, resting on my elbows. I watch as he straddles me, making me lie back completely as he begins kissing my neck.

The director yells, "Cut!" and Jacoby climbs off of me and helps me up. We redo that part of the scene a few more times before we're naked on top of the covers. My ass faces the camera as Jacoby and I lie side-by-side, facing each other.

We have a heavy makeout scene that leads to lots of touching and rubbing before our hands slide down and simulate hand jobs. We take a break between shots so Sean can bring us items that we'll use to make the movements seem authentic without touching each other. The scene will only show us from the torso up, but it has to look like we're giving each other hand jobs.

I have my arm around his shoulder, my hand gripping his hair as our movements quicken. Jacoby's mouth opens as he moans, his eyes stuck on mine.

I grunt in response, biting my lip as I nod. "Yes."

"Oh god," he cries out, face contorting.

I mimic his sounds, make the best fake orgasm face that I can, and then we do it another two dozen times before we're done.

CHAPTER EIGHT

THE NEXT THREE WEEKS GO BY QUICKLY. I'VE GOTTEN closer to Jessica and a couple other people on set. Jacoby hangs out with us occasionally, but mostly because we feel pressured to keep the lie alive. We've recorded a couple more videos, and based on most of the social media comments, people love us together.

We're off this weekend, so Jessica invited me to go to a bar with her and two other cast members in the next town over. Jacoby turned down her invitation, which is fine by me.

Three hours into our night, we're having a good time. The bar isn't big by any means, and most of the crowd has at least a decade or two on us, but we play pool...terribly. Darts prove to be even worse. The only good thing we do is take shots—off each other's bodies.

We walk down the street at eleven, looking for another bar Jessica said would have karaoke, and I drape my arms around both her and Naomi while Mila clings to Naomi's other arm.

Once inside the second bar, we find that they're not doing

karaoke, but they do have a jukebox, so we create our own karaoke night at the table while continuing to down drinks.

"So, what do you think of Jacoby turning us down?" Jess asks. "Think he doesn't like me?"

"Pfft. He doesn't like anybody."

Every set of red-rimmed eyes at this booth find my face. Fuck. I'm too drunk.

"What?" Mila questions.

"I mean, anybody except me, of course."

Jess rolls her eyes. "I tried talking to him last week, but I was so nervous, because he's so hot and, you know, Jacoby Hart. I probably made an ass out of myself, and now he never wants to talk to me again."

"I doubt that's it," Mila says. "He's really nice, just quiet."

"Has he said anything about the rest of us?" Jess questions, her words slung together.

"What do you mean?"

"I mean, y'all talk, so like, has he said anything?"

Naomi leans into Jessica. "Someone has a crush," she sings.

"Shut up," Jess says with a laugh.

I shake my head. "He hasn't told me anything."

"Ugh, boys are so lame. Y'all don't gossip or talk about girls?"

"Not after Rome stole Faye from Jacoby," Mila says, elbowing me.

"I didn't!"

They all burst into laughter before Jess says, "I'm surprised he even forgave you for that. How can y'all be friends?"

"Because you can't believe the stories the media puts out."

"Mmhmm," Naomi murmurs.

"Anyway, let's not talk about him. He didn't want to hang out with us, so his loss. If he wants to be a boring old man in his hotel room, that's fine."

A song Mila requested on the jukebox comes on and all three girls flee onto a small dance floor and start dancing together. The waitress brings us the round of shots Naomi ordered plus our drinks, so I grab my beer and take a gulp.

My brain is a little foggy, and my vision isn't the clearest, but with all the talk about Jacoby, I pull out my phone and bring up his number.

I only have it for work purposes.

And drunk purposes, apparently.

> Why ar you not with us?

> The girls want to know no tme.

I stare at the screen until I see the dots pop up, and then I take another drink.

> Based on your wonderful spelling, I'm going to assume you're drunk.

> Noooo

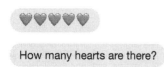

How many hearts are there?

I bring the phone up close and then pull it away. I squint my eyes and then widen them, trying to count the hearts.

7

Wrong. Five. Who's driving you?

Why didnt yu come. I thnk Jess likes you

Several minutes later, my phone rings and I stare at it for a few seconds before I answer. "Hello?"

"Roman, who's driving you back?"

"Oh, hey, Dad. We have a driver." I take another shot. "Why are you so concerned?"

"If you die, this movie doesn't get made, and I really like it, so I'd rather keep you alive until we're done."

"So romantic." He sighs and I laugh. "I can tell you're rubbing your head like you do when you're annoyed by me."

"Stop annoying me then."

"It's kinda fun."

"Are you having fun right now?" he asks. "Who are you with?"

"Jess, Mila, and Naomi. They're dancing."

He's quiet for a second. "You're not dancing with them?"

"Too drunk, I think."

"Hmm. So, Jess likes me?"

"I think so. Lord knows why."

He snorts. "Interesting."

"Why? You interested in her?"

"I don't know."

I take another drink and stand up. "Well, I can hook you up if you want. Oh fuck."

"What's wrong?"

"Nothing. I stood up. Definitely drunk."

I make my way to the bathroom, only bumping into two chairs along the way.

"I gotta take a piss. I'm putting the phone down."

"Great."

Once I'm done, and I'm at the sink washing my hands, I pick up the phone and put it to my ear.

"Miss me?"

"Tremendously," he says without enthusiasm.

The phone slips from my ear and shoulder and falls into the sink.

"Oops. My phone went into the sink kind of like your ass when I pushed you too hard." I laugh, but Jacoby remains quiet. Probably because he doesn't have a sense of humor.

"What kind of bar did you find in Ennis, anyway?" he questions.

"We're not in Ennis. It's some town like fifteen minutes away. We were at this spot called Frontier Saloon, and now we're a block away at some place with a jukebox."

"Sounds like I'm missing out on quite the night. A saloon *and* a jukebox?"

I snort and stumble into the wall. "It's too bad you're a dick who hates me, because you're kind of okay sometimes."

"*You* hate *me*," he says. "I'm just matching your energy."

"I don't even understand you."

"Cause you're drunk. And ignorant."

"Okay, well this was fun, and as much as I'd love to continue to get insulted by you, I think I'm gonna go."

"Roman."

I end the call and spend a few minutes splashing water on my face before I push open the door, nearly knocking someone down who was about to come in.

"Sorry."

I scan the dance floor but don't see the girls, so I make my way back to the booth and spot Mila's long dark hair and Jessica's strawberry-blonde head back in their seats.

"Look who's here!" Jess squeals.

My eyes slowly pan to the other side and find Eric in my seat next to Naomi. Eric plays one of our friends in the movie.

"Oh. Hey, man."

"Hey," he says with a smile. "Jacoby said y'all were having a good time out here."

"Jacoby?" I question.

"He's outside," Jess replies. "Parking, I think."

"What? I'll be back."

I rush out of the bar, shoving the doors open before looking right and left to figure out where the parking lot is. I go right and travel the length of the building until I come to a lot around the side.

I'm not even sure what car he'd be in, but there's not a lot here, so I stroll through them, searching for a stupid, handsome face behind the windshield.

"Looking for me?"

I spin around at the sound of his voice as he leans against a black SUV.

"What're you doing here?" My words come out a little slurred.

"Making sure you make it back to the hotel since you clearly can't handle your liquor."

"I can *handle* it. I'm drunk, but I'm not blacking out."

"Yet."

"What's Eric doing here? Were y'all hanging out?"

"I asked him to look after the girls while I take you to the hotel."

"Wow. Am I grounded?"

"Come on, Roman," he says, pushing away from the vehicle.

"You look...comfy," I say, taking in his joggers and gray hoodie.

"I was in bed."

"With Eric?"

"What?" he questions with a laugh. "No. You're so drunk. Come on."

He opens the door for me, and I pause right in front of him. "What if I wanna keep drinking?"

"I don't think it's a good idea."

"But if I do?"

"Then I'll wait for you out here."

"Why?"

"Because someone needs to look out for you, and the girls are drunk, too."

"Why not go inside and have fun?"

He shakes his head. "Get in. I'll let Eric know that I have you, and he'll hang out with the girls and make sure they get back okay."

I slide into the seat and watch him round the front of the

car. After he sends a text, he starts the engine and pulls out of the parking lot.

"If you're gonna throw up, let me know."

"I'm not gonna throw up. I'm drunk but not drunk-drunk."

"Ah."

I shift in the seat to face him, my head resting on the leather. It takes some effort, considering it's dark and my vision is impaired, but I can still spot the tension in his jaw.

"Are you always uptight?" I ask.

His eyes flicker over toward me before focusing back on the road. "You think I'm uptight?"

I bark out a laugh. "Uh. Yeah."

He's quiet for a little while before he speaks again. "I don't know. I've always been this way, so I never thought of it as something abnormal."

"You never seem to loosen up or actually have a good time. Is it just because you're around me? Is there another version of you that laughs and dances?"

His lips twitch. "Believe it or not, I have laughed a time or two."

I snort and slouch in my seat, facing the windshield again. "I can't even see the road."

"It's a good thing I'm driving then." Silence settles between us before he speaks again. "Why did you get so drunk?"

"It's December."

"Yeah," he says, drawing out the word in confusion. "December is for getting drunk?"

I rub my head and sit up a little, facing the side window. "December isn't my favorite month. That's all."

"Hm," is all I get from him.

"Do you like Jess?" I ask.

He's quiet for a while. "Not in the way she likes me, probably."

"She's cute," I say.

"Yeah. Maybe you should date her."

"She said she doesn't date co-stars, but it seems she'd make an exception for you."

"Jealous?" he asks in a teasing tone.

"No. Everyone likes you."

"Except you."

I sigh. "Yeah. Except me."

JACOBY

CHAPTER NINE

"WHERE'S YOUR KEY?" I ASK A VERY DRUNK ROMAN.

"Mmm, in my pocket, I think. Or wallet. Oh shit," he says, eyes attempting to go wide. "It's in my jacket. At the bar."

I roll my eyes. "Of course it is. Come on."

"Where we going?"

"To my room. It's right here."

I remove the keycard from my pocket and unlock the door, holding it open. I glance at Roman who sways slightly as he watches me.

"You're gonna go get another key for me, right?"

My eyes bulge. "I am doing no such thing. I've done enough by bringing you back here. You will sleep on the couch and get your own key in the morning."

"The couch? You know I'm six foot two, right?"

"You know the couch is a pullout bed, don't you?"

His jaw drops as he strolls forward. "Mine isn't. Is your room better than mine?" He enters the room and starts looking around. "I think your living area is bigger."

"It's not."

"How would you know?"

"We're right next to each other. There's not gonna be much of a difference."

"Except the couch."

I shake my head and kick off my shoes before removing my hoodie. In the kitchenette, I grab a bottle of water and snatch the Tylenol bottle off the counter.

"Here," I say, shoving them at him.

He looks down at the items quizzically before mumbling, "Thanks."

Roman plops down onto the couch, struggling to get his boots off before removing his thick sweater and throwing it on the floor. He then removes a thinner long-sleeved shirt only to reveal another T-shirt underneath.

"Were you afraid you were going to get sucked into a game of strip poker or something?"

He takes off that shirt and still has a tank top underneath.

"It's fucking December in Montana."

I dip my head in acknowledgement. I left the hotel in just sweats, a hoodie, and a T-shirt, only to regret it as soon as I was outside. But I knew I wasn't going to be out for long. I climbed out of bed when Eric invited me to grab some fast food, and then Roman started texting me. Once I realized he was drunk, I told Eric to text Mila and find out where they were so we could head over.

"There's extra toothbrushes and stuff in the bathroom. Do whatever you need to do, but I'm going to bed."

Roman stands up and disappears into my bedroom before I hear the bathroom door close and the water turn on.

With a sigh, I make my way to the living area and move the table so I can unfold the bed. I grab an extra blanket and pillow from the linen closet and toss them onto the middle of the mattress. Right before I head into my room, I decide to bring the trash can closer to the bed—just in case.

I push down my sweats and remove my shirt, folding them up and placing them on the dresser.

"Fuck!" Roman curses from the bathroom.

I go to the door. "You okay?"

"Ah fuck."

I open the door and find him in front of the mirror, rubbing at his eye.

"What're you doing?"

His one uncovered eye looks me up and down before he removes his hand and stares back into the mirror.

"I have contacts in."

"Oh god," I say with a sigh. "Did you poke yourself?"

"I think I scratched it."

"I take it you don't have your case."

"They're disposable."

"Well, that's good. Do you...uhh, do you need me to help?"

He sighs, his shoulders slumping over as he rests his hands on the countertop. He meets my gaze through the reflection, one eye squeezed closed.

"I guess."

I make my way over and wash my hands first. He stumbles back when he turns to face me.

"You can't move."

"I can't help it."

"Good god," I say quietly. "Sit on the counter, would you?"

He bites his lip, fighting off a smile. "You're so grumpy."

"Just do it."

65

"All right, all right." Once he's seated, he looks at me. "Happy?"

I shake my head and step between his parted thighs. I go to the eye he didn't injure first, pulling up slightly on the eyelid. Before my finger gets close, he starts rapidly blinking.

"Stop it. I haven't even touched you yet."

"It's instinct. If someone's finger is going into your eye, you're going to blink."

"Well, either let me do it, or scratch your fucking eyes out trying to do it yourself."

"Geez. Okay."

He attempts to widen his eyes as much as possible, but then they begin to squint as I get closer and he just looks ridiculous.

I laugh. "Stop. I'm serious."

Roman laughs too and then quiets down. "Okay. I'm sorry. Just…be fast. You're so close to me."

"I'm sorry for attempting to help you."

I have my thumb right under his eyebrow, pulling up, and with my other hand, I put my index finger on the white part of his eye and slide the contact until I can pinch it and remove it.

"There. One is done."

"Now you're a little blurry."

"I wasn't before?" I ask with a laugh.

"Shut up."

I drop the contact in the trash and take my place in front of him again. "You ready?"

He's staring at me, eyes red and glassy. "Do you wear contacts?"

"No."

"You have a pretty eye color. What is it? Gray? Blue? Green?" He leans in closer, squinting. "Is that a little brown?"

66

I laugh. "They're blue-hazel. They appear different depending on the lighting."

He sits back. "Hm."

With raised brows, I ask, "Any other questions? Or can I get this other contact out so I can go to bed?"

"Your hair is curly," he states simply.

"Yep. Do you need my whole genetic background so you know why I look the way I look?"

He shrugs. "I mean, we should know things about each other, right?"

With my hand on his face, I pull up his eyelid and repeat the process. "My dad is three quarters Black, one quarter white. My mom is mostly white, mixed with Syrian and Lebanese. I have a sister. We talk fairly regularly. I have not dated anyone since Faye. I reacted the way I did to you the day you came up to me because I had already heard you had plenty to say about me before then. I wasn't exactly thrilled." I pull the contact from his eye and step away to throw it in the trash.

"Wait. What? What did I say?"

I sigh. "It truly doesn't matter anymore, Roman."

"It does if it's why you hate me, and I can't think of anything I'd say that would've been taken negatively. I...I admired you. I was a fan."

I give him a small smirk. "Was?"

He slides off the counter as I'm walking by. "What did I say?"

Looking him straight in the eye and nowhere else, I decide it's best not to have this conversation right now. Probably ever. I know he's persistent and annoying, and he'll likely bother me for the rest of the time we're filming, but it's not something I'm willing to talk about.

"Goodnight, Roman."

I go into my room and climb into bed, giving him my back. He's slow to leave the room, but eventually he does, and once he's stopped squirming on the pullout bed in the living room, I close my eyes and try to sleep.

CHAPTER TEN

As soon as I wake up, I go to the bathroom to take a shower and brush my teeth, but as I'm looking for something to put on, the scent of bacon and sausage filters into my room.

Pushing open the door, I step into the living area and find Roman standing in the kitchen, uncovering dishes of break- fast foods.

"Uh, hello."

He looks over at me, eyes scanning briefly. "Morning. I ordered breakfast."

"I see that. I thought you'd be in your own room by now. Or, at the very least, still asleep."

"I told you I wasn't that drunk, and I was starving, so I figured if I'm gonna eat, you should eat, too. Don't worry, I got dairy-free options. Go put some clothes on."

"This is *my* room, you know," I say with a sigh before turning and closing myself in my room to change.

Once I come back out, he's sitting at the small table with three different sized plates in front of him with a variety of food on each.

I lift the lids on some of the dishes left on the kitchen counter and bring them over to the table. While he scarfs down an omelet smothered in cheese, I rip off a corner of toast and pinch some eggs between it and pop it into my mouth.

He reaches for a glass of orange juice and takes a big gulp before eating half a piece of bacon in one bite.

"Why are you acting like the food's gonna run away?" I question, ripping off another piece of toast.

"Because I'm starving, and I'm sure you're gonna try to kick me out any minute, and I'd like to leave with a full stomach."

I shake my head and continue eating. Once he's finished his omelet, bacon slices, sausage, and glass of orange juice, he sits back and reaches for his glass of water.

"Done?"

"Almost," he says with a smirk. "Hey, quick question."

"Hmm?" I say, stabbing a sausage with my fork.

"What did I say about you that made you hate me?"

"Roman, please."

"But I never said anything about you. Who said I did?"

"Does it matter?"

"It's going to bother me now. I've hated you because I thought you were a smug asshole who thought he was better than me, but if you were only reacting to something you thought I said, then maybe we can put this past us. Be friends."

"Well, the world already thinks we're friends."

"You don't actually want to be?"

"No." I say it quickly. Much too quickly. I see him jolt back in surprise. "I mean—"

"No, you said what you meant," he replies, standing up.

"Roman."

"It's fine, Jacoby. I'm gonna head downstairs to get a key to my room. I'll see you on set."

Behind me, I can hear him putting his shoes on. I fight with myself about what to tell him, but it's probably better that he leaves.

His heavy, booted footsteps approach but come to a stop right next to me. I peer up at his dark eyes and watch his protruding Adam's apple bob when he swallows.

"You know what, Jacoby? You're a real asshole."

I turn and face him, resting my arm on the back of the chair. "Oh, am I? *Me?*"

"Yes, you. Because I was willing to put everything aside to try to be your friend."

"It's interesting that the guilty party is always willing to leave everything in the past."

"Guilty party?" he questions, brows furrowed. "What the fuck am I guilty of?"

I stand, ending up toe-to-toe with him, forcing him to take a step back. "You've said some real foul shit, Roman, and the fact that you can't remember means maybe you should lay off on all the drinking."

"Oh, fuck you," he says with a cruel laugh. "I get drunk one time around you and now I have a drinking problem?"

"No, it seems you've had one for at least a year now. I saw the videos and photos of you. It was around the time you had plenty to say about me but can't remember."

"If you're not gonna fucking tell me what I supposedly said, then I'm going to assume you're full of shit. I *liked* you, Jacoby. Past tense, but I fucking liked you. Or at least the idea of you. I was with the rest of the world, falling for Hollywood's new heartthrob. I was a fan. I *wouldn't* have had anything bad to say, so you're mistaken. But honestly, go fuck yourself."

"Roman, wait," I say, catching him by the wrist as he begins to storm off. His angry eyes drop to my fingers around his arm and then slide back up to my face. "What do you mean *falling for*?"

He shakes me off him, his eyes scanning my face under pinched brows before he swallows and lets out a humorless laugh. "Get over your fucking self."

Then he marches to the door.

"No. That's not what I meant," I say, following him.

"You sure do say a lot of shit you don't mean then. Learn to speak your truth, sweetheart."

He yanks open the door, and I grab the knob. "God, you're so infuriating. If you would just please—"

"No," he says simply, stomping down the hall and toward the elevator.

CHAPTER ELEVEN

THE NEXT TIME I SEE ROMAN, IT'S ON SET THE FOLLOWING day. Right before we're due to start shooting scenes where Andrew is visiting William at his college campus. It's a steamy scene where we basically find every hidden spot to kiss and touch each other, having just spent months apart.

Having to do this with Roman is hard enough as it is, but, after our fight and not speaking to each other since then, it's going to take a lot of professionalism to put it aside and act like I'm in love with this stupid asshole.

When he spots me, he burns holes into my head with his piercing gaze, his jaw clenched tight. *Great.*

After speaking with Mike, the director, and Sean, the intimacy coordinator, we take our spots and begin.

To create what will be a montage of stolen moments and passionate kisses, we start in William's dorm room while his roommate is gone. I shove *Andrew* against the closed door, smashing my mouth against his as his hands roam up my sides and around my back. He walks me backward to my bed where he pushes me down and undoes my pants, kissing down my stomach.

After a change of clothes, we film another scene in the same room, this time of me nipping at *Andrew's* neck before bending him over my desk.

The next scene is in the school library, where they really push the limits of getting caught by touching each other under the table, through clothes. The camera will zoom onto our hands as we rub and grope one another. Though, we were given barrier materials to wear to keep from actually feeling too much of the other person's hand.

We rush to a hidden alcove to makeout, hands exploring and lips tasting.

Another scene is outside, behind a tree, and the final one is in *William's* truck, where *Andrew* gives him a blowjob as he drives down the street.

We get through each shoot like professionals, but in between, we don't speak to each other. Roman gives me a few looks, and based on the intensity of them, I'm assuming he's plotting how to murder me.

"All right, guys. We're gonna break and we'll see you at seven-thirty."

We slam the doors to the truck, going our separate ways.

Before we're due to start filming the most intimate scene of the movie, Sean calls us both to set while everyone is still gone.

"I want to go over the scene before the cameras start rolling," he says, standing near the bed. "This will show nearly everything without revealing your most private areas. Roman, I do believe your bottom will be shown, and the side of yours, Jacoby. There will be a lot of tight shots, but the movements and expressions need to be perfect. It's very, very intimate. Extremely up close and personal. You will have your protective garments on, but if you have any concerns or questions, I'm here to help.

"Roman, when you get on top, you're going to rock slowly. The camera will leisurely pan from your face down to your waist. Your hands will need to be placed on his sides, maybe around the middle of his ribs. We may need to adjust, but we don't want your arms blocking your hip area as we'll focus on the body movement there."

"Okay," he replies with a nod.

"Jacoby, for you, it's going to be mostly expressions at first. Your hands will eventually reach out for his waist, fingers skating up his abs. When it's time to flip over, you'll grab him here and here," he says, showing me on Roman's body where to grab. "You'll both have to help to make the movement seamless, but don't worry if it takes a few times. They won't show you from the waist down."

"Okay," I state.

He continues explaining the scene and then a few people trickle back in before we start shooting.

We film a slow and romantic undressing scene before we wind up on the bed. Roman has to straddle my legs, his body movements slow and sexy as he simulates riding me. We keep eye contact as my hands lightly grip his hips, and then he releases a groan as he drops his head back.

I watch his Adam's apple as he swallows, and I swallow too. He drops lower, bracing himself on his arms as he gently rubs his nose against mine, closing his eyes.

"I've been waiting for this moment."

My tongue darts out to lick my lips as I run my hands up his back. "Me too."

The director tells us to stop, and we end up re-recording to get close ups on certain parts and re-do a couple things, then we film the part where I roll us over and rock into him.

When I get him to his back, he lifts one of his legs as I

hold onto it, pressing it closer to me. I move forward and he closes his eyes, his teeth sinking into his lip.

"Look at me," I whisper.

His eyes flicker open, lust reflecting in their depths as his lips part. I lie over him, my face nuzzling into his neck.

He arches, inhaling deeply through his nose before whispering, "Jacoby."

I freeze, my heart slamming against my chest as my breath stutters. I pull back to see his slightly widened eyes before he melts into the bed, his head turning toward the camera. "Sorry."

I let go of him and back away, giving him a tight smile when he looks at me sheepishly.

"Let's start from the roll over," the director calls out.

We film the scene over and over again. Each take gets better, but the first time is caught in a web of thoughts.

Yes, we're acting. No, this means nothing. He was caught up in the moment and a slip of the tongue is all it was. I've done it before. Almost every actor has to have called someone by their real name in a scene.

But my name on his lips, whispered huskily and desperately, is something that will remain with me for a long time, because even though he doesn't know it, I've had a crush on him for years.

CHAPTER TWELVE

A LITTLE OVER TWO YEARS AGO, ROMAN WAS MAKING A name for himself outside of the teen comedy show, *In School Suspension*, he'd been on for a few years. He landed a really good supporting role as Luna Miller's son in *Broken* in which he had me enraptured every time he was on the screen.

There was also a short indie film titled *X Marks the Spot*, where he played a sociopath who led the cops on a goose chase as they tried to find the teenage son of one of the police officers.

He was incredible, and I quickly became intrigued by him. I had already had a couple well-received films under my belt, and I thought I could use some of the perks of being a celebrity and get some info about him.

I was, and still am, in the closet. I had and have no clue about how he may identify, but I wanted to be his friend— acquaintance at the very least. I just wanted to know him.

We had a mutual friend, and when I knew Lance was going to be hanging out with Roman, I told him to bring me up in a casual way and if he showed interest, get his information and I'd reach out.

It had the potential of being extremely awkward, but I trusted Lance to figure it out. Turns out, it ended up worse than awkward. Lance told me that someone else in their group had been talking about me, but he caught on toward the end of the conversation when he heard Roman say, "Fuck no. Why would I like that guy? I'm not gay. Gross. What the fuck?" Lance pushed his way into the convo to get more info, and said it was clear Roman and a couple of his friends were laughing and making fun of me. He said some of the jokes bordered on homophobia.

Knowing what Roman had said left a bitter taste in my mouth and informed me he held no interest in getting to know me.

It was maybe eight months later that he approached me at an event, but his words that were said behind my back were still very much in the forefront of my mind. At that time, I figured he was being fake and wanted to get close to me for the sake of a role he was trying out for in a movie I was already cast in. Instead of arguing or having a confrontation in front of dozens of cameras, I simply gave him a tight smile and walked away. I didn't think I was being rude, but I know I didn't go out of my way to be friendly either.

"Hey, how are you?"

I'm snapped out of my thoughts by Jessica's question. I turn and find she's walking alongside me as I make my way to wardrobe.

"Oh. I'm good. How about you?"

"Good," she chirps with a smile. "Nearing the end of our time here. It's crazy, right?"

"Yeah. Went by fast."

She nervously tugs on the strings of her hoodie, and when I glance over, I notice she's biting down on her bottom lip.

"Um. I know there's gonna be a wrap party, but Naomi

and I were thinking about having a little something just for us."

"Oh yeah? Who's us?"

She smiles. "You know, me, you, Naomi, Mila, Eric, Marco, Steve, and Rome."

"Oh." I nod my head. "Yeah, maybe."

Jessica nudges me a little with her elbow, peering up at me with big brown eyes. "Come on. It'll be fun."

I spot Roman walking toward us, already dressed and ready for our next scene. His eyes lock onto mine, his face stoic. Then his eyes drop to Jessica, and a smile stretches across his face.

"Hey, Jess."

"Hey, Rome. Convince Jacoby to come to our party."

Roman stops short and Jessica's steps come to a halt, too. I freeze in place, wishing I didn't have to play the part of Roman's friend right now.

His dark eyes scour my face. "Is he being a boring old man again?"

I look up to the sky, shaking my head slightly. "I'm not boring."

"No?" Roman questions. "Then why don't you want to party with us?"

"Maybe I don't like to be around certain drunk assholes."

Roman's jaw clenches, but he forces a smile and looks at Jess. "I told you he doesn't like anyone."

My gaze bounces between them both. "I do like people. I just…"

"Think you're better than them?"

Once again, my eyes fall to Jess. She's looking at us with a very confused expression. Roman's no longer playing the part of being on friendly terms with me.

"Definitely not, Roman. I, unlike others, tend to like people until given a reason not to."

He widens his stance, slipping his hands in the pockets of his black jacket. "Huh. Did we all give you a reason to not like us, and that's why you're refusing to hang out with your co-stars?"

My nostrils flare. "Not everyone."

"What's going on here?" Jess finally asks. "Did y'all get into a fight? Are the internet rumors true?"

Both Roman and I drop our staring contest to look at her.

"What rumors?" I ask.

"You know, that you still hold a grudge against Roman for dating Faye. That y'all have a competition type thing going on. That you basically don't like him."

My eyes flicker over and find Roman already watching me.

"I thought people loved seeing us together on set," he says.

Jess pulls out her phone. "Well, yeah, some do. Others still talk about the love triangle situation and wonder if y'all are gonna end up fighting it out." She turns and holds up her phone. "Look."

Roman and I gather behind her, gazing down at her screen. "What's this?" he asks.

"A poll on Twitter."

"Do you think Jacoby is over Rome stealing his girl?" I read it aloud before standing up straight. "Honestly, I don't give a shit about that. I don't know why people are so focused on it."

Roman's eyes look me up and down slowly before he focuses back on Jessica's phone. "Most people believe you are not over it."

"Then there's this," Jessica says, pointing to something on her screen.

"When was this?" Roman asks.

She shrugs. "Whoever's in charge of the *Another Life* social media accounts posted it.*"*

I inch my way back over and find a candid shot of me and Roman on set. He's talking to someone else that can't be seen in the photo, and I'm on a chair nearby, looking up at him like he hung the moon.

I swallow, not realizing I've been so unguarded. What other photos exist?

"They love this one of you two. People are shipping you."

"What?" Roman asks with an unbelievable laugh.

"And then there's this post where they bring up the interview Jacoby gave where he said he hoped you didn't play his brother."

I sigh, running a hand through my hair. "It wasn't an interview that I *gave.* It was a random question shouted at me by someone on a rcd carpet. I was caught off guard and slightly unsure what they were even talking about."

"That's bullshit," Roman barks, looking at me.

"Believe what you want. I have to go."

"So, you guys aren't friends or...?" Jessica lets the question hang between us, but nobody answers.

I pull my gaze from Roman and walk away, letting him deal with responding to that.

CHAPTER THIRTEEN

REGARDLESS OF WHATEVER DISDAIN ROMAN HOLDS FOR ME for whatever reason, he's a good enough actor to not let it be obvious amongst everyone else. Jessica is probably the only one who questions the authenticity of our friendship, but to her credit, she hasn't brought it up again since our little blow up last week.

We get through our scenes like professionals, and we interact with each other on low levels around the cast and crew. We've taken photos together and with others, and also made sure to record little snippets for our personal social media accounts.

The fans go crazy for it. Any photo I post of the two of us is immediately inundated with comments from people speculating about our relationship. If anyone doubts our friendship or whether I'm still mad about the Faye fiasco, the amount of people who don't seem to care outnumber them by the thousands.

When we're released for the night, I bury myself in my jacket as I trek to my trailer for my things before I'm to be driven back to the hotel. An arm slips through mine before I'm halfway there.

"Please come over tonight."

I look down at Jess whose nose is red from the cold. She pops out her bottom lip in a pout, pulling a laugh from me.

"I'm sure you'll have a good time without me. Roman's not completely off the mark when he says I'm boring. I'm not one for drinking and dancing. But also, don't tell him I told you that."

She laughs. "Prove him wrong. Come have a drink. If you want. No pressure. But come have fun. I am pressuring you to do that. We've had this incredible experience together and we should celebrate."

"We're not quite done yet."

"Yeah, but let's party with everyone under thirty now and be professional with the rest of them next week. You're not old, Jacoby. I'm twenty-seven and I still know how to have fun. Let's party like the college students we're playing."

We come to a stop in front of my trailer where she peers up at me expectantly, hope brimming in her eyes.

"Okay, fine. But I make no promises on how long I stay. Roman can be insufferable."

She squeals and wraps her arms around me briefly before stepping back. "My hotel room. 712. Around ten o'clock."

I nod. "I'll be there."

At nine-thirty, I step out of my shower and dry off before looking through my closet for something to wear. I won't have to leave the hotel so I don't need to worry about dressing for the weather. I throw on a pair of jeans, a dark gray long-sleeved shirt, and some tennis shoes.

After putting a little moisturizing curl cream in my hair, I spray a couple spritzes of cologne and slide my key card into my back pocket.

In the hall, I press the button on the elevator to take me down the couple of floors, but before it reaches my level, a door opens up to my left and Roman steps into the hall.

God help me.

"Oh lord," he says aloud when he spots me. "You're actually going. Well, color me surprised."

I take in his outfit—a green shirt that looks like it may be made of silk. There are splashes of gold and orange flowers against the emerald color. He's got the first couple buttons of his shirt undone, and he's paired it with a nice pair of black slacks. A gold watch circles his wrist. He's a bit all over the place. This, on anyone else in the world, would probably look ridiculous. He makes it work.

"Looks like you got the color part covered."

He snorts. "You're just mad you can't pull this off."

"Who wears jungle-themed shirts? Except, of course, children."

The elevator doors open up and we step inside. "I guess it's the Colombian in me."

"You're Colombian?"

"Half."

"What's the other half?"

He rests against the bar on the opposite side of the elevator, his gaze penetrating. "You want to be my friend now?"

"I don't know what I want with you," I reply honestly. "Mostly I just want to choke you so you stop talking."

His teeth sink into his bottom lip as he grins at me. "If you don't want me to talk, stop asking me questions."

"I'm trying to be nice," I say through gritted teeth.

He chuckles. "Do you usually choke the people you're *nice* to?"

One brow goes up. "Sometimes."

His smile falls and curious eyes watch me. My heart bangs against my ribs, and I'm grateful when the elevator doors open.

Halfway down the hall, his phone rings from behind me. "Hey, Emmy. I'm on my way to a party right now. Yeah, call me later."

"I take it Emmy is Emerson. One of your alphabet girls."

Roman laughs. "You're almost right, Jacoby. Almost."

I don't get to question him because he pushes open the door that's kept cracked by the door guard lock.

"Party's here," he announces as he struts in, arms spread wide and up in the air. "And the party pooper," he continues, pointing to me.

I roll my eyes but greet Jessica and Naomi with a smile.

"You made it!" Jess squeaks. "I thought for sure you'd bail last minute."

"We have shots," Naomi says, grabbing a couple of small, neon-colored plastic cups. "The blue and green cups are dark liquor. Whiskey and bourbon. The pink and red are clear liquor. Just vodka, really."

"We also have some beer in the fridge and juices and sodas for mixers. Eric ordered some wings and pizza, and he should be up here soon with that," Jess says.

"To the first guests," Naomi says, grabbing a pink cup and holding it in the air.

Jess picks up a blue one and does the same while Roman grabs a green one and sniffs it. "Is this Crown?"

"Yeah, it's Crown Apple which is why I put it in the green cups," Naomi says with a grin.

"Want one?" he asks, looking at me over his shoulder.

"Yeah."

His brows lift in surprise but he doesn't say anything. The four of us tap our little plastic cups together and down the first shots of the night.

Within fifteen minutes, Eric and Marco show up with the food. Steve and Mila stroll in a few minutes after, looking like they might've been making out right before. Mila's lipstick is a little smudged, and Steve's hair is mussed up, and they both can't stop smiling and laughing at each other.

Jess has the music up at a decent level. Considering her closest neighbors are in this room, there likely won't be any complaints. The lights are low, and the TV is on but muted.

After eating a half dozen wings, I mix some whiskey with a Coke and stand near Eric.

"Hopefully you don't end up having to babysit again," he says with a nod toward Roman, who's downing another shot with Jessica and Marco.

"Bastard didn't even have a hangover."

Eric laughs and it gets Roman's attention. He stays locked on me for a few seconds before he turns away.

Progressively over the next hour and a half, everyone starts getting a little drunker. I had another shot with everyone about an hour ago and have the remnants of my first drink settling in the bottom of my cup right now.

While Roman attempts to get someone to do a body shot off of him, I find my way out onto the balcony. It may be cold, but I need a breather. It only takes a few minutes before I'm ready to go back inside, but before I can, Roman joins me.

"What're you doing out here?"

"Just…" I can't think of a reasonable excuse. "Just hanging out."

Roman laughs. "You want to go back to your room so bad, don't you?"

I glance at him, a small smile tugging at my lips. "I'm not about to be the first one. You'll never let me hear the end of it."

"Are you an extreme introvert where social settings fill you with anxiety?"

"I'm an introvert, but I can function. It's not anxiety that I feel, but…self-consciousness, I guess."

"Self-conscious?" he questions, blowing into his hands. "What do you have to be self-conscious about?"

My lips quirk. "Plenty."

"But you're—" I turn around to face him, raising a brow as I wait. "You know, Hollywood's heartthrob."

"There's that word again," I breathe, looking out over the snow-covered land.

"You don't like it?"

"Do you know what the definition is?"

He shrugs. "Someone that everybody thinks is attractive."

"A man that women find attractive. Words like *hunky* and *sexy* are thrown around. You have the ability to make women scream."

"Whoa," Roman says with a smile, holding his hands up.

"I mean at movie premieres and such," I say, giving him a look. "They line up to get a glimpse of you."

"What's wrong with that?"

"I'm an actor. I take it seriously. I want fans and admirers of my work. Not my face." I sigh. "Look, I'd never say this to anyone else, and if you tell anyone, I'll deny it, but it's not that I don't appreciate that people find me attractive. But is that all I have to offer? I don't think so. When they talk about me, I want them to discuss my acting skills, my dedication to the craft, my commitment to a role. I don't care if women think I'm nice to look at."

"Why would you deny saying that?"

"I don't want to come off ungrateful. I'm aware my looks play a part in my popularity, but it comes off a little shallow, right?"

"I mean…it's Hollywood," he says with a shrug. "But I get it." He's quiet for a little bit. "If you tell anyone what I'm about to tell you, I'll deny it."

I turn and face him. "I'm intrigued. Go on."

He chews on his lip like he's really debating on whether to actually tell me. "I watched *Unforgivable Sin* like fifty times. And it wasn't because of your looks. I've always thought of you as an incredible talent. Some people are meant strictly for action roles. Some are always typecast as the goofy, sarcastic character. You, you can do it all. You bring emotion and depth. You're fucking hilarious. You're intense. You're vulnerable. You've showcased it all, and you're still so young. And as much as you may not like it, you *are* attractive, but it's not all you are. Don't let it get to you."

I absorb his words and let them soak in. They mean more to me than I could properly express, so I simply say, "Thank you."

His smile starts crooked and grows into a wide grin. "You're welcome. I still hate you."

"Mm. Seems like you're a fan."

He shakes his head, fighting off a smile. He opens his mouth to say something, but his phone rings.

I watch as he pulls it from his pocket and touches the screen. He holds it in front of him, so I know it's a FaceTime call.

"Emmy!" he shouts with a big smile on his face.

I turn and head for the door so I can leave him to his call

with his ex, but before I can slide it open, he extends his arm like he's calling me over.

"Say hi to Jacoby."

I force a smile and prepare myself to see another blonde-haired, blue-eyed ex-girlfriend, but when he angles the phone toward me, I'm met with the face of a man. A blond man, but a man, nonetheless.

CHAPTER FOURTEEN

"HEY," I SAY, SOMEHOW STUTTERING, THROUGH THE THREE-letter word.

"Jacoby Hart. Holy shit," the guy on the screen says.

"I'll leave you to talk," I say, looking at Roman.

Our eyes linger on each other before he remembers he's on a call.

As soon as I step inside, I'm enveloped in the warmth of the stuffy room, and make my way to the bathroom. After relieving my bladder, I wash my hands and try to wrap my head around Roman and Emmy. Emmy has to be Emerson, right? I mean, he doesn't have to be the same one. His name could be Emerald or Emmanuel and Roman just calls him Emmy. It's probably not the same person. And I shouldn't care either way.

But could Roman be bi?

I shake my head and turn off the water. It doesn't matter.

Once my hands are dry, I open the door and find Roman leaning against the wall. I stop short and then continue. "It's all yours."

"You good?" he asks, eyebrows raised slightly.

"Yeah. Of course."

"Are you about to leave?"

"Probably."

He nods once, stepping away from the wall. "Emerson got a kick out of seeing you."

My heart pounds. "Emerson." I repeat the name back to him, making sure I'm not hearing things.

"Yeah. Bleach blond guy on the phone?" he says with a smirk.

"Right. Yeah," I say slowly, surveying him carefully.

He watches me like he's waiting for me to ask him something—to force him to clarify what I'm thinking.

"I guess I could've been nicer."

"Well, that's just not you, is it?" he says with a teasing grin before walking into the bathroom.

"It's not you either," I say to myself before turning around and walking to the living area.

Before I can open my mouth to announce my departure, Jessica rushes up and puts her arm around my waist.

"Jacobyyyyy." She draws out my name in a pitchy squeal. "Eric's being mean to me."

Eric gives me a look. "I told her to drink some water. Yes, I'm an asshole."

Jess grabs my arm and looks up at me with hooded eyes. She's clearly drunk, and it's probably best she does drink water instead of whiskey.

"Wow, Eric. Let the girl drink," I say.

"Yeah," she pipes in, sticking close to my side.

Eric knits his brows at me.

"Let me go get some shots, okay?" I tell her, sitting her down on the couch before handing her an open bag of chips.

"Thank you! You're the best."

Roman emerges from the hall, looking around. "Who's the best?"

"Jacoby," Jess says. "He's getting us more shots."

"Is he now?"

Roman follows me to the counter in the kitchenette where I have Eric lining up the colorful plastic cups.

"Make sure you eat those chips!" I call out, making eye contact with Jess.

She's already chewing. "Yes, sir!"

"I'm not giving her more alcohol. She's already fucking wasted. Pour water in these, pretend it's alcohol when you drink it. She may not notice at this point. Pour some apple juice or something in it for flavor.

"Apple water?" Roman questions with a disgusted look. "Squeeze a drop of lemon juice in it. She needs something that'll make her screw up her face. She'll assume it's liquor because it'll have that bitter taste."

"That works. They have one of those lemon concentrate things over here," Eric says, grabbing the yellow and green bottle.

"Guess you're sticking around, huh?" Roman asks, sliding up next to me to help pour the drinks.

"Just for a little."

Between the three of us, we end up with eight shots, and surround Jessica on the couch.

"All right. Here we go," I say, handing her the first shot of lemon water.

"Yay!"

The four of us clink our cups together and drink it down. We all watch her, waiting for her response.

She purses her lips. "Ooh. What is that?"

"Uh, Jacoby made it. You know he probably likes weird drinks," Roman says.

I give him an exasperated look. "Let's do another one!" I say, handing her the next cup.

She takes it and we all drink our faux liquor shots.

"This tastes a little weird."

"Sorry," I say, biting my lip. "I mixed some stuff up that you had over there."

"Oh god. Am I gonna get sick?"

"No, no. It wasn't anything crazy."

"Should we play a game?" she asks, eyes going wide with excitement.

I look at Eric and Roman, hoping for help.

"What kind of game?" Roman asks instead.

"I don't know. What are they doing?" she asks, pointing to Mila, Naomi, Steve, and Marco.

"They're playing slapjack," Eric says.

"Bo-ring!" Jess calls out, standing up only to fall back into my lap. "Oops."

I hold onto her and lean back. "Wanna go get something to eat with me?"

"Like a date?" she asks.

My eyes find Roman who's holding in a laugh.

"Let's go to the kitchen."

"Oh. Okay."

I pile two slices of pizza on a plate and warm it up in the microwave before placing it in front of her. Next to it, I leave her a glass of water, and then warm up a few more wings for myself.

She smiles at me as she chews. "I bet you're really tired of taking care of drunk people."

I chuckle. "I didn't really take care of Roman. I just made sure he made it back to the hotel safe."

"That's taking care of him. He said you helped him with his contacts."

My chest feels tight. "Oh. Yeah, it wasn't a big deal. The dumbass was about to poke his eye out."

She laughs before taking another bite. "I don't believe the rumors."

"Which ones?" I ask, licking sauce off my thumb.

"That you hate him."

I look over her shoulder and find Roman watching me as Eric talks to him. He quickly averts his gaze.

"Only sometimes."

"You guys have really good chemistry. People will see it when this movie comes out."

After she finishes her first slice, she wipes her mouth with a napkin. "I think he has a crush on you, too," she says with a drunken snort.

My chest feels warm and my stomach clenches. I don't know how I'm even supposed to approach that comment, but curiosity gets the best of me.

"Who? Roman? No way."

She peeks over at him before looking up at me. "He talks about you a lot."

"Yeah. Probably talks shit."

"You know what they say about the thin line between love and hate."

My eyes skate over his body as he leans against the wall, a wide smile on his face as he talks to Naomi. I don't know how long I look, but it's too long. Jess follows my gaze before picking up her second slice.

I clear my throat. "You said he has a crush on me *too*. Who else does?"

She blushes, giving herself away. "I don't know. You don't really date, though, do you?"

"Not really. No."

"Are you—"

Panic seizes my lungs. All of a sudden I'm hot and sweating, and my stomach is in knots. I can't let her finish that question. I can't keep staring at Roman. I have to leave.

I pull my phone from my pocket and lie. "Oh. It's from my sister. I have to take this. I'll see you tomorrow, okay?"

"Oh. Yeah," she replies with a nod.

I quickly say goodbye to the whole room before rushing out into the hall. My finger jams at the elevator button like pressing it fifty times will make it come faster.

Was she about to ask if I was gay? She caught me watching Roman. This is why I hate going out and drinking. It loosens your inhibitions. It makes you let down your guard. Everyone will see the real you.

The elevator arrives and takes its sweet time to open the doors. Roman appears at my left, emerging from the room.

No, no, no, I think to myself, rushing into the elevator to slam my finger on the number nine.

Heavy footsteps echo in the hall. Fast. The doors are closing, and I can almost breathe a sigh of relief, but then a large shoe slides between the doors, forcing them open.

I let out an exasperated sigh.

"What's wrong?" he asks.

"Nothing. Why?" I reply with a bite.

"You said your sister called." His eyes scan me, noticing I'm not on the phone. "I thought there was an emergency."

"Well, there's not."

He finally comes all the way inside and lets the doors close.

"Roman, you can't come after me. What are they gonna think?"

His brows draw in. "Who? Jess and them?"

"Yes, of course."

"That I cared about my friend who may or may not have

had a family emergency. What's wrong with you? You look so panicked. Are you sure nothing happened?"

The doors open on the ninth floor and I storm out of the enclosed space. "Yes, I'm sure."

I'm not sure. Did she realize?

"Did you make up a fake family emergency to get out of the party?"

"No, Roman," I say on an exhale, pulling out my key card. "Can you leave me alone, please?"

"If you lied about your family being hurt or something, that's some real fucked up shit, because—"

I push open the door at the same time I explode. "God-dammit, Roman! I just said I had a call. What the fuck is it to you anyway?"

He follows me in. "You didn't have a call, though. Why are you so jittery?"

I slam my key on the table and whirl around, staring at him.

"Is this because of Emerson?" he asks.

"What?"

He slides his hands in his pockets, his shoulders slumping forward. "I know you remember me saying I'd been with an Emerson. You just had no clue it was a guy until tonight, right? Are you freaking out? Because…well, because of this movie and us and…I don't know. What's going on in your head?"

I let out a slightly maniacal laugh as I spin around and run my fingers through my hair, taking steps toward the window. "My god. I don't know. I don't know what I'm thinking."

"I don't want you to feel weird about it. I thought I could open up to you since you told me about your feelings on only being seen as a pretty face. I don't know." I spin around and find him with his fingers interlocked behind his head. "I don't know what I was thinking."

"What are you telling me right now?"

He drops his arms and walks toward me. "I haven't told people. Emerson knows. Obviously."

"That you're…" I wait for him to finish it for me. I have to hear him say it to know I'm not crazy.

"Bisexual."

I let out another humorless laugh as I walk aimlessly around the room. "Bisexual. You're bisexual."

His loud steps let me know he's getting closer. "Don't fucking laugh about it. I thought you'd be cool about this considering you took this role." Roman's large hand lands on my shoulder to spin me around.

"But you…you said. I—"

Roman looks at me like I've lost my mind, but he's crowding my space and has forced me into a wall. His brows are furrowed and his jaw tense, and he's unbelievably close. So close I can smell the scent of his cologne and feel the soft exhales of his breath.

My eyes fall to his lips and then back to his eyes. "I… I'm…I don't have a problem with that," I say quietly.

His eyes scan my face. "Good."

Seconds pass. *One. Two.* He's still watching me. *Three. Four.* There's something in his gaze that makes my heart squeeze. *Five.* He takes a step back but I reach out and clasp my fingers around his wrist.

He glances down at my hand, his gaze frozen at the contact. I wait for him to look me in the eyes, but it's like he's afraid to move past this point. When he finally allows his eyes to travel away from my fingers around his wrist, it's a slow journey. He traces my forearm, bicep, shoulder, collarbone, and then I finally look into the dark depths of his eyes.

We communicate with nothing more than the expressions on our faces and miniscule movements. His confusion is showcased by the dip in his brows and slight frown on his lips. I shake my head slightly, giving the tiniest shrug to let him know I'm confused but going with it.

He rotates his wrist to pull out of my grip only to then wrap his fingers around my forearm. We get locked into a staring contest that neither of us wants to pull away from, asking permission and awaiting rejection all at the same time.

When he leans in just slightly, I grab ahold of his arm and pull him the rest of the way. His body slams into mine, and then our mouths connect for the first time as Jacoby and Roman, and it's the most magical moment of my life.

ROMAN

CHAPTER FIFTEEN

My lips brush against his, softly at first. Nervous, confused, and shocked; they forget how to work until he sucks in a shuddering breath, releasing a quiet moan.

He clutches my shirt in his fist, keeping me close to him. I rest my hand on his hip, lightly gripping him there. When he opens his mouth to suck in a small gasp, I let my tongue dance across his bottom lip before sliding it between his teeth to taste and explore more of him.

It doesn't take long before our slow and cautious kiss takes a turn and we become feverish and full of desire.

Jacoby wraps his arms around me and spins, pinning me to the wall. I reach up and rest my hand on the side of his neck before running my fingers through his hair.

His tongue glides over mine, and he kisses me like he hates that he's doing it—hates that he's enjoying it so much.

When he finally pulls away, he rests his forehead on mine, both of us reduced to heavy breaths and straining erections.

"Fuck." He backs up and avoids looking at me.

I stand up straight and wait a few seconds. "So—"

"I don't know," he replies instantly, turning around and removing his shirt to reveal an undershirt underneath.

"You're…"

"Gay? Yes," he spits, kicking off his shoes. "And I'm pretty sure that's what Jessica was about to ask me at the party. That's why I left."

I walk toward him. "What do you mean?"

"She was talking about how I don't date and then started to ask if I was gay, I think. I cut her off and said I had a call. She caught me looking at you. I know she did. It was too much."

My brows draw in as my eyes bounce around, trying to keep up with all the thoughts firing off in my brain. I don't know where to start.

Once he has his shoes off, he makes his way to the couch and sits down, his eyes finally landing on me.

Slowly, I make my way closer, choosing to sit in a chair across from him. "So, you *really* didn't care about the Faye thing."

His face remains stoic for a few seconds, and I begin to think maybe I messed up starting with that, but then he laughs. His smile is wide and his eyes light up in a way I'm not sure I've seen before. He runs a hand through his hair as he shakes his head, his laughter dying down.

"Faye was a beard. I needed her to keep the rumors at bay."

"Were there rumors?" I ask, never having heard anything before.

"Nothing that spread wide. Friends were always curious why I'd never go out with a woman, or never showed interest in women. Considering I'm, you know—"

"Hot?"

He laughs. "No. Well, kind of." He waves a hand through

the air. "I was hoisted up as this eligible bachelor, you know? I *should* be dating all the Hollywood starlets. Why wouldn't I be taking advantage of my *status*, you know? Anyway, I like Faye. Going on dates with her wasn't a chore. We're really good friends."

"Does she know?"

"She does now. She didn't in the beginning."

I nod. There's still a lot to question, but my mind is spinning from the kiss, and it's all I can think about.

"You kissed me."

His brow arches slightly as his lips curl up on one end. "You leaned in first."

"You grabbed me."

He rolls his eyes. "Okay, so what's the question?"

"You like me?"

Jacoby runs his fingers across his forehead in a nervous gesture. "I liked you almost three years ago."

My brows lift. "What?"

He shakes his head. "I was a fan of your work. I was attracted to you." His shoulders raise with a shrug. "I wanted to know you. I had a friend who was friends with one of your friends. I knew he was going to be out with you all and just asked him to see if he could get your information so I could reach out."

I shake my head, confusion etched on my face. "Why didn't he?"

"Well, apparently someone brought my name up that night. Your response was to question why you'd like me because you weren't gay and that it was gross. I guess there was some laughter and jokes between you and your friends afterward."

I stare at him, noticing the hurt in his gaze.

My lips begin to curl up and I shake my head as I stand,

pacing around until I come to a stop behind the soft high back chair.

"Okay, so this is going to be hard to explain." He raises his brows as he nods his head once, waiting for me to continue. "Well, so, funny thing…" I let out a small chuckle as I brush my hand through my hair. "Um. Well, I told you I was a fan of yours, right? Like, I watched your movies, as well. I guess I was too vocal in my praise for you, and I had friends questioning why I was so *obsessed*. Their words. I was *not* obsessed."

He grins. "Mmhmm."

"Anyway. They would tease me about having a crush on you or whatever. Just dumb stuff. That night, I don't remember how the conversation started, but yeah, someone mentioned your name. I had already been harassed about liking you for a while and I was around new people, and I just said it. I didn't realize how it would come off. I was halfway to drunk, and nervous about being with some other actors who were far more established than I was, and I…I was dumb. I think the comment was from some actress who liked you and she was going on and on about how sexy you were, and your eyes, and smile, and who knows what else, and when someone asked if I liked you I said what I said, because I was deflecting. I *was* attracted to you, and I was coming to terms with my bisexuality while deep in the closet, and…" I shrug. "I'm sorry."

He's quiet for a while. "So, you *are* a fan? And slightly obsessed."

I snort and walk around the chair to sit back down. I ignore his comment and say, "Are you saying we could've been friends three years ago?"

He shrugs. "Maybe. Who knows?"

"And now?"

Jacoby sits up. "What do you mean?"

"Well…I don't know. Are we friends now? Or?"

"We can try being friends," he says, fighting a smile.

"Platonic friends?"

"What are you really asking, Roman?"

The way he's looking at me has my heart racing. Suddenly it's hard to maintain eye contact, so I pretend to be focused on the lining of the arm of the chair.

"I don't know, just wondering."

I hear him make a noise, but he doesn't say anything. Instead, he stands from the couch and takes a few strides to get to me. My gaze flickers up when he stops near my chair.

"You usually have plenty to say," he tells me. "Don't lose your words now."

I stand, facing him as I swallow down these newfound nerves. "I guess I don't know how to talk to you unless I'm giving you a hard time."

His eyebrow quirks, his lips twitching. "Hmm."

I shake my head, a smile stretching across my face. "I didn't mean it like that."

"Too bad."

My eyebrows shoot up, surprised by his boldness. I've only ever thought of him as some stuck up, pompous jerk.

"Have you…had many experiences before?" I ask, getting an air of confidence from him.

"Yes. Very, very discreet experiences that were protected by NDAs. And before I was famous, I had a few, minor experiences."

"You've been acting for a decade."

"I've been gay my whole life."

I nod. "Okay, so, you know what you're doing then."

He laughs. "Don't you? You were with Emerson."

"I've *only* been with Emerson."

Jacoby cocks his head slightly. "Are you still?"

"No! No, no. We're not together. We were each other's firsts. We sort of did our experimentation with each other and then we gradually did more and more."

He studies me for a few seconds. "Okay." He nods once, his eyes lingering on my mouth for a few seconds before looking me in the eye. "So, did you have a question?"

"I have a lot of them," I say with a chuckle, nervously running my hand through my hair.

"Do you need to ask them now or can I kiss you first?"

I swallow. "Oh."

"You're clearly not gonna do it. You can't even say you want to."

"Well, I—"

He steps forward and prevents me from stuttering through a response by hauling my body against his and planting his lips on mine. His tongue slides into my mouth as his fingers splay across the middle of my back.

I moan against his lips, my hands roaming up and down his sides and back, not knowing where to touch him and yet wanting to touch every part of him.

"I would've said it," I say between kisses.

"You would've danced around it," he replies before angling his head and parting my lips with his tongue. "Like you were already doing."

I pull away slightly. "I was getting there." I plant small pecks across his neck.

"So, where are you going now?" he questions as my hand travels over his hip and toward his ass.

I freeze in place and he chuckles.

"Shut up," I say, cupping his ass and erasing any space between us as I bring us close enough to feel just how much we've been enjoying our kiss.

When our erections grind together, Jacoby moans into my neck before gently biting on the flesh. A spark of electricity shoots down my spine and I grab his head and keep him in place.

"Yeah."

His tongue swipes over the skin before he repeats the bite.

Pulling away, he looks at me. "I can't leave a mark. Makeup might get suspicious when they have to cover it up."

"I have other areas you could suck on."

Once again, Jacoby's brows lift, amusement playing on his lips.

"I didn't—" I think to say I didn't mean that, but I go with it. "You know what? I'm not opposed."

Jacoby lets out a full laugh, and the sound of it makes my smile grow wider.

"I feel like I've never heard you laugh until today. Outside of acting."

He takes a step to the side and rests his butt on the arm of the couch. Crossing his arms, he says, "I always feel like I'm acting. There are very few people who know the truth, therefore I'm not comfortable being myself around everyone."

I nod. "Well—"

Before I get the next word out, there's pounding on the door.

Jacoby and I look at each other with furrowed brows. The top three floors of the hotel are reserved for people working on the movie, so it has to be someone we know. Without a word, he makes his way to the door. The knocking continues the entire time, and when he pulls it open, Jessica's voice filters in.

"Hey, I wanted to check on you. Is everything okay?"

I watch as his posture stiffens slightly. "Oh. Yeah, everything's fine. Are you okay? Where's Eric?"

"Back in the room. I couldn't find my phone, but I wanted to make sure you were okay."

"Oh. Well, that's nice of you. I'm fine. Thank you."

There's an awkward silence, and I wonder if Jess is hoping for an invitation to come in. She can't see me and I doubt Jacoby wants her to know I'm here, so I remain still and quiet and wait to see what comes next.

"Okay," she says. "I guess I'll head back to my room."

"Do you need me to walk you back?" he offers.

"No. No, it's okay. I'm gonna try to find Rome. I'll uhh see you later."

When Jacoby closes the door, he leans against it and his shoulders slump.

"She really likes you," I say quietly, walking closer. "Now I kind of feel bad."

He sighs. "Well." His shoulders rise and fall with a shrug and he doesn't elaborate.

"I guess I should go if she's gonna be looking for me."

"Your room is right next door. If she's looking for you, she's still in the hall. I'd give it a minute."

"If you want me to stay, just ask."

He rolls his eyes and pushes away from the door. He grabs two bottles of water and tosses one to me. We talk for a couple more minutes before making sure the coast is clear. I pause at the door, wondering if I should kiss him again, but our situation is so weird. We went from hating each other over misunderstandings to making out. We're not together. We can't be. We're both hiding huge parts of ourselves, but we're clearly attracted to each other. I have no idea what will happen, if anything, past tonight.

"Goodnight."

He smiles. "Goodnight, Roman."

CHAPTER SIXTEEN

I DON'T SEE JACOBY UNTIL WE'RE ON SET AND READY TO FILM an argument scene that leads to passionate declarations.

We both have each other's phone numbers, but after I left his room two nights ago, he didn't reach out, so I didn't either.

"Ready to fight?" Jacoby's voice hits my ear as he approaches from behind, stopping in front of me.

"Huh?"

"The scene."

"Oh. Yeah. Should be easy."

He grins, his eyes flickering around. "Unless you like me too much now."

My heart gallops in my chest. "Please. You're not that good of a kisser."

His gaze drops to my mouth. "Hmm."

Then he's gone, turning around and walking away, leaving me desperate for more of his attention. What the hell happened to me?

In place, we get ready for the director to call out *action* and when he does, Jacoby begins.

"You can't force me into this, Andrew. You know how I feel about you. You have to! It's just not as easy for me."

"I'm not forcing you to come out, William. I just want to know where I stand. We've been doing this back and forth thing for almost a year now. I come here and we sneak around. You come to me and we're open and free. I love both. I love every second I spend with you, and because it's you, I'll wait. I'll wait for as long as you need, but I have to know I'm not wasting my time."

"Oh. I'm sorry for wasting your time," he bellows.

"That's not what I said and you know it. Every time I attempt to tell you how I feel, you run away. But haven't you noticed that I'm always chasing you? I'm not giving up."

"I'm fucking terrified, Andrew! Your family and friends accept you. I could very well blow up my entire life. And then what? What will I have then?"

I walk forward and let my fingers skate down from his elbow to his fingers, interlocking mine with his. "You will have me. You're guarded. I understand that. But you don't have to be guarded with me. I want to be the person you feel at home with. I want you to be open and vulnerable with me because you know I won't judge you. I'm your safe space, William."

He squeezes my hand, releasing a shuddering breath as his eyes water. "I know. I'm sorry." His free hand runs through his hair. "I tried talking to my parents the other day, and I didn't get much out before they made it very clear I'd be unable to have a conversation with them. They are who they are. They won't accept me when I tell them, and that hurts. They adopted me. They gave me a better life than I would've had, and to know they'd give me up based on who I love breaks my heart."

I reach up and wipe a tear from his cheek. "I will love you unconditionally."

He studies my face, eyes scanning every inch. "I love you."

We come together for a kiss and the director calls out, "Cut!"

"What're you doing for Christmas?" Jacoby asks me as we eat lunch at one of the tables set up for the cast.

I twist the cap on the water bottle in my hands. "I don't know. I'm going to see if my sister's free."

"Where do you live?" he questions, taking a bite of a watermelon cube.

"Sherman Oaks area. You?"

"Pasadena."

"It'll be nice to be back in California and away from all this snow."

He laughs. "You're supposed to have snow for Christmas."

"I disagree."

"If we weren't packing up here to finish filming in California, I'd definitely prefer spending the holiday here."

"That's probably because you're crazy."

"There's just something nice about being in a cabin with the snow falling outside, a fire lit in the living room, and the smell of apple cider and cinnamon filling the room."

I gawk at him for several seconds. "Holy shit, you're a romantic."

"Shut up," he says, his cheeks turning pink as he looks around to make sure nobody is listening. "It's not romantic, it's cozy."

"Oh my god, you're adorable."

"Stop or I'm going to throw food at you," he says, gazing up at me.

I laugh and he throws a roll at my face. I catch it and take a bite. "Thanks."

After a couple minutes, I swallow and lick my lips. "So, I was thinking—"

"Uh-oh."

"Fuck off," I say with a chuckle, throwing my half-eaten roll back at him.

He catches it before biting into it. "Thanks."

I roll my eyes and shake my head. "Anyway, I was thinking maybe we should get together again…soon. Before you fly out."

For some ungodly reason I feel my cheeks warm up, and my chest tightens as my heart tries to escape.

He leans back in his chair, eyes focused on me as I pretend to not notice. I look at my food, but he's hard to ignore even in my peripherals.

"Look at me."

The command is spoken in a quiet but firm voice and I'm finding I like this other side of him. This side I didn't know.

I move my gaze from the plate in front of me to his face, and my stomach does a flip when I see his expression.

Confidence. Lust. Unmatched beauty.

"You want to spend the night with me."

It's not formed as a question. He already knows the answer. He just wants me to confirm it. He wants to force me to say the words.

There's been no discussion of long-term secret hookups. We haven't even mentioned wanting anything to come of this. All I know is I'm attracted to him. I have been for years, and now that I know it's reciprocated, I'd like to explore it even just a little. Even just once.

My tongue dances across my bottom lip, and his eyes watch the movement. I force confidence I don't feel and say, "Yes. I'd like to spend a night with you."

"Tonight?"

I nod. "Okay."

He stands up and takes his plate, peering down at me with an intense and promising gaze. Holy shit. I don't know what I just got myself into, but I'm both excited and nervous as hell.

"See you later," he says.

"Yeah. See you."

He strolls past me and it takes everything in me to not turn around and watch him disappear, but Jess walks around shortly after and plops herself into his abandoned seat.

"Oh my god, I'm still so embarrassed."

"About what?" I ask, forcing myself not to think about tonight.

"How I got super drunk and was attempting to flirt with Jacoby. Do you think he knew? Think he's gonna avoid me now?"

I shake my head. "I think he's fine."

She reaches over to my plate and takes a grape. "Well, I definitely don't think he's into me. Doesn't really seem to be into anybody. Do you know if he's dating anyone? I was going to ask him but he got a phone call."

I remember his panic when he thought she was going to ask if he was gay. I'll be happy to let him know that wasn't the case.

"I don't think so," I say, clearing my throat. "He's pretty private, though. You know? Also, what happened to *I don't date my co-stars*? Was that just you trying to let me down easy?" I tease.

She barks out a laugh. "I really don't, but he's Jacoby Hart."

I sigh. "Yeah."

"He's hot."

"Yeah."

She cuts her eyes to me. "Oh really?"

"What?" I sit up and reach for my water.

"You into your friend, Rome? Because I've been getting vibes."

I choke out a laugh as I stand up. "You're hilarious. No. I'm not *into* him. What does that even mean? And everyone knows he's hot, just like they know I am."

She follows me to the trash can, scoffing. "You talk about him constantly."

"He's my…friend."

The word feels weird on my tongue. We've never been friends, and now we're about to step into something else.

"Well, I wouldn't blame you, but the unrequited love shit is for the birds. So, be careful. Also, are you…" she trails off and I turn to look at her.

"Am I what?"

She shakes her head. "Never mind. It's fine. I'll see you later."

For the rest of the day I overthink every conversation I had where I brought up Jacoby. I didn't realize it would be noticeable to people that I had this *fixation*. If that's what it is. I thought I was doing what I needed to do and letting people think we were really close and got along. I need to be careful that people as perceptive as Jess don't read more into it.

Especially now.

I've been toying with the idea of coming out, but it's scary for anybody to do so, and as an actor who's trying to make it big, I'm afraid it'll do more harm than good. And I hate that I feel that way, but the world isn't perfect.

JACOBY

CHAPTER SEVENTEEN

I DON'T KNOW EXACTLY WHAT ROMAN WAS ALLUDING TO when he said he wanted to spend a night with me, or should I say, I don't know how far he's willing to go.

I'm more experienced than him when it comes to intimacy with men, but I don't know much about his history with Emerson and what he's comfortable with.

Regardless, I'm willing to do whatever he wants to do, even if it means we end up dry humping like teenagers.

Roman doesn't know the extent of my attraction to him, and it's not something I feel comfortable bringing up to him, because we've had a rocky history, and we're hardly on a smooth road now. We cleared up some misconceptions, but we don't know much about each other. However, I don't have to know everything about him to know he's the most attractive man I've ever seen. His confidence and swagger are hard to ignore. When he's on a red carpet—or at any event—my eyes find him immediately. Without trying. He's magnetic and charming, and has a smile that could turn anyone to Jell-O. I feel like he's the exact opposite of me, and part of me envies him.

However, I've noticed an interesting thing about him since our kiss. He's not quite as confident around me as I thought he'd be. His usual bravado turns into timidness, and his big mouth stutters through words. And something about that sends a thrill up my spine.

I'd love to get to know more about him, but every fiber of my being is saying to fight that thought. What will it do aside from make things more complicated? I already struggle with forcing fake relationships with women to keep the media and gossip sites from questioning why I'm single. I act every minute of my life so nobody finds out who I really am. I live in fear that if it ever gets out my career will tank.

On top of that, there're my parents, but I try not to think too much about what their reaction would be.

A knock on the door pulls me out of my reverie. I've showered and done all the preparation needed for whatever tonight brings. I have Netflix on in case it's just watching a movie and making out. Condoms and lube are in the bedroom in case it escalates, and there's food and drinks in the kitchen so we can eat and talk if that's what he wants to do.

Wearing only a T-shirt and sweats, I walk to the door and pull it open. Roman's wearing a neon yellow shirt that's had the sleeves cut off and a pair of black joggers. His facial hair is growing a little thicker since he's able to change it for the next scenes we'll film in California.

"Hey."

I grin and step back, allowing him in. "Hey."

After closing the door, I turn and find him awkwardly standing in the middle of the room, his palms running up and down the sides of his pants.

"You okay?" I ask.

"Yeah," he says too quickly in a voice too high. He adjusts. "Yeah. Fine."

"Want a drink?"

"Please."

I snort and make my way to the bar. "What do you want? Whiskey? Beer?"

He's at my side, studying the small bottles of liquor in the mini fridge. "I'll take this and this," he says, grabbing a Jack Daniels bottle and Coke can.

I close the fridge and watch him take a drink from the liquor bottle before swallowing a large gulp of Coke.

"You want some?" he asks.

"No, thank you." I walk over to the couch and sit down, turning on a movie. "You seem antsy."

"Do I?"

I nod, my lips pressed into a small grin. "A little."

"I guess I'm slightly nervous."

"Why?"

He angles his head over his shoulder, his gaze drinking me in. "I don't know."

"We don't have to do anything. You just wanted to hang out, right? Let's hang out."

Roman gives me a weird look that I can't decipher, but he slowly makes his way over to the couch and sits next to me.

I slide my eyes to him and see that he's doing the same. He turns his attention to the TV first and I follow suit.

Out of the corner of my eye, his head swivels to look at me again, and his hands won't stop rubbing against the couch.

Turning to face him, I ask, "Are you sure you're okay?"

"Look, I just need you…I don't know what to do or what is expected, so I'm all in my head and I don't know—"

I grab his hand and look into his eyes. "Nothing is expected. Tell me what you want."

His eyes bounce between mine before dipping to my mouth and then coming back up. "I want to kiss you."

"What else?"

He inhales deeply and quietly. "To touch you."

"Okay, well you should know I'm very agreeable. Whatever you want to do, I'm okay with."

Roman swallows before licking his lips. "Is there anything you're *not* okay with?"

"Are you about to get real kinky on me?"

He laughs, releasing some tension in his body. "No. Not yet, but you already told me you like choking."

I grin, my chuckle spilling out. "Well, I can control myself."

Roman's gaze darkens slightly. "Yes, you're very in control. I like that."

I cock a brow and things start coming together. "Hmm."

There's something quite endearing about his nervousness, and since I can be myself around him now, I love how our roles have flipped. I'm the confident one. The one with the bravado. Behind closed doors, with him, I can be me without any acting.

"Roman, come here," I say, jerking my head slightly. He scoots closer until our legs are touching. "Now kiss me."

He hesitates only briefly before leaning in and planting his lips on mine. I rest one hand on his thigh and he moans so seductively that it makes my cock twitch, stirring to life.

Our tongues twirl and dance before I suck his into my mouth. He lets out another sinful groan that sets my body on fire.

"Get on top of me," I tell him.

He straddles my lap without question and my hands find placement on his hips as I angle my head up for another kiss.

Roman swipes my lips with his tongue before plunging it

into my mouth. He rocks forward and my grip tightens on him.

"Sorry," he says, thinking I meant for him to stop.

I shake my head and reach into my pants to adjust myself. "No. Don't be. Do it again."

He listens, grinding himself onto me as our mouths connect in another kiss. His lips brush softly against mine before his tongue dances with mine once more.

I run my hands up his back and then back down until I get to his ass.

"Your lips are so soft," he says breathlessly before kissing me again. His hands travel down my chest, touching everywhere he can. "I need more."

"Take off your shirt," I tell him.

He sits back and removes the bright material as I do the same with my plain white tee. His body is sculpted to perfection. Lean and muscular. Skin bronze and flawless. And a thin trail of hair leads down below his waistline.

My skin is a little lighter than his, there's no visible hair, and my body is just slightly softer and less toned. I workout and keep in shape, but I've never been known for my muscularity.

"Get up. Let's go to the room," I say, smacking him on the thigh.

He climbs off of me and waits for me to get up before following me into the bedroom. He kicks off his shoes before I step up to him and wrap my arms around his waist.

"Tell me when you want me to stop. Got it?"

Roman nods, looking at me with round eyes.

I push down his joggers and find he's not wearing any boxers.

He bites his lip. "I normally don't wear them. That wasn't just for tonight."

With my eyes still on his, I reach down and let my fingers dance along his shaft. "And here I thought you were thinking about me with this decision."

He pulls in a shaky breath. "Well, I was definitely thinking about you."

My fingers close around his erection, the skin smooth and hot in my grip. "What were you thinking about?"

"Th-this," he stutters. "You touching me. Me touching you."

I move my fist downward, planting kisses on his neck. "What else?"

Roman moans and thrusts into my hand. "Tasting you."

"Mm. And what about me tasting you?"

"God, yes," he says, throwing his head back as I nibble on the flesh.

"Get on the bed for me, Roman," I say with another teasing stroke.

He pulls away and steps out of the pants that are hugging his ankles before lying across the bed. I don't make him wait long, only taking the time to remove my own bottoms before crawling between his legs.

I kiss up his right thigh and along the crease of his groin before swiping my tongue across the underside of his head and then enveloping it in my mouth.

"Holy shit," he breathes, fingers pulling at the covers. "Oh god, yes."

I moan around his length, taking more and more of him into my mouth. He reaches down and threads his fingers through my hair and we make eye contact.

"Oh god," he says again, dropping his head back down as I use my hand and mouth in tandem.

I reach up and use my free hand to cup and play with his

balls while my saliva coats his length. I take him deep, nearly choking on it before I pull away.

"Oh my god," he cries.

I release him from my mouth and plant licks and kisses down his shaft and scrotum before letting my tongue dip low under his sac.

He peers down at me as he sucks in a shuddering breath. "You're too beautiful to be doing such filthy things."

My lips curl up into a grin before I lick across his perineum again. "Should I stop?"

"Fuck no."

I chuckle before licking lower, my tongue searching for a spot just out of reach. Unsure if he'll be uncomfortable, I move back up and take one of his balls into my mouth while my hand continues to stroke his length.

Roman releases a string of words that don't form a cohesive sentence before finally saying, "Please. Stop or I'm going to come."

I ease away and look up at him, giving his own words back to him. "I wouldn't be opposed."

"I feel like I'm thirteen and can't control myself. I want to do more before, you know, I can't. You're just so good."

Crawling up his body, I leave a trail of kisses on his torso before flopping over on my back at his side. "All this praise. I better soak it in before you start hating me again."

He turns to his side, his eyes scanning my body. "I only hated you because I wanted you to like me."

"Hmm. Make me like you then."

Roman gets on his knees and tugs my boxer-briefs down. With his eyes focused on my erection, he wets his lips and adjusts his position.

Now straddling me, he reaches out and holds me in his fist,

his grip soft at first. His hand travels upward and then back down. Dark eyes flicker up to look into mine. He's still nervous. Still cautious. I have to challenge him and give him what he's used to.

"Scared?" I question with a raised eyebrow.

His eyes narrow before his head descends and his lips wrap around me. It doesn't take long for me to realize Roman really knows how to use that mouth of his.

"Oh yeah," I moan, reaching down to run my fingers through his hair. "So good."

He makes a noise of approval as he continues on, flicking his tongue at the tip and driving me crazy in the process.

Roman turns me into a writhing mess that can only grunt, moan, and gasp for breath. When he grips my hips with both hands and bobs his head up and down, I can't take it anymore.

"Okay, okay, okay," I say, reaching for his wrists.

He pulls away, lips wet and glistening. God, he's stunning.

"Scared?" he asks.

"Scared I'll drown you in a few seconds if you're not careful."

He sits back and bites his bottom lip. "I know how to swim."

I cock a brow. "Fine." Interlocking my fingers behind my head, I stare at him. "Don't leave a mess."

With one hand and his mouth, Roman seems to challenge himself to do even better than earlier. He moves his tongue in ways I can't fathom. My brain short circuits with every tug and slurp, and before I know it, I'm crying out.

"Roman," I breathe. "Ro-man."

He hums around me, hand moving faster, and then I'm shattering. My world comes apart as my body convulses, and my throat strains with a roar.

Roman continues to mewl and moan as he makes sure to leave no mess behind. When he pulls away and gives me a smug smirk, I grab him by the shoulders and push him to his back. There's no way he's not about to come apart for me too.

I lower my body over his and completely devour him. I don't let any fraction of skin go unnoticed or untouched by my lips, tongue, or fingers. I rub, kiss, lick, and suck on every inch until he's pleading to god. His legs try to clench around me, and his hands tug on my hair as he whimpers and cries for more.

"Jacoby, I'm…I'm…"

I moan around him and wait for the dam to break. When it does, his body tightens, muscles flexing, and his yell seems to echo around the room.

Warm liquid lands on my tongue and I quickly swallow it down and continue to suck him into my mouth. I tease his tip, lapping up every drop until he's nearly convulsing.

When I collapse next to him, both of us breathless and sweat-slicked, he exhales loudly and says, "Well, I am a fan."

I chuckle. "I already knew that."

"This is completely different. I'm a fan of your mouth."

"Only that, huh?"

His head flops over and he gives me a lazy smile. "Can't stroke your ego too much."

"No, you did plenty of stroking."

We laugh and continue lying together on the bed, stark naked, without a worry or thought about what comes next.

CHAPTER EIGHTEEN

"Why are you all smiles?" my sister, Fallyn, asks as I stare down at my phone.

"Huh? Oh. I'm not."

She scrutinizes me for several seconds. "Who is it?"

"Who is who?" I ask, tucking my phone in my pocket.

"The person you're texting that's making you smile like a crazy person."

I laugh and reach for my mug of apple cider. "Nobody."

"You're gonna lie to me on Christmas Eve?"

I purse my lips at her. "Anyway. How are things with you?"

She gives me a look but must decide not to push any further. "Everything is good. I'll be working on a zombie movie in the next few months."

"Oh yeah? That's cool."

"Yep. Gotta put these skills to work."

"Well, you're pretty talented, so I'm sure you'll do fine."

She scoffs. "*Pretty* talented. More like the most sought-after special effects makeup artist in Hollywood."

"According to…"

She throws a balled up napkin at me. "Shut up."

My phone buzzes in my pocket, and I immediately reach for it, but my sister's assessing eyes make me freeze.

"Oh just get it. You're acting like a teenager who has to reply in the first ten seconds."

She stands up, folding her gray sweats over at the waist before walking to the kitchen. As she loads the dishwasher, I pull out my phone and read the message.

I should've stayed in Montana. It doesn't even feel like Christmas in California.

See? I told you. Do what I do. Turn the AC down really low, put on some sweats and a robe, make some cider or hot chocolate, and turn on Christmas movies.

Even in Montana I'd have it warm inside. No thanks to freezing my balls off.

Wouldn't want that, would we?

"All right. Who is he? Do I need to put on my detective cap?" Fallyn asks, strutting to the couch with a cup of hot chocolate.

I get up with my cider and join her, both of us putting our slippered feet on the coffee table. "No. It's complicated and something I shouldn't be doing, and might not even actually do. I just—" I stop talking and take a sip.

"Oh, well, thanks for that info."

"It's Roman," I say.

"Roman...Black? The guy you're filming with right now?"

I sigh. "The one and only."

"Oh my god," she says with a laugh as she drops her feet to the floor. "What?"

I suddenly remember that he's not out. I put my mug on the table and let my feet touch the carpet.

"Shit. Please don't say anything. Nothing's really even happened."

She waves her hand through the air. I know she won't. Fallyn's never been one for gossip, and when it comes to sexuality and coming out stories, she's not one to play around. She was outed by someone who used to be a friend. She believes, just as I do, that everyone should be able to come out on their own time and in their own way if they want to.

"You talked so much shit about that guy while also completely lusting after him. Didn't you say you were afraid to film the movie with him because you couldn't control yourself?"

"First of all, I can control myself, and I also talked shit privately. And apparently it was due to some misunderstanding. Kind of. I don't know. It's a whole thing."

"So, he's into you too? Or y'all are just texting? Please don't fall for a straight guy again. Last time was bad enough."

"We're maybe becoming friends. I don't know."

"Please be careful, Jac. Not only do I not want you to be broken-hearted, but if you're not ready for the world to know about you, then you have to take precautions. Have you got him to sign an NDA? Because everything might be cute now but what about in a month or two? What if he starts talking? If Mom and Dad find out this way, you know—"

"He wouldn't," I say, cutting her off, "But anyway, I don't want to get into it. It's nothing."

She gives me a skeptical look but turns her head toward the TV. "He *is* pretty cute."

My lips curl up into a grin, but all talk of Roman ceases, and my sister and I watch *Home Alone* (one and two) before going to bed.

I'm staying with her at her place in West Hollywood for the holiday before reuniting with the rest of the cast and crew in LA to finish our final scenes for the movie.

After my night with Roman, he hung around for a little while before going back to his room, and we haven't seen each other since. We've texted a few times though, and I find myself looking more and more forward to when his name lights up my phone screen.

Just as I'm getting under the covers, my phone goes off. I look at the screen and laugh. It's a photo of Roman wearing a hoodie with an annoyed look on his face.

I'm freezing and it still doesn't feel like Christmas. You have terrible ideas.

> Do you have hot cocoa?

Am I nine?

> Some part of you might be.

Is that the kind of conversation you want to be having?

> Merry Christmas, Roman. I'll see you the day after tomorrow.

Ah. Figured. Merry Christmas. See you.

CHAPTER NINETEEN

I WAIT OUTSIDE THE TRAILER FOR MAKEUP, HAVING SHOWN UP fifteen minutes early since all I was doing was pacing around my own trailer. It's only been four and a half days since I last saw Roman, which is nothing. And yet, I have stomach tightening nerves over seeing him again. Well, not nerves, per se, but excitement. Curiosity, perhaps.

We still haven't discussed anything about what we did or what it could mean. I think we both understand our predicament, so avoidance of serious topics seems to be what we're doing. However, I don't know how he'll act around me now. I'm not sure how I'll act around him.

I'm used to putting up the wall and being conscious of every movement, word, and gaze. But now that Roman's navigated around that wall, I wonder if it'll be harder for me to erect another. Will he pretend nothing happened? Will he make it more difficult for me to pretend nothing happened? And what the hell do I actually want?

The door swings open, and Roman descends the few steps.

Him. I want him. That's the first thing I think of when his eyes rake over my body in such a lascivious way.

"Hey, Heartthrob," Roman says with a look meant only for my eyes. "Waiting on me?"

"No. Just waiting for Malissa," I say, gesturing toward the trailer.

He drinks me in again, his gaze leisurely roaming every inch. When our eyes finally connect, I grin.

"How was Christmas?"

"Fine," I answer. "Did you spend yours with your sister?"

He shakes his head. "She was working."

"Parents?"

His eyes change slightly and he forces a grin. "Don't keep Malissa waiting. I'll see you soon."

He walks away, and it takes me several seconds before I realize I'm watching him do so. I quickly spin around and head inside to get ready.

An hour later, I'm on set with the actors who play my parents, filming the scene where I come out to them. It's an emotional moment that has William in tears as he expresses his truth and hopes his family doesn't disown him.

I feel slightly similar to William—not that my parents are religious, but that I have a fear of telling them the truth because I don't know how they'll react. Fallyn was forced out of the closet years ago, and my parents were shocked, angry, and confused.

Granted, maybe that's due to the fact that Fallyn was only seventeen and had been messing around with a woman my mother knew who was nearly a decade older than her. Fallyn's friend at the time told all their mutual friends, it traveled around the school, and it ultimately led to a teacher reaching out to our parents.

Fallyn's relationship with them has been strained for

years, and I'm not sure if it's because she's a lesbian or because they just can't get along.

I'm not sure how they'd feel about me being gay. My mom has questioned me about girls I'm dating or when I'll get married and have kids, and I've always given her answers that were palatable. *Soon. I haven't met the one yet.*

But really, I'm just blatantly lying.

I get lost in the scene as I pretend I'm coming out to my own parents. Once we cut from there, we take some time to get set up for the next one with Roman.

In what's used as Andrew's house, I walk in and march right for him, lifting him in my arms as I smile with unshed tears in my eyes.

"I told them. I told them, Andrew."

"You did?" He wraps his arms around me as I set him back down. "Oh my god. How was it?"

"I cried. My mom cried. Dad was fairly stoic, but it was fine. I didn't allow much room for questions or anything. I just told them I'm gay, and I always have been, and that I've finally found someone to love." We move to the couch and sit side-by-side. With his hand in mine, I look into his eyes. "I told them I hope they can accept me and that I still want to be in their lives, but that my life and my future includes you now."

His hand cups my cheek and his lips press against mine in a kiss before the director cuts.

"One minute, guys. We're gonna reset and start over. The lighting is off."

Roman's thumb grazes over my hand and I realize we're still connected. I slowly pull away and meet his gaze before he stands up.

"What're you doing later?"

I shake my head. "You?"

"Are you asking if you can do *me* later?" he questions quietly with a smirk.

I stand and slip my hands into my pockets. "Only if the answer is yes."

He swallows but doesn't get a chance to reply before we're back to work.

After what feels like forever, we break for lunch.

"Want to eat together?" he asks, looking straight in front of him as we make our way to craft services. "In my trailer." His eyes flicker in my direction briefly.

"Yes."

I watch as he tries to bite down on his lip to keep from smiling, and my smile grows wider.

CHAPTER TWENTY

On the walk to my trailer, I feel like every eye is on us and that they know exactly what we're going to be doing as soon as the door closes. We wave and nod at a few people we pass, and as far as everybody's concerned, we're just good friends. Co-stars. This isn't abnormal.

How I feel is though. My stomach does flips, and sweat prickles along my hairline. Does he know why I invited him to have lunch here with me? He has to, right? It's not simply to eat.

What if he doesn't know? Should I pounce on him? Give him a warning? What the hell are we doing?

I walk inside the trailer and put my food on the counter. The door clicks behind me, and I turn around and stare at him for three long seconds before he lunges forward with one long stride and closes the distance between us. His hand goes to the side of my neck, and our lips clash together.

"Oh, thank fuck," I mutter against his mouth before I hold his face in my hands and taste the mint on his breath.

My hands move to his body, exploring the planes of his sides and back as he walks me to the couch.

I fall to my ass and then he's between my legs on his knees, reaching for the button and zipper on my jeans.

"Oh. So you have been waiting for me."

"Shut up," he says, yanking the material down.

"Okay." His mouth envelopes my shaft in warmth and wetness. "Ohhh kay. Yes. Fuck."

Jacoby is a fucking cannibal. He consumes me, and I welcome every single second of being his victim.

He completely dismantles me. I'm not whole. I'm fragments of a person, unable to form words or reasonable thoughts, and hardly able to breathe. In an embarrassingly short amount of time, Jacoby has my body convulsing as I reach euphoric bliss.

"Oh god!" I yell.

His hand comes up and clamps over my mouth, and I cover it with mine, knowing I need help to keep from alerting everyone on the property that I've just had my mind blown. Or…something blown.

He slowly removes his palm as he continues his movements. Once I'm completely spent, he eases back and gazes at me with those unique and beautiful eyes. Then he swallows.

"You're incredible," I say, completely blissed out.

He smirks and I reach forward and clasp his face in my hands and kiss him without a care in the world. What's better than tasting a man who tastes like you? Fucking nothing.

"Okay, your turn," I say, pulling up my pants.

"We don't have time," he replies, reaching into his jeans and adjusting himself. "We have to eat and be on set in fifteen."

I pout. "What if I promise to be fast?"

He snorts. "I don't want it to be fast." Reaching down, he grabs my hand and pulls me up. "I want you to be slow and deliberate. I want you to worship me."

My stomach does a somersault as my heart thumps hard against my ribcage. "I'll get on my knees right now."

His smile is slow, and the look in his eyes is tender as he reaches up and caresses my face. "Do you want to come over tonight?"

"To your house?"

"Yes."

"Okay. Yeah."

He gives me a quick but soft kiss on my lips. "Good. Let's eat."

We scarf down our food as quickly as possible, our eyes never straying far from each other. The sexual tension between us is palpable. When I look at him, all of my thoughts are X-rated and I know he can read them in my eyes.

I burst through the door, hoping the outside air will help blow away every filthy thought in my head.

The shutter of a camera goes off behind us, and we both spin to find Keisha there taking photos.

"Just doing my job," she says when spotting our confused faces. "Smile!" We're barely able to obey before the camera goes off. "Sheera wants another video from you two in the next few days. Just talking about how filming is almost over and you're excited and hope the fandom is also excited, and blah blah blah."

"Okay. We'll do it," I reply with a grin.

"Awesome. See ya."

"She's a sneaky one," Jacoby says.

"It's a good thing I didn't grab your ass like I was thinking."

"Oh, is that right?" he questions, turning his head to look at me.

"I'm thinking about a lot of different things. All of them are raunchy and disgusting."

His brow arches as his lips quirk into a grin. "I hope you can tell me later. You might clam up as soon as we're behind closed doors."

"Please. I just...I'm. I don't know. You make me nervous."

"Why's that?"

"You're more yourself when it's just us, and it's not the you I'm accustomed to. I'm used to you being quiet and stiff."

"Which one do you prefer?"

I glance over at him, noticing the wicked glint in his eye. "The one behind closed doors. The real you."

Jacoby glances around. The next few scenes take place outdoors, in an apartment building, and a restaurant, so we're in the city blocks backlot surrounded by tons of makeshift buildings. There are people milling around and equipment set up where we'll be filming next, but Jacoby surprises me by grabbing a hold of my arm and steering me off our path.

We cut between buildings, and he forces me into an alcove away from any prying eyes.

I open my mouth to ask what's going on, but he slips his tongue between my lips and steals the words from me. His kiss is forceful and passionate. He wraps his arms around me, holding me close.

"I like every version of you," he says when he pulls away. "The cocky loudmouth that parades around in jungle-themed clothing and acts like he doesn't have a care in the world.

144

And the one who quiets down and waits for me to tell him what to do, because he's too shy and nervous to make the first move."

"Hey, fuck you," I say, giving him a soft shove.

He smirks. "I said I like it."

"I can make the first move."

"I'd rather tell you what to do, so shut up and kiss me one more time before we have to go."

My eyes study his face for a few seconds before I submit and do what he says.

Fuck. I like when he tells me what to do, too.

CHAPTER TWENTY-ONE

AT THE END OF THE NIGHT, I STAND IN THE BACK AS JACOBY finishes up one of his scenes. Jess is beside me, both of us enraptured by his talent.

When the director cuts, I still don't take my eyes off of him. "He's amazing, right?" I say in awe.

"He is." It's silent for several seconds before she speaks again. "Sooo, funny thing."

"Hm?" I muse, still watching him as he talks to the director.

"Eric kind of kissed me yesterday."

"What?" I swirl around and look at her. "Eric?"

She grins. "Yep."

"What about your *rules?*"

"It's not like I asked for it!"

"But it was consensual?"

"Well, duh, but I wasn't planning on it happening."

"First you lust after Jacoby," I say, pointing in his general direction. "Then you kiss Eric. You know, I'm starting to feel hated for some reason."

"Oh stop," she says with a laugh. Jess bites on her lip for a few seconds, her eyes wide and excited as she bounces on her toes. "The kiss was so good, though!"

"Naughty, naughty girl."

"Sometimes breaking rules is fun."

Movement catches my attention and I spot Jacoby walking over. "That's certainly true," I reply to her.

"What's going on over here?" Jacoby asks, eyes bouncing between the two of us.

"Just talking about breaking rules and kissing people you work with," Jess says.

His eyes widen slightly as his brows lift. "What?"

I give a gentle shake of my head when he looks at me. "Nothing. Jess is going around kissing people."

"Wow. One person, Rome. And *he* kissed *me.*"

I notice Jacoby visibly relax when he realizes we weren't talking about us.

"Well, I'm gonna get going. I have plans tonight."

He gives me a nod that would suggest he's simply an associate of mine and not the man who told me he wants me to worship him after having my dick in his mouth.

"Hot date?" Jess asks.

Jacoby turns around and continues walking backward. "Not that hot."

Bastard.

"I'm sure you'll have the best night of your life," I say with a grin. "Have fun."

His eyes narrow in on me. "You too."

Once he's gone, Jess turns to me. "He's dating?"

I shrug. "I dunno. I guess."

"What is up with men and their friendships? Y'all don't talk and tell each other everything? Are you even friends?" she asks with a laugh.

The truth is, I don't know what we are.

"I told you, he's private. He just does his own thing. I'm sure it's nothing."

The words leave a bitter taste in my mouth, because there's a chance that's true. This could be nothing. We could have sex and then it'll be over, never to happen again. Because what could come of this? Jess is right. We don't communicate very well, and this seems like something we should definitely discuss.

Maybe later. After we do whatever it is we're going to do.

That thought alone fills me with panic. What do I need to do to prepare myself? Is he a top? Bottom? Vers?

I say goodbye to Jess and head to my trailer to pick up my things. While I'm in there, I pull out my phone and decide to get some information from Jacoby.

> Uhh, so this is awkward, but...what should I expect tonight?

What do you mean? I thought I made it clear what to expect.

> Well, sure. But we haven't really discussed the logistics.

Logistics?

> Who goes into who? God. The fact that you make me spell it out is annoying.

I was planning on talking to you when you got to my house, but since you're so impatient, we can discuss now. You've only been with one guy. What did you do? And if I'm so annoying, don't come. Yes, it's a double entendre.

Wow. Really funny. Anyway, I topped. And you?

I've done both.

Do you have a preference for tonight?

I'd prefer you stop texting me all these questions. Who even said we were going to have sex? You owe me a blowjob.

Oh, so I'm only being used for my mouth?

And your hands. Can't have a good blowjob without using your hands.

I hate you.

I don't get an immediate response, so I end up just staring at my phone and contemplating saying something else.

A couple minutes later, the door to my trailer swings open and Jacoby stands there with amusement on his face.

"You know, they say hate sex is the best sex."

I scrape my teeth along my bottom lip, drinking him in. "I'd still have to know who, you know…"

Jacoby rolls his eyes and drops his bag on the floor before

strutting forward. Yanking me up from the couch, he wraps an arm around my waist and brings me close.

"Since you're clearly nervous and worried, you can just give me what you owe me and be on your way. How about that?"

He plants a couple kisses on my neck, his nose nuzzling under my ear.

"No. I want more than that."

"Then tell me what you want," he says against my throat, still teasing me with kisses.

"I thought we…" I let out a moan as his tongue dances across my Adam's apple. "I thought we determined that I like it when you tell me what to do."

"Yes, but you have to decide this. I'm not going to do anything you're uncomfortable with." He pulls away to look me in the eye and reads my expression for several seconds. "Okay. Tonight, you top. Is that okay?"

I nod. "Yes."

"Good." His lips form a small grin. "Now come on, my car is waiting."

He walks away and grabs his bag, leaving me scrambling to get mine so I can follow him.

"I was planning on showering and stuff."

"I have bathrooms at my house, Roman. You can use one."

"I can't believe I'm going to Jacoby Hart's house," I tease.

"Please don't use my full name like that."

"In that case, you can call me Rome."

He gives me a look before he opens the car door and slips inside. "No, thank you."

"Why?" I question, getting into the seat next to him. "Everyone does."

His eyes flicker forward toward the driver. "Well, not me."

"Do you try to be a stubborn ass all the time?"

"I guess it's just natural," he says with a shrug.

My phone vibrates, so I pull it out and look at the screen. It's a message from Emerson.

> I can't wait till you're done filming so we can hang out again. It's been so long. What are your plans for next month?

> You know I don't make plans. Why, what's up? What do you wanna do?

> Anything. I've just been a lame ass who does nothing but work and sleep. I need some fun in my life.

> Well, that's definitely me.

> I know. ;)

My body tenses up with the wink emoji. Emmy and I haven't done anything in a while, but there is a lot of history between us. We experienced a lot of the same firsts at the same time, and we held each other's secrets.

I look up and find Jacoby's eyes watching me.

"Change of plans?" he asks coolly.

"No," I reply, turning off my phone. "Are you being nosy?"

"Would only be returning the favor."

"Anyway. All is good."

"Hmm."

The ride to his house is quiet, and for some reason, I feel guilty.

JACOBY

CHAPTER TWENTY-TWO

WHEN WE GET TO MY HOUSE, I SHOW ROMAN WHERE THE other bathroom is so he can take a shower, and then I go to my own and do the same. I try not to think about his text exchange with Emerson, or why it made me feel…angry and jealous.

I told Roman I'd meet him downstairs since I'll be doing a little more prep work than he has to, so once I'm showered, dry, and moisturized, I slip on a pair of lounge pants and a T-shirt and head to the living room.

Roman's standing behind the couch, wearing only a towel around his waist as he types into his phone.

My feet carry me quietly across the natural stone floor until I'm at his back.

"Lose your clothes, sweetheart?"

He jumps, dropping his phone to the couch. "Jesus. You're so quiet."

I bend forward and grab his phone, handing it to him. "You're not texting *Emmy* are you?"

Roman spins around and rests his ass on the back of the couch. "Jealous?"

"That you're talking to the one and only man you've had sex with right before you're about to do the same with me? No, of course not."

He crosses his arms in front of his chest. "It's not like that. We're not still sleeping together. In fact, it's been a while."

I playfully let my fingers run along his skin above the towel. "How long?"

"Since we had sex? Almost a year."

"And anything else?"

"There's been little things here and there. I think the last time was around seven months ago. We're mostly friends."

"Mostly," I repeat, my fingers sliding under the cotton material.

He sucks in a breath, eyes watching mine. "And you?"

"Fourteen months ago was the last time."

"Damn."

My brows lift. "Mhmm. And to get the important but less sexy talk out of the way. I've been tested. I'm negative. I always use condoms."

"Yeah. Same," he says, swallowing as my hand travels lower, loosening the towel.

"Good. Let's go to my room."

CHAPTER TWENTY-THREE

JACOBY TURNS AND STRUTS UPSTAIRS, AND I FEEL LIKE AN excited puppy following his owner for a treat.

He seems so calm and relaxed while my heart threatens to leap out of my throat in anticipation.

I don't think he realizes that just because I've done this before doesn't mean I'm not absolutely losing my mind. I mean, he's only the second guy I have hooked up with, *and* he's Jacoby Hart. I've been a fan of his work for years. I've been attracted to him for a long time too, and this happening is almost too good to be true.

Walking into his room, my feet immediately come into contact with gray carpet that's soft and plush. A large crystal chandelier dangles above the foot of the king-sized bed, and two gray chairs are up against the opposite wall, separated by a small table with a lamp in the center. To the right of the bed leans an oversized full length mirror that's framed in silver.

Everything is variations of gray, white, and silver. It's very luxurious while also maintaining a simple vibe.

"Your house is very nice."

"Thank you."

"I really like—"

"Roman," he says, cutting off my nervous chatter. "Come here."

I walk over to where he's standing near the bed. He closes the space between us and puts his hand to my neck as he brings his lips to mine. His tongue slides into my mouth, stealing my breath away.

Jacoby undoes the towel at my waist, letting it fall to the floor before his hand curves over my hip and cups my ass.

I moan into his mouth as I grind against him. "You have too many clothes on."

"Take them off of me."

My heart begins to gallop and I reach for the hem of his shirt and pull it up over his head. Still staring into his eyes, my thumbs slide into the waistband of his pants and tug them down.

Deciding at the last minute to drop lower as I pull the material past his thighs, I end up on my knees as he steps out of the pants.

Peering up at him, I take his length in my hand and stroke before opening my mouth and tasting him.

"Oh yeah," he moans, his fingers instantly threading through my hair.

I commit to his request of worship, and moan appreciatively as I take him deep into my mouth, twirling my tongue around his shaft before focusing on his tip.

The muscles in his thighs flex as I hold onto them while my mouth moves up and down his shaft.

"Hold on. Come here," he says, breathing heavily as he backs up to lie on the bed.

I instantly climb between his legs and continue devouring him. I reduce him to grunts and strings of cuss words as I take as much as I can, coating him in my saliva. My hand moves faster with a stronger grip as I suck on his crown. His breathing picks up, his stomach rising and falling with each deep inhale. The desire to drive him to completion is stronger than ever. I don't even care if this was supposed to be fore-play, I want to be his undoing.

"Okay," he pants, reaching for me. "Wait. Oh god."

I keep going for a few seconds before easing away. "Just trying to worship you," I say with a smirk.

"Yeah, well, good job," he says with an exhale. "There's lube in this drawer," he says, pointing to his right. "Condoms, too."

I get up and get both, finding my way back between his legs. As I cover myself with the condom and then coat the latex with the slick liquid, Jacoby gets the bottle and pours some into his palm. I watch with rapt fascination as he readies himself for me. It's the single hottest action I've ever seen, and he does it without a fraction of embarrassment or insecurity. And his eyes remain focused on me as I leisurely stroke myself.

"You're so fucking hot."

His lips quirk up slightly. "So are you."

"I want to do that," I say, nodding toward his hand.

"Yeah?"

I bite my lip and nod. "You're driving me crazy."

He removes his hand and gives me the bottle of lube. I generously coat my fingers and scoot in closer. I press where he was just pressing, slowly and carefully entering him.

His back arches and his head goes back as his eyes flutter closed. "Yes," he says, drawing out the word. "So much better when you do it."

I lean over him and kiss his collarbone as my hand continues to work. I harden even more against his hip, my breaths coming in pants.

"I want you so bad."

His fingers dance along my back. "I'm ready."

I shift until my mouth is hovering over his, leaning down to plant feather-soft kisses on his lips. His hand slides into my hair and pulls me closer, his tongue gliding across mine.

"Your mouth," I breathe. "Your lips. Tongue. Everything. It's so good. I could do nothing but kiss you and be happy."

He smiles against my lips. "As much as I appreciate that, I'd really love it if you'd do a little more." He wraps his legs around me. "You've driven me to the brink of insanity, and I'd like to be committed now."

I chuckle and kiss him again. "Okay."

Easing away, I grab a hold of myself and make sure to use more lube on both of us before I begin to slide in.

Time slows down and the world ceases to exist around us. Inch by inch, I get closer to him, watching his face contort and his flesh redden. His mouth opens as he takes in slow and deep breaths, and I have the thought that he may be the most beautiful thing I've ever laid eyes on.

As our bodies merge, I hover over him, my hands holding me up. "I can't believe this is happening."

His fingers run up my sides, squeezing my lats. "Keep moving." I rock my hips slowly, afraid to hurt him. He bites into his bottom lip and nods. "Mmhmm. More."

I hook an arm under his knee and push it farther up as I lean into him, giving him more of me just like he asked.

"Oh god," he moans.

His words and the way they're said—unfiltered and shaky—send goosebumps down my arms.

Jacoby's hands travel around my lower back, finding a home on my ass. He pushes me deeper and we both inhale at the same time, our gazes locked on each other.

He arches, his face a perfect example of euphoric bliss. He reaches for my head and brings me closer to his mouth.

When I think he's about to kiss me, he whispers, "Fuck me," against my lips and my entire body reacts.

My chest feels warm and tight and my stomach does a flip. My hips move back and forth, the pace picking up.

"Yes," he cries. "More. Harder. Oh fuck."

"You're a needy little shit," I huff, pushing my hair from my forehead as I get back to my knees.

I spread his legs even more and focus on where our bodies connect. When he reaches down to stroke himself, my gaze flickers between both scenes.

"Holy shit."

"It's so good," he says between breaths.

The visual is making fireworks go off in my brain. It's too much. Too sexy. Too good. I'll finish much too fast if I continue to watch our bodies work together.

My movements slow, but Jacoby won't have that.

"No," he demands. "Faster. Deeper."

I listen, my teeth grinding together as sweat beads across my forehead. "It's too good. I…I—"

"Get up," he says.

"What?" I question, pulling away.

Jacoby doesn't give me answers. He simply gets up and pushes me to my back, quickly climbing on top of me.

"Oh. Ohhh," I say as he straddles my waist and fully seats himself on me. "Oh shit."

I grab his hips as he moves. Up, down, back, and forth. His hips rotate and rock, and he rises and falls, and holy shit, my brain is about to explode.

"Not yet," he tells me, his chest expanding with deep breaths.

"Fuck. You feel so good." My hands curve around to his ass. "I can't...my mind...oh my god."

He grabs himself in his right hand and strokes as he continues to move. His head drops back, and I focus on his throat and the sheen of sweat down the center. Even that's sexy.

"Jacoby." His name emerges from my mouth in a grunt.

"Wait for me," he says, completely breathless.

"I can't."

"Fuck."

As soon as I see his muscles flexing and feel him clench and tighten up, there's no more control left in me. I cry out first, my orgasm exploding out of me and into him, and then he lets out a roar. Our noises create a symphony of pleasure and release.

Warmth hits my stomach as his body shakes above me, and if I wasn't so completely spent, I'd take the time to revel in the mess created by what we just did.

But all I can think about is the fact that it just happened—that it was real. And not only that, but it was one of the best experiences of my life.

CHAPTER TWENTY-FOUR

After we get cleaned up and dressed again, Jacoby leads me to the kitchen where he opens the fridge and pulls out Tupperware dishes filled with food.

"Hungry?"

"Always."

He removes a couple of plates from his white cabinets, and scoops what looks like some sort of pasta onto them.

After putting one dish into the microwave, he puts the Tupperware back into the fridge and grabs a couple of cans of Coke.

"So," he says, leaning onto the counter. "That was fun."

My lips curl into a grin. "I'd say so. When do we get to do it again?" I wiggle my brows at him.

"Unless you're planning on bottoming, not tonight."

I smirk. "Ah. I see."

The microwave goes off and he takes the plate out and places it in front of me as I sit at the breakfast bar. He swivels to get a fork and bring it back to me.

"Here you go. It's vegetable pasta."

"Thanks." I take the fork and start poking around. "You

seem…lighter. You're basically floating around the kitchen. Is that because of, you know," I say, looking down at my lap.

He gives me his signature eye roll as he turns around. "You're awfully full of yourself."

"No, but you w—"

"Don't," he says, cutting me off.

I laugh and take a bite of the food. "Anyway." I swallow it down. "I mean it. You seem different. Comfortable."

"Because I'm in my home, with someone I don't have to hide from."

I nod and continue to eat, digesting his words. Jacoby does come off very rigid and serious, and while I thought that was just who he was, it sucks to know that it's only because he's constantly worried about how others perceive him.

My phone vibrates in my pocket, and I don't miss the quick gaze I get from Jacoby when I pull it out to read the screen.

"It's Eric," I say, giving him some peace of mind. "Apparently he and Jess kissed and now I'm the middleman, and they're both trying to talk to me about it."

"Wow," he says, his brows lifting as he walks around to sit next to me. "You're a relationship mentor?"

"I know a few things."

"Except how to tell me you want to kiss me."

I give him a sidelong glance. "Anyway. People like talking to me."

"Why?" he questions, taking a bite.

"Are you being an asshole or actually asking? I can't tell."

He smirks. "I assume you make people feel comfortable."

I shrug. "I'd hope so. I'm pretty laid back. I know I'm, what did you call me? *Flashy*. But I'm also chill and easy going."

"You *can* be both. How else do you explain those red carpet outfits?"

I chuckle. "Which ones are you talking about specifically?"

"One was a red leather jacket, but you didn't have anything underneath and it was open."

"Oh yeah. I liked that one."

"What about that aqua colored outfit where the shirt sleeves looked like they were kept together by strings?"

"Strings?" I question. "That was a designer blazer that was meant to look like that, and they weren't *strings*. But I'm sorry you don't know fashion."

He snorts. "No, I like that about you, even if I tease you. You're comfortable in your skin. You're you. Always radiating this positive energy and just living life to the fullest. I've always cared too much about what other people think."

I swallow and shift slightly, unsure how to respond. He doesn't know what prompted my style change and cocky, bad boy persona. He thinks I've had this perfect, happy life where I've never been concerned about anything, but it's not true. I just don't know that I can open up right now.

"Hey, you make the classic black suits look good. I think I even saw you in a blue one once," I say with a smirk.

"Shut up." He laughs, shaking his head.

"Let me respond to Eric real quick. He's texted me like four times." He nods and continues eating as I type out a response. "He wants advice on how to go forward. Should I tell him to just be an ass and push Jess to finally kiss him to shut him up? Worked for us."

His lips quirk as he huffs. "At least you admit to being an ass."

"Look, I'm a pro at this now. I'm seasoned in kissing people you shouldn't and secret…hookups."

Jacoby tenses up before standing and taking his plate to the sink. "Yeah, I was thinking."

I put my phone down, nerves tightening my stomach. Nothing good comes after *I was thinking* especially in the tone Jacoby has.

"Thinking what?"

"Well, my sister brought it up, and it's probably a good idea. I've done it before, so it's nothing new. Nothing crazy."

"Just spit it out, Jacoby."

"I think you should sign an NDA."

I stare at him in silence for a long few seconds, waiting for him to laugh or say he's kidding. He wants me to sign an NDA?

"I'm sorry. What?"

"We can backdate it to cover everything from the night of Jessica's party. I don't want anyone finding out about—"

"Us?"

"Me," he corrects. "But that would include us, yes."

"And you think I'm going to run my mouth about you? You do know I'm not out yet either, right?"

"Yes, but I can't take the chance of you telling anyone about me. You talk to more people. You're more personable, and everyone clearly goes to you for stuff," he says, gesturing at my phone. "It's more likely you'll say something than me."

"And now I'll be under threat of legal action?" I stand up. "Are you kidding me?"

"Roman, please."

"No. Fuck that. Fuck you, Jacoby. We just...we had...you know what?" I turn and look for my shoes. "After what we just did you want to bring this up?"

"It's just a precaution. I've done it before."

"I really don't want to be lumped in with all your

previous secretive booty calls or whatever the fuck you wanna call them."

"This would protect you too."

"I don't care. I really don't give a shit, Jacoby. It never even crossed my mind to ask you something like this. I trusted you'd keep it to yourself until or if we decided we wanted to say something about it. Hell, we haven't even discussed what the fuck we're doing or what it means. And you expect me to sign this and then go on fucking you? You really know how to take the sexy out of something, don't you?"

"Roman, it's not like that. I'm just being careful."

"Yeah, well, no need." With my shoes on, I march back to the counter and grab my phone, staring him in the eye. "We're done, and believe me I will *not* be telling anyone about this lovely encounter, or any of the previous ones. You'll have to trust me because I am not signing a fucking NDA."

As I storm toward his door, he calls out, "You don't even have your car here, remember? Where are you going to go?"

"I have a phone. I'll figure it out. Bye, Jacoby."

I slam the door with more force than necessary and fume all the way down the street until I can order an Uber.

CHAPTER TWENTY-FIVE

"I CAN'T BELIEVE WE'RE OFFICIALLY DONE," JESS SAYS AS WE walk into the upscale bar that was rented out for our wrap party. "I'm gonna miss you."

I drape an arm around her shoulder. "You have my number. We'll make plans to get together soon."

"I'm gonna miss seeing everyone. This was such a fun cast. I'm doing an audition next week for a ten episode arc in a primetime drama, and I'm afraid they'll exclude me since they've been at this for four seasons already."

"Which show is it?" I ask.

"Suspicious Acts."

"Ooh. That's a good show. I'm sure they'll love you, though."

"Where's Jacoby?" she asks, looking around as we walk up to the bar.

I shrug and try to keep from clenching my teeth. "Don't know."

Her eyes burn holes into the side of my face as I wait for the bartender to make his way down. I glance down and back at the bottles of liquor.

"What?" I question.

She sighs. "I may have told Jacoby that I think you have a crush on him."

"What?" I exclaim, whirling around to stare at her with wide eyes. "Why would you say that? And when? But most importantly, why do you think that?"

"I told you!" she says, standing up straight. "You talk about him a lot. You watch him any time he's around. It seems obvious, but you've never said you're…you know." She doesn't finish, her eyes scanning the nearby vicinity.

"I've never said what?"

"If you're into guys," she says quietly, barely moving her lips. "But you don't have to tell me," she says, holding up her hands. "I just wanted you to know what I told him just in case it made him start acting weird around you. That wasn't my intention. But for the last several days he hasn't been around almost at all."

I attempt to relax my shoulders a little. "You think he's not around because he thinks I have a crush on him?"

Her lips downturn as she shrugs. "I didn't mean to make things weird. Stupid alcohol had me saying things I shouldn't. I also basically told him I had a crush on him, too."

"It's fine. I don't think he cares or maybe he doesn't believe you. I don't know." I shrug. "He hasn't said anything to me about it."

"Which means he probably thinks it's true," she says, slapping a hand on her forehead. "God. If he thought I was way off base he would've been like, 'Did you know Jess said you had a crush on me? So weird, right?' But he hasn't, so maybe that's why he's been pretty scarce lately. Damn. I'm sorry, Rome."

I smile down at her. "It's fine. He hasn't acted weird

toward me. He probably chalked it up to drunken nonsense. No offense."

She rolls her eyes. "Well, speaking of drunken nonsense, let's get drunk."

The bartender finds us and we order our drinks plus some shots to take to Eric, Naomi, Mila, and Marco.

Music blares from the speakers and people sway and jiggle on the dancefloor while others stand around high top tables with food and drinks.

An hour into the party, as I'm dancing with Naomi, I spot Jacoby walk in. My lips quirk slightly when I see what he's wearing.

Not dressed in his usual black or blue suits, he's got on a maroon button up shirt and a pair of black slacks.

Damn. The shirt looks really good on him though.

I try to ignore him and keep on dancing. The alcohol running in my veins has me feeling hot, so I've taken off my royal blue blazer and unbuttoned the white button up to reveal the tank top underneath. My sleeves are rolled up just under my elbows, and my once formal attire is looking a little casual now.

After the song ends, Jess runs up to me. "Let's go say hi to Jacoby so I know I didn't fuck up y'alls friendship by being a drunk ass."

I grumble, but now I feel like I have to pretend this friendship thing is real for her sake. I can't tell her I'm pissed that after we had sex he wanted me to sign an NDA. I can't tell her that I think about him way too often because I *do* have a crush. Or did. That it was turning more into *really liking* him until he made me mad again.

Did I even tell her that I *don't* like him and that I'm *not* into guys? I think I'm just now realizing that I didn't even bother to deny it.

"I'll just tell him you don't like him. Problem solved," she says with tipsy confidence.

"Please don't say anything. I'm telling you there's nothing to worry about."

Jacoby's at a table, taking a sip of his drink as his eyes bounce around the room. Some guy is at his side, but he leaves before we get close. I hurry my steps to beat Jess to him, and his eyes stay locked on me until I'm in front of him.

"Just go with it. I'm still mad at you."

His brows dip and his lips part to question what I'm talking about, but then Jess arrives and I force a smile.

"Hey, you made it. We were wondering where you were," I say.

Jacoby's lips struggle to form a smile before his eyes flicker between the two of us. "Oh. Yeah, just running behind."

"Nice shirt," I say with a grin. "Nice to know you can choose other colors besides black and blue."

"Yeah, that color looks good on you," Jess says.

"Thanks," he replies, looking down at it. "I guess I've been hanging out with Roman too much. His desire for flamboyant clothing is rubbing off on me."

"Well, I'd never wear that, but sure, you can blame that on me."

Jess smacks me. "Be nice."

"Ah, he's used to it," I say, clenching my teeth and forcing a smile. "Aren't you? And this guy," I say, walking around to wrap an arm around his shoulders. "This guy can dish it. You just haven't seen him in action."

"Nah," Jess says with a smile, shaking her head. "Jacoby's a sweetheart."

Jacoby shrugs me off of him. "Hear that?"

"Jess!" Eric shouts from the bar, waving her over.

"Oh. I'll be right back," she says, rushing off.

I immediately step away from him and go to the other side of the table.

"What's going on?" he asks.

"Jess thinks you're being scarce because she told you I had a crush on you, and now you feel weird around me. I tried telling her that's not the case, but you didn't hang around any of us during the last week of filming, and well... this is me acting like everything's fine. You're welcome."

"Does she think..."

"Whatever she thinks is about me not you," I say with a sigh.

"And you're fine with that?"

"I really don't care. Maybe I'll come out soon. I don't know," I say with a shrug.

"Roman, I still think we should talk. I didn't mean—"

"It doesn't matter what you *meant* to do, it's what you did. You didn't mean to what? Tell me to sign an NDA? Because I'm pretty positive that's what you intended. You didn't mean to hurt my feelings? Well, that was done, too. You didn't mean to come off like a giant asshole? Well." I shrug.

The guy that was at the table earlier shows up with a plate of finger foods. "Here you go. I'll be right back with more."

Jacoby nods at him before he leaves.

"Who's that?" I ask, gesturing with my head toward the man walking away from us. "One of your NDA-signing booty calls?"

He sighs, shaking his head. "Please don't call them that."

"You with him?"

"Roman."

"No, it's fine. I'll see ya later."

It's a thousand percent not fine, and jealousy coils in my stomach as I head for the bar to try to drown it.

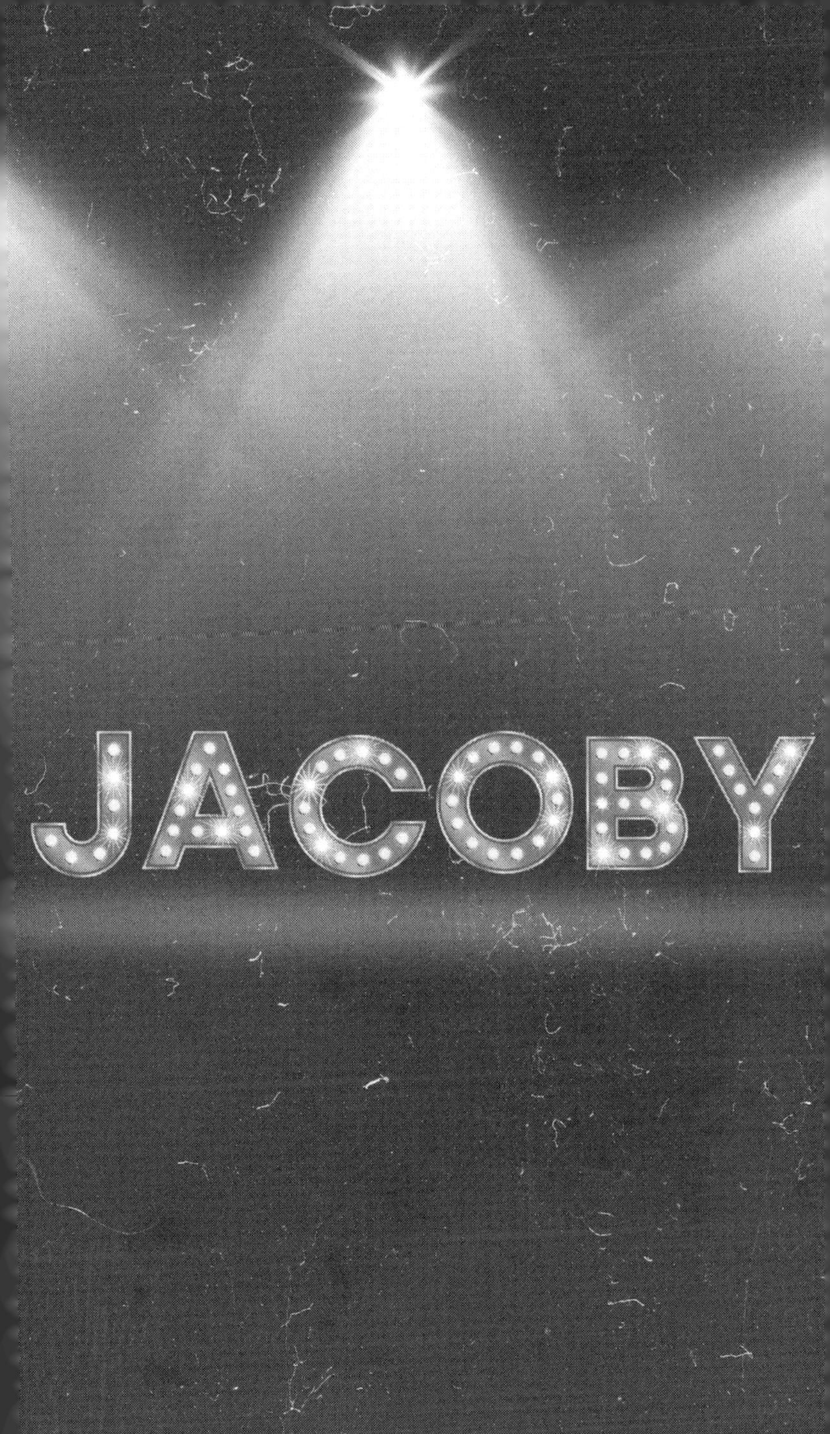
JACOBY

CHAPTER TWENTY-SIX

I watch Roman as he downs a couple of shots with some of the other cast, and it's obvious he's trying his hardest not to look at me. When he does, he scowls, his jaw clenched as his eyes bounce between me and my assistant, Grant.

We need to find time to talk, but now probably isn't the best time, considering he's halfway to drunk and angry as fuck. The last thing either of us needs is for us to get into a heated and loud argument about what happened at my house last week.

Did I go about things the wrong way? Probably, but there isn't really a good way to tell the person you just slept with to sign an NDA. But my fear is real, and our relationship—or whatever it is—isn't defined. We're not in love. Sometimes I feel like we hardly like each other. We're simply attracted to each other.

Roman is extremely talkative, and knowing he's been talking to Jess and Eric about whatever it is they're doing and joking about being a pro at secret hookups just made me instantly nervous. I don't think he'd do anything maliciously, I really don't, but it could happen.

Would I actually sue him? I don't fucking know. I don't know why I said it, but it's what I've done before and it just came out.

I turn to Grant, who's talking to someone at a nearby table, and let him know where I'm going. I push my shoulders back and slip a hand into the pocket of my slacks as I make my way across the dancefloor so I can get to the bathroom.

After a few nods and hellos to some people, I find myself behind closed doors and away from the music. Once I'm done relieving myself, I'm at the sink washing my hands when the door flies open, letting in the raucous noise from the bar.

"You know, I was thinking," Roman starts as he makes his way to the urinals. "If you're so worried about being found out, why would you bring a guy here with you? Even if he did sign an NDA?"

I sigh and turn off the water, making my way to the paper towels. "I'm not *with* him. He's my assistant."

He goes silent until he's done peeing. "Oh."

With a shake of my head, I lean my shoulder against the wall and watch him wash his hands. "Roman, I still think we should talk."

"Nah, that's okay," he says, shaking his hands above the sink before walking to the paper towels. "I'm done. It doesn't matter anymore."

"Oh, you're *done?* But you were at the bar drinking to keep from thinking that I was with someone else. You were in here about to question me over my assistant, but you're *done?"*

"Yes. I'm done. I can still feel jealous and not want anything to do with you. All you've done is piss me off and confuse me since we started working together."

"And the same goes for you, but I didn't intend for this to end."

"What *did* you intend?" he asks, crossing his arms in front of his chest as he stands less than a foot away from me.

I let loose a frustrated growl. "Goddammit, Roman. I like you. As infuriating as you are, I like you. I don't know. I wanted to see where things went. I wasn't making plans, I was just going with it."

He seems to soften, but only briefly. "I can't. I won't sign an NDA. It makes this"—he gestures between us—"feel cheap and inauthentic. If I'm going to really give things a chance with you, it's going to mean something. It's going to be real "

"It would still be real."

He shakes his head, stubborn defiance etched in his features. "No. I'd rather—"

"What?" I ask, stepping closer. "Find someone else? Go back to Emerson?"

His eyes travel down my face before flickering back to my gaze. "Maybe."

I close the distance between us, forcing his back against the wall. "It wouldn't be the same, and you know it."

"It would probably be better."

My lips quirk as I push in even closer, my hips against his. "Your quivering breath says otherwise." I nip at the flesh below his ear. "We both know you like the way I handle you."

His chest rises and falls with quick breaths. "Are you sure you wanna be this close to me?" he asks in a husky tone. "There's no contract between us."

My nose drags along his jaw before my lips hover a hairsbreadth from his. "Roman. Please don't take this away."

His intake of breath is audible, and his desire for me can

be felt against my thigh. I remain still, waiting for his permission. Eager for his acquiescence.

Roman's hands finally come up and grab a hold of my hips, and now I'm the one with shaky breaths as I rest my forehead against his.

His facial hair scratches my skin as he skates past my cheek and brings his lips to my ear. "If you want to fuck me, it will be without a contract and only when you've begged me enough times for me to know you truly want me."

I ease back to look him in his eyes, and he drops his hands from my body. We're locked in a staring contest as I try to determine what I want to say, and then the bathroom door flies open.

CHAPTER TWENTY-SEVEN

"SORRY, I HAVE TO PE—"

I step away quickly. Too quickly, probably. Jess stands just inside the bathroom with a confused look on her face.

Roman stands up straight, getting away from the wall. "What're you doing in here?"

"I have to pee," she says, eyes ping-ponging between the two of us as her brows knit in the center. "The women's bathroom is full."

She disappears into a stall and Roman and I share a worried glance. I contemplate just fleeing, but I don't know if that'll help or worsen things.

The toilet flushes and the door opens, and Jess is armed with questions.

"What's going on with you two?" she asks matter-of-factly as she turns the water on.

"What do you mean?" we both say at the same time.

She gives us both the same look. It's filled with skepticism and frustration.

"You're friends, then you're not talking, then you're friendly again, then it looks like you hate each other, then it seems like you really like each other, and whatever I just walked in on looks a lot like toeing the line of both." She shuts off the water and grabs some paper towels. "I've been thinking that maybe I ruined y'all's friendship by telling you that I think Roman has a crush on you, but I don't believe I have anything to do with whatever it is you two have going on. I'm not here to pry or force you to answer questions, but if you think the tension between you isn't palpable, you're wrong. If you think I can't see the way you both watch the other person, I'm here to tell you that my vision is 20/20. And if you think you're keeping your"—she twirls her hand in the air in our direction—"concoction of feelings from everyone, you're wrong. People have been wondering what's up with you two for a while. They may not be as suspicious as me, but if you're trying to keep everyone in the dark about something, do better. I'm gonna go enjoy the rest of the party."

She tosses the paper towel in the trash and struts between the two of us. Roman follows her, and the two of them leave together.

I stare at myself in the mirror before slamming my palm against the wall with a grunt of frustration. When the door opens and a couple other guys walk in, I give them a nod and walk out.

I don't want to be here anymore. I can't. Not now that I think everyone here can see something brewing between Roman and myself. I'm so angry, but it's not like I can place that blame on anyone in particular. I'm just angry at the situation. At myself.

"Hey, I'm gonna head out," I tell Grant when I get to the table.

"Everything okay?" he asks.

"Yep."

"I'll get the car pulled around," he says, already moving toward the door.

As I wait, Jess approaches. I swallow, my heart lodging itself in my throat because I'm not ready for this conversation.

"Hey," she says in a soft tone. "I'm sorry if I made you uncomfortable. I didn't want you to flee, but I want you to know you can trust me and I'm here if you ever need to talk."

The sincerity and genuine expression on her face nearly has me ready to break open and spill everything, just in the hope that I'll feel a little lighter.

"I appreciate that," I say. "But you know, everything's fine."

She gives a smile that lets me know she doesn't believe me. "Not even an amazing actor like yourself can make me believe that."

Jess turns away and walks back toward Roman. His eyes linger on me for a few seconds before I cut and run, making my exit.

In the car, I call Faye, because she's the only one I can talk to about this right now. Once she informs me she's at home and it's okay to stop by, I have Grant drop me off at her house so he can go home.

"Hey there, handsome," Faye greets when she opens her door.

"Hey, gorgeous."

We embrace and hold onto each other for several long seconds before disappearing into her house.

"I have tea and liquor. Which do you prefer?"

"Tea is fine. Thank you."

I follow her into the kitchen and watch as she moves around the space in her silk pajamas and pink slippers. Her long, dark hair falls in loose curls to the middle of her back, and her glasses sit atop her button nose.

"So, what's going on?" she asks, pouring the hot water over the tea infusers in our glasses.

"I've found myself in an interesting situation."

"Uh-oh," she says, putting down the teapot and spinning around. "Boy troubles?"

"Aren't all our troubles boy troubles?"

She snorts. "Yes."

"So, there's this guy…"

"Of course," she says, leaning over the counter with her chin resting atop her hands.

"He's bi, but he isn't out publicly."

"Also an actor?" she questions with a raised brow.

"Yeah. And we've started…something. I don't know what to call it. We're just messing around."

"And?"

I sigh and rub my forehead. "Is the tea ready yet?"

"Don't stall," she says, standing up and removing the strainers from the glasses. "Keep going."

"After having sex, for the first time, I may have asked him to sign an NDA."

Faye slowly spins around with a strainer in her fingers and her jaw hanging open. "You didn't."

"What?"

"Jacoby Hart."

"It's not like I haven't done it before."

She shakes her head as she goes about finishing the tea. It

isn't until she's placed the colorful glass in front of me that she speaks again.

"Right after you had sex? Like, immediately?"

"I mean, we were getting something to eat."

I bring the cup to my lips and slowly sip, avoiding her gaze.

"What else?"

"Oh, is this keemun tea?"

"Yes, stop asking questions and start answering."

"I said we could backdate it to the time when we kissed for the first time, but Faye, I'm protecting us both."

"Honey. There's a right and wrong time for these things. You picked the worst time. All your other NDA hookups know beforehand. You were already kissing, and doing who knows what else with this guy before throwing a contract at him? Come on."

"He knew I'd done it before. I didn't think it would be a big deal, but I hurt his feelings and now he's done with me."

She cocks her head and walks around the island in the kitchen, reaching for my hand. "Come. Let's go sit. Take off your shoes."

I toe my dress shoes off and leave them in the kitchen before she brings me into her living room. We pass huge plants that stand on either side of her cream-colored couch that's covered with orange and cream pillows.

There are hand carved antique lamps that replicate a Korean house pavilion on the end tables that give off a soft, warm light.

I love how much of herself and her heritage she put into her place. Faye has always been so open and inviting, and a thousand percent authentic. I admire and adore her, and though she'll give it to me straight, I know I can come to her with anything and still be loved.

"So, you're not thinking about coming out anytime soon, right?"

"I always figured it would be something I'd worry about *later.* After this movie, after that award ceremony. You know? Just *later.* I know there are plenty of people who are out now, but we don't know their internal struggle or what could possibly be going on in their personal lives. Some media sites might praise them for living authentically. There will be people who will be happy for them, but there's always a dark side, right? Your closest friends or family. Little comments you hear in whispered tones. Secret bigotry that's better hidden but that you still feel."

"I know it's scary, but I don't want you to live like this until you're ready to retire from acting. You're so young, and you could be working for another thirty years or more. Are you never going to fall in love? Get married? Live your life the way you want to?"

"The idea of no longer hiding or being afraid that someone will find out is amazing. I'd love to have that sort of freedom, and I'd like to think my acting ability will keep me getting jobs and that my sexuality won't affect that, but there's a slight worry. Plus, my parents."

She nods and takes a sip of her tea.

"They're fine, you know? Fine, but not thrilled that my sister's a lesbian. They don't want to know who she's dating or get to know any girlfriends. They don't say anything mean, but they don't seem to accept it either."

"Hmm."

"And anyway, besides all that, this guy…" I shake my head and sigh. "He's a handful."

"Ohh," she says, raising her brows.

"Not like that…well, yes, like that, but also he's extremely infuriating. One second I think I hate him but then

I want to do disgustingly delicious things to him. He's so loud and outgoing. My complete opposite. But when it's just us… he's different. I don't know," I say, shaking my head as I put my tea on a coaster. "My head's fucked up and I don't know what to do."

"You really like him," she says, her lips pulling in at one corner.

"I do. I was starting to anyway. I didn't want it to end but I was afraid. He talks to so many people, you know? What if he said something?"

"You said he's in the closet, too?"

"I know, that's what he said. I can't explain fear. It just exists and it grows and infiltrates rational thinking."

"You don't think an apology would work?"

I rest my elbow on the back of the couch as I hold my head in my hand. "He said he'd only continue if we did so without an NDA and once I begged him enough to make him believe I truly wanted him."

"Oh, my. I think I like him already."

I snort, wishing I could tell her that she knows him. "I don't know if he's who I should come out for."

"No," she says in a serious tone. "Don't come out for *anybody*. When you come out, it needs to be for yourself."

"I'm not sure I'm ready yet."

She reaches for my hand and squeezes. "Then don't do it."

"You know I love you, right?"

"Ah, yes. I am quite loveable."

I move in closer, wrap my arm around her shoulders, and we spend the rest of the night talking and laughing.

And it's exactly what I needed.

PART TWO

ROMAN

CHAPTER 28

IT'S BEEN THREE MONTHS SINCE I'VE SEEN JACOBY. WELL, face-to-face anyway. He's been on TV, promoting a movie he filmed prior to ours, and now we're set to take photos and sit for an interview for a magazine issue that'll come out a couple months before our movie does.

To my surprise, he never reached out after that wrap party. I definitely expected him to, and I'm not sure if that's narcissistic of me or just hopeful, but I was waiting for him to at least text.

Sure, I never did either, but I was still holding on to my anger.

The week following our wrap party, photos started coming out of Jacoby and Faye being out together, so there's rumors of a rekindled relationship and gossip about mine and Jacoby's friendship.

Of course, we haven't been seen out together, so it fuels the story that we're still fighting over the same girl. However, the social media team for *Another Life* have been posting behind the scenes photos and videos that were taken while filming. The hope is that this will keep the hype up on the movie and put an end to the rumors. So some people believe we're just as close as ever, some choose to believe we hate each other over Faye, and others are hoping we're secretly together, which sort of makes me laugh.

As I wait for the shoot to begin, I scroll through social media and find photos of Jacoby and I from when we were filming the end of the movie. Fans get a hold of behind the scenes pictures, or even scenes filmed on public streets and put together edits. I click on the comments of one video and read through them.

Oh my god, the way he's touching him.

They're low-key fucking. At least I hope so.

Y'all are crazy. You can see the tension in Jacoby's face. He hates him.

Wrong. That's sexual tension. He wants to jump his bones.

They are so cute!

I can't wait for this movie.

Did you see the way Roman looked at Jacoby's mouth?? Lord have mercy. If someone looked at me like that I'd be on my knees.

I'm feral.

I want my boyfriends to be boyfriends!!

I laugh, shaking my head, and then stumble across some thirst trap edits of Jacoby at the Venice film festival. Everything is in slow motion as he smiles and poses for cameras. He winks at someone in the crowd, and I hate what that wink does to me as I watch.

"Hello."

I jolt, nearly dropping my phone as I look up and spot Jacoby right in front of me.

"Shit."

He doesn't grin, he just watches me as I turn off the phone and pocket it.

"How are you?" he asks.

"Fine." My heart is still racing slightly, but I push my shoulders back and give him what I hope is a casual once-over. "You?"

"Great."

His tone implies differently, but I don't question it.

"Well, good. So, I guess we're back to being fake best friends for the interview."

"I guess."

"Anything new I should know? Dating anyone?"

I regret the words as soon as they leave my mouth. They come out bitter and jealous, but they don't taste good for another reason. We both know even if he's "dating" someone, it's not real.

He flattens his lips into a straight line. "Nope." Looking away, he asks, "Are you? I've seen you've been photographed with Malia recently."

"Ah. Keeping an eye on me?"

His head swivels back and his eyes stare into mine. "It's not like I'm watching fan edit videos."

My jaw drops as I realize he saw what I was watching. "I didn't search for it, it was just in my feed."

"The feed that caters to your likes." His lips finally twitch into an almost grin.

Before I can continue arguing, his assistant comes up to him. "We're ready."

Shortly after, mine approaches and informs me of the same thing. We've both been dressed and made up for the pictures, so we make our way to the set and get started.

We start with shots of both of us in front of a white background, with the direction of maintaining stoic expressions. We switch outfits and backgrounds and have more of a playful shoot. We're directed to pretend like we're playing a card game, but I bend half the deck and let them go flying at Jacoby. He laughs and brings up his arms to block them, and the director thinks it's fantastic.

After another outfit and scene change, we take turns with individual photos. I chat with my assistant, Pilar, on the sidelines as the photographer directs Jacoby into positions. He's on a chair in one of his classic black suits, but the top few buttons are undone, and the makeup artist and hairstylist are in front of him making slight changes.

His hair is mussed up and not in its usual pristine condition. I can't take my eyes off of him as he moves, removing the jacket for the next set of photos as someone comes to help roll up the sleeves of his shirt in just the right way. They're taking apart his normal put-together facade and I find myself fascinated.

He's told to slouch and lean, when he's usually so stiff and proper. They undo the buttons on the shirt, revealing a tank top underneath, and he's handed a glass of liquor to hold onto as he sits on the floor in front of the chair with his legs bent.

His eyes find mine briefly before he's staring back into the lens.

"Holy shit," I say under my breath, taken away by his beauty.

"What's that?" Pilar asks, typing into her phone.

"Oh. Nothing."

Except I'm thinking I want to renege on what I told him before. He doesn't have to beg me, because I'm damn near ready to beg him. For what? Anything. A kiss. A touch. Just a reminder that what we had was actually real. That it wasn't a fever dream.

The stubborn part of me wants him to crawl back to me though, and my anger still bubbles under the surface.

Once he's done, it's my turn. My photos are taken in a similar way, but my starting outfit is what I'm known for. Bright colors and eye-catching designs. They slowly strip me down, changing my positions and hair, but as my eyes dance around, I notice Jacoby isn't watching. And that bothers me.

When I'm down to the last shots, my button up completely open and exposing my naked torso, I lie across a vintage couch with one leg planted on the floor and the other dangling over the end.

Movement catches my attention, and I watch as Jacoby comes to a stop in the back. The way he's looking at me makes me swallow, because he's not looking at my face. He's drinking in my entire body, and it sets me on fire.

The photographer gets my attention and snaps a few more.

"Oh, wait. Jacoby," he calls out, spinning around with the camera in his hand. "Is Jacoby still dressed?"

"He's here," someone says.

Jacoby walks forward, still mostly in what he was wearing for his own shoot, except he put on a T-shirt.

"Come. Take this off," the photographer says, touching the shirt.

Jacoby removes it and hands it to someone nearby.

"Shoes off for both of you."

Assistants come to set to take what we discard as the photographer seems to come up with a new idea on the spot.

By the time he's ready to take pictures again, we're both barefoot, and my shirt is still open but now the button of my pants is undone. Jacoby has on his undershirt that reveals his broad shoulders and toned arms, and black slacks. I'm directed to lay just as I was before and Jacoby sits in front of the couch. The photographer tells me to let my hand fall over Jacoby's shoulder, so I do it.

After a couple dozen or so shots, we're done and invited to look at some of the photos. The first thing I think of when I see the most recent shots are that it looks like we just got done hooking up, which makes me think of our last time together.

"Looks really good, right?" the photographer says with a wide smile.

Jacoby's studying them intently. He stands up straight and smiles. "Yes. Very good. Thank you."

His eyes land on my face and I try to read the emotion in his gaze but I can't. He's gone before I can even think about it.

With one final peek at the pictures on the screen, I know that one from this collection will end up safely tucked away in my house somewhere.

CHAPTER 29

AFTER I'M CHANGED, I GET READY TO MEET UP WITH JACOBY in another room on a different floor of the building. We'll be interviewed by an outside party, and then we'll interview each other in what's supposed to be a fun, carefree sort of thing.

"You have thirty minutes to eat and take care of anything else you need to before I bring you over to the interviewer," Pilar says. "They have sandwiches and other things set up over here," she tells me, pointing toward an open door. "I'll be back soon."

"Thanks."

I make my way into the room she pointed out and find a couple tables and chairs and a small loveseat. There's food set up on a long countertop and a fridge with a variety of drinks.

I grab a finger sandwich and eat half of it in one bite, then put a few more on my plate. As I'm picking up baby carrots with tiny tongs, the door opens and Jacoby and his assistant walk in.

Turning my back on them, I scoop some ranch onto my plate and finish eating my first sandwich.

Jacoby whispers something to the other guy, and by the time I turn to take a seat at one of the tables, his assistant is gone.

I give him a quick inspection before continuing to eat my food as he gathers his. When he turns to sit down, I lean back and watch him, waiting to see if he'll choose to sit with me or at the other table.

He debates it, his eyes scanning me before flicking toward the empty table. He decides not to sit with me, but chooses to face my direction, watching me as he picks up his sandwich.

I shake my head and continue to eat, choosing to give him the silent treatment rather than my usual sarcastic comments.

Halfway into the thirty minutes we have before the interview, he finally speaks.

"Roman."

I glance up, leaning back in my chair with one leg outstretched. "Jacoby."

"I'm sorry that I hurt your feelings. I'm not used to having to worry about that."

"You're used to being an uncaring asshole?"

He twists his lips as he levels me with a stare. "I'm not used to having anyone in my life who cared enough to be hurt by anything I did or said."

I sit up straight, emotions tugging at my heart. "Well. Okay. Thank you for the apology." I swallow, knowing I need to say more, but feeling conflicted about the whole situation.

He seems to realize that's all he's going to get, so he gives me a nod and picks up his plate to throw in the trash. God, I hate when he's so controlled like this. So stiff and not himself.

"I'd still like to hear you beg."

He turns around, his eyes showcasing a bit of shock. "Not gonna happen."

"You don't want me?" I tease, giving him a smirk.

His blue-green eyes drink me in from head to toe, cataloging every inch of me. My body warms under his slow perusal. He's looking at me as if I'm naked, and I quickly want to be.

When his gaze lands on my face, he gives a slight shake of his head. "That's not what I said."

My tongue darts out to wet my lips, and it feels like we're back to our old ways. He has me under his spell, and I'm willing to do anything he wants as long as he tells me exactly what it is. But that can't happen. He has to beg me. He has to prove how much he wants me before I just drop to my knees. I'm not the one in the wrong.

I force a bravado I don't feel, since it's my go-to anyway. Fake it and nobody will know just how hurt and broken you are.

Standing up, I take a couple steps toward him. "So, you *do* want me?"

He swallows. "I've wanted you since before I knew it was a possibility to have you."

I freeze in place, not expecting that answer. "Then why—"

Jacoby cuts me off. "I'm afraid, and you're not someone to keep hidden." He shakes his head. "I can't—"

"All right, let's start heading up," Pilar says, bursting into the room.

Jacoby straightens up and looks at Pilar over my shoulder, but I stare at him a few seconds longer.

"Yeah, we should get going," he says after clearing his throat.

He walks past me, giving me a sidelong glance before disappearing through the door.

"Come on, let's go," Pilar says.

In the middle of the interview, I still can't stop thinking about what Jacoby said. He's never had anyone in his life care enough to be hurt. That pangs me, and I know it has to leave him with an ache in his chest. But here we are with plastered smiles, talking about romance.

"And how do you feel about bringing these beloved characters to life? I imagine there's readers all over the world that have their own interpretation of how these two men look and behave," the interviewer, Malcolm says. "So, is there any pressure?"

"Well," Jacoby starts, "I read the book when I was chosen for this role, and immediately understood why it's so adored. I fell in love with Andrew and William's story like so many others had. We were lucky enough to be able to have discussions with the author, and I'd ask him if there were any more bits of information that could only live in his brain, you know? He created these people and had backgrounds for them and personality traits, and sometimes not everything makes it to the book, but it's still his vision, and I wanted to know everything. I really put myself in William's shoes, and I hope that everyone thinks I gave him a little justice. Roman and I put everything we had into these characters."

"I read the book as well," I say. "Twice, actually. It's beautiful and heartbreaking, sexy and heartfelt, and because of its large fandom, I definitely felt the pressure. Having

Jacoby as an acting partner in this really helped. He's amazing, right?" I say with a laugh. "Everyone knows that, and to have someone like him work opposite me, it really helped elevate my skills as an actor." I nudge Jacoby's arm. "Can't have him showing me up too much."

Malcolm laughs. "And you two are friends, right?"

"Well, I think the media has kind of run wild with our story. One day we're best friends and another day we're enemies." I glance at Jacoby who's watching me with curious eyes. "The truth of the matter is, we weren't exactly friends when this movie started filming. We had run into each other a few times, but that's about it."

"Really?" Malcolm questions. "I've seen some behind the scenes footage, and you guys seem really close."

"Yeah, well, we got close. I'd say we're friends now, but it's not like we grew up together or anything."

"Like you mentioned, the media has had a field day with some stories about you two. One particular rumor that had a spotlight on it didn't just include you two, though. Is that not true either?"

Jacoby chuckles. "We already know what this is about, and no, there were never any problems between us when it came to a specific actress."

"Definitely not," I add.

"Okay, I heard the director put you two in a cabin for three days so you'd be more in the headspace of William and Andrew. Is that true, and if so, how did it go?"

We both laugh and Jacoby starts. "Yes, it's true, and it was fine. This one showers way too long."

"And this one can't drink regular milk."

Jacoby rolls his eyes. "We didn't have a TV, so we just cooked, went over the script, and..." He shrugs. "We got to know each other a little better."

I glance at him and nod. "Yeah."

"I imagine it was good that you did get along and became friends. With a film like this, where there are so many intimate scenes, did you ever feel worried about how it would come across on camera?"

"No, I was never worried," Jacoby replies, messing with his tie. "We're actors, and regardless of whether it's a fight scene, a crying scene, or a sex scene, we're doing our job and giving the best performance possible. I could've hated Roman and still made you believe I didn't."

I snort. "What he said is true, however, I will say this—it was nice knowing I could go to Jacoby with some trepidation, and not for any other reason except I had never done scenes like this before, and he'd offer advice and make me feel comfortable and confident. I don't imagine every actor is like that, and again, that's why I'm glad he was the one I was working with. He really did make me better, and I'm excited for everyone to see that when they watch the film."

I feel his gaze on me, but I can't look at him. Not now. Not while Malcom is watching our every movement.

"The director is a gay man, the author is a bisexual man, and you two are perceived to be straight. Did you ever think that maybe—"

"I'm going to stop you right there, Malcolm," Jacoby says, making Malcolm's eyebrows reach for his hairline. "Our sexuality is not the point of this interview."

"I suppose you're right, but there are people out there who question why these roles weren't given to queer men."

"Again, to think that, would be to presume. And I do believe gay actors should get roles, but I don't believe they should *only* be given gay roles. There aren't enough queer movies being made, and to limit them to only those roles would mean they wouldn't work very often."

"To your point," Malcolm continues, "since there aren't many queer movies, don't you believe that queer actors should get those parts? Why you?"

I stare at Jacoby in shock. He's fuming. His jaw is clenched and his nostrils flare with each intake of breath. He's trying not to lose it, but I can tell he's mad.

"I believe that's a question for the casting director or perhaps the director of the film himself," I say, chiming in. "Mike trusted us with these characters, as did the author of the story. We are doing what actors do and transforming into people who aren't us and have experiences that maybe we don't. I was never the son of an alcoholic mother, and yet, I played one. And back to what Jacoby said, when people question the sexualities of others they don't know, you could be forcing them into an uncomfortable situation. It's best to tread lightly." I relax in my seat a bit more and give him a forced smile.

Malcolm clears his throat. "Yes. Now, to discuss what you just mentioned, you played the son of an alcoholic mother. In that role, you gained critical acclaim. I read that you pulled from your real life when acting in the scenes after your mother died in the film. Do you normally recall your own personal tragedies or traumas to really reach that level of emotion?"

Where I was first grateful for the change of direction, I'm quickly uncomfortable again. I know he's doing his job, but it doesn't mean I was prepared for this question.

My assistant speaks up. "I don't know if we're going to answer that," she says, looking at me.

"It's fine." I suppose it's time to mention it. "Not always, Malcolm. Some actors will pull from real life to get the tears or anger needed for a scene, and some can just do it." I shrug. "For *Broken*, I didn't necessarily seek out memories of my own trauma, it came naturally. My parents died in a car accident, and though I never had to deal with what it's like growing up with a parent who was an addict, I knew what it felt like to be broken. I had experienced gut-wrenching pain and loss. I had been angry and lost, and when I had to grieve for a parent in that film, I knew what that felt like. I had experienced it, you know?"

"I imagine that was very tough."

My eyes flicker to Jacoby who's watching me with a shocked and sorrowful expression. I ignore it because I can't deal with that right now. The pity is something I still can't handle.

Malcolm finishes up his questions and the rest of the interview goes smoothly. We get another brief break before Jacoby and I are due to have a more lighthearted interview with each other.

"You handled that well. You okay?" Pilar asks.

"Yeah. I'm fine."

"You don't ever talk about that, and if you want me to make sure it gets cut, I can."

"No, it's fine," I say with a flat smile. "I'm gonna use the bathroom."

I walk off, wanting some time to myself. Pilar is right. I never bring up the deaths of my parents. As you'd assume, it's a hard topic and not one I've dealt with really well.

They died three years ago, right before I filmed *Broken*, and before I became a well-known name in the industry. My way of dealing with that trauma is to ignore it. I don't discuss them or what happened. I pretend like everything is fine.

My *flashiness* as Jacoby refers to it, was born from their deaths. I wanted to be someone else. I wanted the persona, because if I'm in bright colors and bold prints, that's what people will talk about. If I'm with high-profile actresses at premieres and fashion shows, they'll take photos and discuss what I'm wearing.

I forced my happiness when I was sad. I wore bright colors when I was grieving because wearing black reminded me of their funerals. I started partying a little more, and during the month of December, I drink more than usual. Not to a point of a problem, but because they died in December and the holiday season is hard.

Everything I've done and do is in an effort to move past the pain, not acknowledge the broken parts of me, and act like I'm fine and happy. People won't question you if you're always laughing and enjoying life. If you're down or sad or quiet, the questions begin, and as soon as someone asks if I'm okay, it's a reminder that I'm not.

CHAPTER 30

"HAVE YOU SEEN ROMAN?" I ASK HIS ASSISTANT.

"Bathroom, I think. But I'd give him a minute."

I stop and look at her. "Is he okay?"

"I'm sure he's fine, but…" She shrugs. "He doesn't talk about personal things, and that was very personal for him. He may need a moment."

I nod and wander off, my heart forcing me to find him while my head says to listen to his assistant and leave him be.

A few minutes later, I walk into a bathroom in the hopes it's the right one. When I spot Roman, he's leaned over the sink, his hands clutching the sides of the porcelain in a tight grip as he stares at the running water in a daze.

My steps pull him out of his thoughts, and I watch as he slips on his mask. The pain in his eyes disappears and he forces his easy going grin as he begins to wash his hands. "Almost done for today."

"Yeah," I reply.

"I cannot wait to go get an actual meal after this. I'm starving. Little finger sandwiches ain't gonna cut it for long, you know?"

I can't pull my gaze from his face in the mirror, and now that I know what he's been through, it's easy to recognize the front he's putting on.

"Roman."

His back goes stiff and he stops washing his hands. "Not right now, Jacoby," he says, shutting off the water.

"I just wanted to say I'm sorry. I didn't know."

"It's fine," he says curtly, marching to the paper towel dispenser. "That's how I want it."

I take a couple steps closer to him. "If you ever—"

"I don't," he says, cutting me off as he tosses the rumpled paper in the trash. "I don't want to talk."

"Okay," I say with a nod.

"I don't want your pity either. I'm an adult. It's been a few years. I'm fine."

He's not, and we both know it, but I'm not going to argue with him.

"Okay," I say again.

"Good. Let's get this interview over with."

He storms out, leaving me alone in the bathroom with a head full of thoughts. I've never had to deal with the death of someone close to me, let alone a parent. To lose both at the same time, so suddenly, has to be extremely hard to cope with. It seems clear Roman hasn't processed his trauma yet. If he avoids it at all costs, I doubt he's given himself proper time to grieve.

A few things make sense now. His demeanor, always being so happy-go-lucky and cheerful, is carefully constructed. He's crafted the way he wants to be seen, hiding the anguish with laughter and jokes.

With me, when it's just us in intimate moments, he's always been different. Quiet, nervous, and seeking direction. I thought it was just a dynamic we had, but perhaps he's really that way, and everything else is just an act.

And his drinking. I remember questioning him about it and he gave me some vague reply about it being December. I'd bet money the accident happened in that month and that's why he struggles more at that time of year.

Considering I don't have time to dwell on this, and I'm unsure I'll ever get him to open up to me, I shake it off and go find him. We have a job to do.

"All right, I'm Roman Black."

"And I'm Jacoby Hart."

"And we're here taking *JP Magazine*'s BFF quiz."

"BFF?" I ask, looking at the camera positioned in front of us. "Is there a different one? Maybe a buddy quiz? Or an acquaintance test?"

"You don't think we'll pass or what?" Roman asks with a grin, holding his cards up.

"Oh, I think I'll get more right than you."

Roman barks out a laugh. "Okay, sure. When I win, by a landslide most likely, you owe me dinner."

"Yeah, yeah. Let's get to it."

He clears his throat as he looks at his first card. "Ah, this is a good one. What was the first movie I ever acted in?"

Roman watches me with a smug grin like he knows I'm going to get it wrong.

"Hmm. The first movie. I want to say it was *Wind and*—"

Roman's eyebrows go up, and now he has me second guessing myself. "What? It's not that one?"

He shrugs. "I don't know. What's your final answer?"

I narrow my eyes at him before I look at the person behind the camera. "Wait. His first acting role? What are the baselines? Does he have to have been in it for a certain amount of time?"

"What is this?" Roman asks with a laugh. "You don't get to ask questions. Just answer it."

"Fine. I think it's a trick question, but you appeared in a movie called *Get Wet*, but the next one was a bit more substantial and that was called *Wind and Waves*."

Roman squints at me briefly before leaning back in his chair. "I guess you got that right."

"Yeah!" I say, thrusting my arm in the air. "Okay, your turn." I look over the questions on the card and read one. "What's my favorite food?"

"That's really the question?"

"Yep."

He crosses his arms, a smile on his lips. "Steak."

I look at him with surprise etched on my features before I narrow my eyes. "How did you know?"

"What if I know your favorite movie and hobbies? Do I get bonus points?"

"No," I say with a chuckle, and then it hits me. These were our getting to know each other questions in the cabin. "Oh! You actually listened to me that day."

Roman laughs, winking at me. "You can buy me a steak dinner later."

"No, you'll be buying it for me."

"Please," he says after a scoff. "Okay, next question. What was my first job before I got into acting?"

My brows knit. "Who knows that?"

Roman looks into the camera. "I bet there's a lot of

people out there that know. Not you, because you're not my BFF."

I shake my head. "Probably like…a movie theater."

"Are you fucking kidding?" he bursts, staring at me with his lips parted. "You just guessed that?"

"It's true?"

He waves his cards at me. "I don't think you should get that point. That was a lucky guess."

I pretend to adjust my tie as I look at the camera. "Or I'm just that good."

"Yeah, right."

"Okay, which movie earned me my first award?"

"That's easy."

"Oh yeah? Which one?"

"*To the Flame*."

My brows jump up. "Good job."

"Good job to you, sir. It was a great movie." I smile and let him read off his card. "What's my favorite thing to do when I'm not working?"

"Oh." I make a face as I think. "Who knows with you? Maybe…shopping? Watching my movies? Uhh—"

Roman laughs. "Watch your movies. Yes. You're correct. Moving on. Which of my movies is your favorite? If you've seen any."

I roll my eyes. "I've seen 'em. But I'm going to say the one we just filmed."

He looks at me with a twinkle in his eye. "Because you're in it too?"

"No, because you were incredible."

My honesty shocks him and his eyes widen. He clears his throat and gazes into the camera. "You guys got that, right?" He looks back at me. "You can never deny it now."

"Never."

His eyes scan over me once more. "Okay, what's your question?"

I glance at my card. "Most embarrassing moment on set?"

Roman laughs. "Well, there is one, but I'm not gonna say that here." He looks at the camera. "You guys don't get that little secret."

"Well, now I'm curious."

"You know it. Or you should if you think about it long enough. But no, we're not talking about that. Let me give you the second most embarrassing moment."

"No, I really want to know the first one."

"Jacoby, no!" he says with a laugh.

I think back to when we were filming, and we did have a lot of fun moments where people would mess up lines or someone would trip.

"Was it when you pushed me into the sink?"

"Oh yeah," he says with a laugh. "Yeah, let's go with that."

I face the camera. "Zero points for that, because it's a lie. Just tell me and stop being a baby."

"I don't mind telling *you*, but telling a million people," he says with a gesture toward the camera. "Not happening."

I tap my finger on my chin. "Was it—"

"Jacoby."

The way he says my name triggers something in me. A memory. When I look over at him, he lifts his brows just slightly, his face a little flushed.

"Oh. Ohhh," I say, realizing. "Yeah, I think I got it."

Roman laughs and runs his hand through his hair. "Jesus."

It was when he whispered my name during our sex scene. Not quite sure that will ever leave my memory. I just don't classify it as embarrassing on my end.

We keep going for a few more minutes before we're out of questions.

"Well, that's it for us," Roman says.

"Bye, guys!"

Once the cameras stop rolling, a couple people who were behind them come up and start removing our mics.

After a few minutes, we're free to leave.

"You gonna buy me dinner?" I ask Roman as we're walking down the hall.

His head swivels and his dark eyes meet mine. "I thought that was for the cameras."

"We're both hungry, right?"

"Just dinner."

I grin. "Of course. What else would there be?"

He presses the button for an elevator. "Nothing." Spinning around, he puts his hands in his pockets. "At least not until I hear a certain word leave your lips."

"What word is that so I know to avoid it?"

He smirks. "Please." The doors open and we step inside. "Followed by *fuck me*."

The doors enclose us in the small space.

JACOBY

CHAPTER 31

"WELL, DON'T WORRY ABOUT THAT. THOSE WORDS HAVE never been uttered by me before."

Roman leans back in the corner. "Really? Never? I have a very vivid memory of you saying those last two to me."

"They weren't preceded with *please*. It was more of a demand than a plea."

"Ah." Roman inclines his head, a smirk on his lips. "I see."

"And usually, it's my partner that says those words. Not me."

"Hmm. So I'm special."

I tilt my head slightly. "You're something."

The doors open and release all the tension-filled air as we spill out onto the lobby floor.

"You drive here?" he asks.

"I took a cab."

"Good. I have my car. You're riding with me."

We leave the building and round the corner to make our way to a parking garage. It's fairly late, but in the city it hardly matters. There's plenty of people walking around, and some of them recognize us and pull out their phones to take photos or record a video.

"There's paparazzi down there. That red car. He's always finding me."

"You have a stalker."

"He's decent enough. Just don't do anything you don't want talked about tomorrow."

"Right. I'm always acting up in public."

He snorts. "You're perfectly calculated. I know."

"As are you, I think."

We disappear into the garage and find his car—a dark gray Mercedes Benz coupe.

"This looks fast."

"Yeah, but I'm careful."

Inside, I sit in the leather seat and fasten my belt while Roman clicks a few things on the screen in the center. Some Latin music comes on low before he buckles his own seat belt and starts up the car.

"So, where we going?" he asks.

"Juanita's."

He looks at me. "Where?"

"It's a hole-in-the-wall Mexican food place. Believe me. It's so good."

"Where is it?"

"It's off 134. Pasadena area."

"Trying to get me close to your house?"

I laugh. "No. It's just a good place to eat."

"Will they be open? It'll be ten or so by the time we get there."

"As long as we're there before eleven, it'll be fine."

"How did you know about *Get Wet*?" he asks after a couple minutes.

"Late night internet sleuthing."

"So, you stalked me."

"I guess you have two stalkers."

He's quiet for several minutes as he drives, and I stare out the window and watch all the lights of the city and cars as we pass.

"You seemed to get upset with the interviewer today," he says.

I harrumph. "I tried to hold my tongue."

"You know, it's going to be a common question."

"Sure. This is my first queer movie. Well, where I play the gay character. I've been in some things that featured queer couples, but this is a first for me. I wanted to do it, and I knew it would come with questions, but I guess I wasn't prepared."

"I want to come out," Roman says after a few seconds. "But I don't want to do it because I feel like I have to because I played this character. I don't want to have people question you and how you feel about that, because I don't want you to feel obligated to answer or come out yourself. I don't want it to be a big deal, but I'm unsure how to go about it now."

My pulse spikes. The thought of coming out is both terrifying and freeing. If he did it, I may get questions about it, especially as we're still promoting the film. It could become a spectacle, but maybe not. Others could, in turn, question my own sexuality even more, but also, maybe not. Roman should be able to do whatever he wants at the time of his choosing, and the fact that he's even thinking about me in a decision like this makes my heart clench.

"I don't think you should worry about me. If you want to, you should."

"It's not like I've been lying. I just haven't dated any guys."

"Maybe you can just show up to an event with a date and have it be that easy."

"Well, it's not like I have a list of gay or bi men who would be willing to be with me, so it's not that easy."

"Do you have a list of women?"

He snorts. "Kind of."

"I hate you," I say with a laugh. "If you come out, I bet you'll have a line of men waiting to be with you."

Roman's quiet for a few seconds. "I might like for you to be at the front of the line."

The low rhythmic music plays as we both fall into silence. I have a million thoughts running through my head, but I can't think of a proper response.

"Hmm."

He makes a noise in the back of his throat but doesn't say anything else. By the time I direct him to the restaurant, guilt has eaten through me.

"Roman."

He parks. "Let's go eat."

I turn in my seat and face him. "I want you. I want you more than I even want to admit to myself. You don't understand the yearning I feel. The last three months have been filled with pitiful inner monologues that vary from reasons why it's best to stay away from you to plans to get you to want to be with me again."

His eyes soften. "Why did you have to ruin everything with that fucking NDA?"

"I was afraid. I still am."

He sighs. "I get it, and I'm willing to move past it, but I won't sign one."

I nod my head once. "I know."

"But I still want more. More from you. More of us. Whatever it means, wherever it leads."

My heart beats rapidly in my chest, but I try not to get my hopes up. "In secret?"

He studies me for a few seconds. "In secret."

CHAPTER 32

IF THE LAST THREE MONTHS PROVED ANYTHING, IT'S THAT I'M not over this thing I have with Jacoby. It feels weird calling it a relationship, because I guess it's not one. It doesn't feel like just friends with benefits either, though.

Whatever we have going on, I haven't been able to stop thinking about it. I've been so angry at him. At first it was for bringing up the NDA at all, and then the subsequent silence we fell into because of that idiotic request. Mostly, I was mad because I wasn't talking to or seeing him anymore. Yes, he was really fucking annoying trying to make me sign a contract, but at the end of the day, my frustration over that doesn't come close to my desire to be with him.

"However," I say, holding up a finger. "We have to be honest with each other."

"Okay," he says slowly, concern creeping into his narrowed eyes. "Have you been with anyone since—"

"No," I say quickly, shaking my head. "I haven't been with anyone since you."

"Neither have I."

"I won't be with anyone else either," I state, brows lifting to let him know I expect the same.

"Right," he says with a dip of his chin.

"If we want to end things, for whatever reason, we have to be honest with each other."

"Okay."

"Anything else you want to add?"

"I think we should skip the Mexican food and go to my house."

A grin sweeps across my face. "Sounds like a plan. Are we going to watch a movie?"

"Sure. Which movie do you want to watch?" he says, eyes alight with amusement.

"Hmm. How about *The Voyeur*?"

"You want to watch a movie where I have lots of simulated sex with a woman?"

"I've watched it countless times already," I say, a blush warming my cheeks.

His lips form a small smile. "Okay. Let's go. Let's see how much of the movie you can watch before you're begging me to fuck you."

I watch as he types his address into my GPS with a smug grin on his face.

"Um, I think you're confused. You're still gonna be the one begging me."

"Okay," he says with a mischievous grin.

"Yeah. Okay."

"Let's go."

As soon as we're inside, I want to pounce on him, but I can't. It would give him way too much satisfaction, and he'd hold it over my head forever. But damn, my body is thrumming for him. He's too controlled and I should've thought of that before.

He steps out of his shoes and leaves them near the door, so I do the same. Jacoby then makes his way to the TV and turns it on before leisurely walking into the kitchen. He's already driving me crazy.

"Want something to drink?" he asks.

"Water is fine."

After a minute, he walks over with a cold glass of ice water and a grin. "Popcorn for the movie?"

I bite down, clenching my jaw. "No, thank you."

He smiles wider. "You can go ahead and find it. I think I'm going to take a quick shower."

"Oh. Maybe…should I take one too?"

His brows lift. "Should you?"

I inhale deeply through my nose. "Well, only because it's been a long day and they put some makeup on me for the shoot. You know?"

Jacoby inclines his head, his expression way too amused for me. "Right. Well, you can use the same one you used last time. I'll leave you some extra clothes."

"Okay."

His eyes travel down my body. "Okay."

As he makes his way up the stairs, I quickly find a coaster to put the glass of water on and rush to the bathroom.

I don't know what to expect tonight. We're both playing this *who's gonna beg for who* game, and I'm already on the verge of losing. Am I begging for him to fuck me or for me to fuck him? I want both. I truly do. I want him to be underneath me, quivering and gasping for breath as he begs me to go harder and deeper. But I also want to be on the receiving end. I want to know what it's like to succumb to the pleasure he doles out.

After using the restroom and doing a thorough scrub down of my entire body, I exit the shower and reach for a towel. I open the door to see if he left clothes and find some folded up pieces on a nearby table.

I snatch them up and close myself back in the bathroom, doing my best to clear the fog from the mirror before drying off and using some lotion. When I unfold the clothes, I find a loose-fitting cut off tee and a pair of blue pajama pants. The material is thin, and the fly doesn't have a button or anything to keep it closed.

My cock is going to pop out of this fairly easy if I get even a little bit hard. He probably did that on purpose.

I fold up my clothes and put them where he had his, and then make my way to the living room.

Realizing he hasn't come down yet, I grab his remote and find *The Voyeur* on a streaming app and press play. After taking a drink of the ice water, I find a soft blanket rolled up in a storage basket and drape it over my lap as I make myself comfortable.

The Voyeur is such a gripping movie. The character Jacoby plays is a man who meets a woman he begins an immediate affair with. They don't do romance or dates, simply sex. A lot of sex—all over his house.

His neighbor watches them since his windows are open all the time. She becomes obsessed and starts sneaking into his house to watch things more closely. She's in his closet and under his bed, listening and watching. She touches herself because she's so turned on, but at the same time, she gets irrationally jealous. She attempts to get his attention, and when she does, she thinks she's won…until the same woman comes over the next week and she watches them have sex again.

Her jealousy turns into full-blown rage, and she'll stop at nothing to get what she wants.

The first sex scene happens ten minutes into the movie, and of course that's when Jacoby walks in.

"Enjoying yourself?" he asks, strolling around the couch in a pair of low slung lounge pants and nothing else.

My eyes trace down his chest and stomach. He's fit and toned, but not bulging with muscles, and he's absolutely mouth-watering.

"Not yet."

He chuckles as he sits next to me. "You into voyeurism?" he questions, nodding at the TV.

"Depends," I answer with a shrug. "It's basically live porn, and I love porn."

"You like watching me have sex?"

"Well, I know this is fake, so it's not like I'm jealous. If you're asking if I can watch you have sex with another man in front of me and get turned on, the answer is no."

He scoots closer to me, his leg pressing against mine. "What do you like about this scene?" he asks in a husky tone.

I swallow. "The way you have her against the wall with your hand around her throat."

"Hmm."

After about fifteen minutes he says, "I don't really enjoy watching myself."

"Then watch me," I say. "Because my favorite scene is coming up and I'm not turning it off yet."

"Give me something to watch and I will."

I turn my head and stare at him. He lifts his brows, daring me. Pushing me.

"What do you say?" I tease.

"Now."

"No."

He begrudgingly turns and watches the TV again. This scene has Jacoby tying the girl's wrists to the bars of his headboard while she's on her knees. She's completely naked, her tits swaying as he thrusts into her. He spanks her ass, making her skin turn red as she moans and screams for more.

The camera pans to the open window where the neighbor is watching from her own bedroom.

"What do you like about this scene?"

"Everything," I say on a breath.

He moves in even closer, turning his body to face me as leans toward my ear and whispers, "Tell me exactly what you like about it."

My next inhale is shaky, and I'm suddenly burning up, but I can't remove the blanket from my lap now. Not without giving away just how badly I want him.

I try to keep my words steady. "The spanking."

"Mmhmm," he murmurs, running his nose on the skin behind my ear. "What else?"

"How red her skin turns."

"And?"

"The way you look. The way your body moves."

"What about the restraints?" he questions, easing away.

"Yes," I say with a nod. "I like those."

"How hard are you right now?"

"I-I'm not."

"Prove it."

He tugs at the blanket on my lap but I tighten my grip. "Are *you* hard?" I ask instead.

Jacoby leans back into the couch and spreads his legs. "Check for yourself."

My eyes travel down his body, and the truth is, I don't have to check. I can see that he is.

"From your own movie?" I ask, trying to joke.

"From being close to you. From thinking about all the things I want to do to you since I know a bit more about what you like."

I lick my lips as my gaze drops to his. "Huh."

His lips curl up slightly on the ends. "If you want them to be done, that is."

I shake my head. "You're really fucking annoying."

"You can just ask me, Roman. It's okay."

Considering I'm about ready to give him exactly what he wants, I decide to do something I hope will turn the tables.

I rip the blanket from my lap and toss it on the floor. His eyes track my movements as my hand reaches inside the fly of the pajama pants.

"You want something to watch? Fine."

He scoots back a little and adjusts his position until he's facing me. I glance over, my hand still hidden inside the pants.

"Well, I'm waiting."

I release myself from the material and bring my fist upward in a slow stroke as I watch the movie play out. After a couple minutes of teasing touches, I look at Jacoby again and find him still watching with rapt attention. It bothers me that he hasn't even reached for himself yet.

"Need some help?" he asks with a single raised brow.

"Maybe some lube."

He leans forward and wraps his fingers around my wrist, bringing my hand to his mouth. From the tip of my middle finger to the base of my palm, he flattens his tongue and wets my hand.

"See if that helps."

My gaze is frozen on his face while everything inside me is on fire. I wrap my fingers around my length as I drop my head back on the cushion and watch him.

"I don't know why you're so stubborn," I say quietly.

"I'm not the only one."

His eyes dart to where my hand moves up and down.

"You know you want to touch me." I moan as I curl my hand around my tip.

"I want to do much more than that."

"Then why can't you just give me what I want?"

He moves quickly, his hand skating across my lower stomach. "I want to give you what you want." His fingers slip under my shirt and his nails lightly scratch across my skin when he draws his hand back. "Why don't you tell me what you want me to do to you?"

My head sinks deeper into the cushion as I close my eyes and suck in a breath. "You know what I want."

Jacoby's fingers dance over my hip and move down, squeezing and teasing my inner thigh. "I want to hear the words leave your lips."

"Jacoby," I breathe, my back arching as his hand travels higher.

He leans in closer, his face against mine as he nuzzles into my neck. His hand passes my collarbone and rests on top of my Adam's apple.

With a squeeze, he says, "Say it."

I swallow and cover his hand with my free one, telling him to squeeze tighter. He releases a rumbling growl in my ear and I snap, releasing myself and pushing him to his back as I lie on top of him.

His hands grab a hold of my hips as I rock against him.

"Fuck," I grunt.

"Roman."

"Say you want me, Jacoby." I grind into him again. "Tell me how much you missed me." I lower myself and bracket him with my arms as I breathe into his neck. "Tell you want to fuck me, and I'll let you."

His grip tightens on my hips as he thrusts upward. "Is that what you want? For me to fuck you?"

I move against him again, moaning as I feel just how hard he is. "Yes."

Jacoby's hands move away from hips and I feel a sharp smack against my ass cheek.

"Oh, god." I fall on top of him, seeking friction wherever I can get it as I whimper into his collarbone.

He releases the sexiest moan I've ever heard and then he says, "Rome."

I lose it at the sound of my name on his lips. The name I've been dying for him to use all this time. "Please."

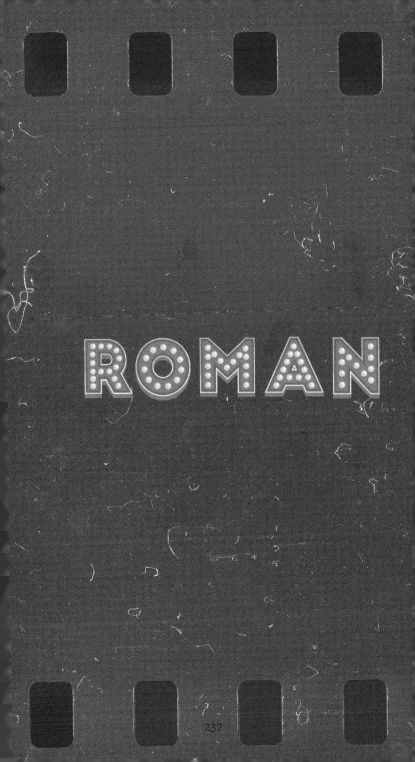

ROMAN

CHAPTER 33

He's pushing me off him in a second, scrambling to get off the couch and drag me up to his room. By the time we're near the bed, he's shoving his pants down his thighs and stepping out of them, quick to do the same for me.

I remove my shirt and drop it with the rest of the discarded clothes before Jacoby pushes me back and has me falling to the mattress.

Scooting back to give him more room, I stare at his body, but mostly one very specific part of it. My tongue darts across my lips as he crawls over my legs and straddles my waist.

"You have no idea how often I've thought about this moment."

"Couldn't be more than I have," I say on a breath as his hand snakes up my chest and reaches my throat.

His grip tightens there as he turns my head to the side and kisses the flesh under my ear. "I've fantasized about you before I even met you."

I arch into him. "Yeah?"

He kisses a path down my neck, all the way to my

Adam's apple. "You're so fucking sexy. I don't know which part of you I want to devour first."

I can only moan in response as he takes his time kissing and licking across my chest and down my stomach.

When he reaches my shaft, his tongue darts out and licks it from base to tip.

"Oh, god," I whimper.

He does it again and again before he finally brings me into the warmth of his mouth, tasting every inch.

I dig my heels into the mattress as I grip his hair in my fingers. My hips move as if they have a mind of their own, but Jacoby doesn't seem to care. He greedily accepts what I give him, making sexy, appreciative noises.

Just as I think about telling him to stop before I completely lose it, he pulls away and drops lower, pushing my legs up and apart. And then I see fireworks behind my eyelids.

He does just as he said he'd do and devours me. His tongue is wicked as it explores, making my toes curl as I suck in a breath and try to remember to exhale.

"Jacoby."

He moans and continues, licking and prodding, turning me into a squirming mess. After what feels like both a blissful eternity and a tortuous tease, he gets to his knees and steps off the bed.

I reach for my aching cock as I watch him dig into his nightstand drawer. He wipes his mouth before finding his place between my legs again.

With painstaking caution and ease, he coats his fingers with the lube and presses where his tongue had just been.

For the next ten minutes, Jacoby uses his fingers and mouth to bring me to the precipice of bliss.

"That's it," he says in a low tone. "You're almost ready for me."

"God," I cry out. "I'm ready. Please. I don't know how long I'll last."

He continues to tease me for another couple minutes before he backs away to cover himself with a condom and some more lube.

"On your hands and knees, sweetheart."

I scrape my teeth across my lip as I stare up at him, then I roll over and straighten my arms, getting into the position he wants.

His large hand lands on my lower back, traveling up my spine and sending goosebumps down my arm. With slick fingers, he teases me once more, ensuring I'm ready.

Jacoby begins to push in, slowly and cautiously, with a deep hum of enjoyment filing the room.

I grip the covers in my fists as I suck in a breath.

"You okay?" he asks, holding still.

"Yes," I choke out.

"Try to relax."

I take in a deep breath through my nose and blow it out as he fully seats himself inside me. Our moans join together in harmony as he squeezes my hips.

"Jesus," he says just under his breath.

The movements are slow and gentle at first, giving me time to adapt. The sensation is overwhelming, and though I feel a dozen different things, pleasure outweighs them all.

He reaches around and takes me in his hand, giving me a few strokes.

"Oh yeah," I whisper, putting my head back.

His hand releases my shaft and grips my hair as he tugs slightly. I release a sinful moan that has him bucking his hips.

"Fuck," he groans, moving a little faster.

"Oh my god," I cry out.

"Your body is fucking incredible," he says, moving his hands to my ass. "*You're* incredible."

He smacks his palm against one cheek and I cry out before taking myself in my right hand and stroking. "Yes."

"You like that?" he questions, voice gruff and full of desire.

"Yes," I say, drawing out the word until it sounds like a hiss.

"Turn over. I need to see you."

Jacoby pulls out fairly slowly, and I quickly get to my back and spread my legs for him. He bites his bottom lip and looks at me like I'm the most amazing piece of art he's laid eyes on. It makes my stomach flip.

After distributing more lube, he hooks one of my legs over his arm and begins to merge our bodies together once more.

"Fuck," I grunt.

"Touch yourself," he commands.

I obey, moving my fist up and down almost in rhythm with his thrusts. After a couple minutes, he drops lower, bringing us chest to chest as his tongue sweeps into my mouth.

I wrap my arms around him, feeling the muscles in his back flex with his movements.

He turns his head and buries it in the nook between my neck and shoulder. "God, you're a dream come true." Jacoby grunts and moans near my ear which is pure fucking audio porn. "I missed you," he whispers just before planting a kiss on my neck and pulling away.

Emotions flood me, so before he fully backs away, I grab him and bring him back to my mouth to give him another kiss.

"You're going to ruin me," he whispers against my lips before straightening his back.

"I'm already ruined," I say right before he thrusts deep.

"Let's make sure of that."

My back arches and my eyes roll back as he moves, his strokes long and deep. His hands hold my thighs apart and I wrap my fingers around my shaft, seeking the release that's been teetering on the edge for a long time.

I open my eyes, and the visual of him with a sheen of sweat on his skin, muscles flexing, hips moving, and teeth digging into his lip as he watches himself disappear into me is what does me in.

"Oh god."

His eyes snap to mine. "Yes."

"Oh. Fuck." I take in a breath. "Jacoby."

"Yes, baby."

That's it. I'm done for. Fireworks explode behind my eyes as I squeeze them shut. Every muscle in my body is tight and flexed as my hand moves faster. My entire being detonates and fractures into a million bliss-filled pieces before I finally come back together with a whimpering moan.

"Oh, yes," Jacoby cries. His pace quickens and his grip on me tightens. "I'm...oh, god. I'm..."

He never finishes the sentence, instead showing me exactly what's happening. His roar fills the room as his cock twitches inside me.

Both of our bodies shake and jerk with the aftershocks of pleasure as we suck in deep breaths.

Jacoby gently pulls away, getting to his feet at the side of the mattress. "I'll be right back," he says, one hand reaching out to touch my knee.

I make some sort of noise that doesn't even resemble a

word and close my eyes. I hear the toilet flush and the sink come on, and then he's nudging my arm.

I open my eyes and find him holding a wet rag. Taking it, I wipe up the mess and then drop my hand with a loud exhale.

He chuckles and takes the cloth, disappearing into the bathroom. I watch his naked body leave and then come back.

Biting my lip, I say, "I'm gonna need you to put some clothes on or I'm gonna want to do more, and I really don't think I have the energy."

Leaning over, he grabs his pants and pulls them on. "Your turn. You look way too sexy splayed on my bed all sweaty and disheveled."

I grin and slowly roll over, groaning in the process. "Fine."

Walking around the bed, I approach my discarded pants but Jacoby grabs them first and hands them to me. "So you don't have to bend over," he says with a twinkle in his eye.

"How sweet," I reply, taking them in my hand.

He reaches out and yanks me into him, his fingers brushing the base of my spine. "Thank you for giving me another chance."

I cup his cheek in my palm and press a kiss to his lips before finding my way to the bathroom.

CHAPTER 34

Oɴ ᴛᴏᴘ ᴏꜰ ᴛʜᴇ ᴄᴏᴠᴇʀs, Jᴀᴄᴏʙʏ ʟɪᴇs ᴡɪᴛʜ ʜɪs ʀɪɢʜᴛ ᴀʀᴍ raised above his head, bent at the elbow and one foot planted on the mattress, his knee falling to the side. I lie with my head on his stomach, staring up at the ceiling while his left hand brushes through my hair.

"I'm in an extremely good mood," I say dreamily.

Jacoby laughs. "So, that's the remedy for your bad moods."

"Yes. Just fuck the attitude out of me."

"Duly noted."

"Unless you're, of course, the cause of my bad mood."

"I'll try not to be anymore, but no promises."

I turn and grin at him. "Can I ask you a question?"

His fingers brush against my scalp. "Yes."

"Not to bring up the past, but what was that email you sent when we were going to the cabin?"

"Not to bring up the past, huh?" he says with amusement.

"I just wanna know. I won't get mad, I promise," I say, turning to my side to look up at him.

"You won't believe me, so let me show you."

He reaches over to the nightstand and grabs his phone, tapping on the screen. He hands it over and I sit up to read the email.

To: FalHart@ymail.com
Re: Douchebag

Fal,

I know I told you this already, but I'm not sure I can do it. We're going to be trapped together for three days. I'm going to have to kill myself to keep from being too obvious, and honestly, I'd rather die than let on that I'm attracted to him. This will not be a good experience for me. I'm fairly convinced he's a homophobe. Not sure what to do, but anyway, I'll check in when I can. Love you.

-Jac

My tongue wets my bottom lip as I hand it over to him. "So, you weren't saying you wanted to kill me and that you'd rather die than do this movie with me?"

He smirks. "I was not."

"But I was still the douchebag."

He shrugs. "I thought so."

"It really sucks that you, and probably other people, thought I was homophobic for my comments. I regret that more than you know. Fear does weird things to people."

"Yes. Like suggesting NDAs to people you really like."

"Really like, huh?" I tease with a small smile.

"Well, sometimes, I suppose."

I playfully smack him in the arm. "Regardless, my fear doesn't excuse what I said."

Jacoby reaches out and rubs the back of my hand. "None of us are perfect. You're not a bad person, Rome."

My eyes light up. "That's the second time in one night."

He smiles and pulls me into him. With an arm around my shoulders, he draws me close to his body and I rest my head on his chest.

As we lie on his bed and cuddle, I have the thought that I never want this to come to an end. That I could do this for ages and be happy.

"So, that email? It was to your sister?"

"Yes."

"It's weird that you email your sister and not text, though. What's wrong with you?"

Jacoby playfully pinches my side. "Shush. I do both, it just depends if she's working or not."

I snort. "I imagine the phone call I interrupted was sort of the same conversation?"

"Yeah."

"So she knows about you and your infatuation with me."

He tugs my hair. "Infatuation? What I feel for you is *not* infatuation, but yes, she knows I'm gay. She's a lesbian, so it's not like she struggled to understand."

I reach up and caress his jaw, a smile on my face. "So, your parents?"

"Well, they know about her, but they aren't really thrilled. They don't discuss her girlfriends or want to get to know them at all. They pretend it's a part of her that doesn't exist. It's caused some issues between them, and Fallyn doesn't really like to talk to them much."

"I can understand that."

"Yeah, so I've been hesitant to come out to them. I already know how they reacted to Fal, and it'll just be repeated. Plus, they'll be even more surprised because I've dated women. I've lied very publicly, and because I'm a celebrity, once everyone finds out it's not like they can deny it to their friends or keep it a secret."

"So, they are top priority when it comes to coming out?"

He's quiet for several seconds, and I wonder if I pushed too far. "I suppose, but more so related to how they'll treat me differently. I know it's wrong, because they're dismissing Fallyn's sexuality, but to think that I'll just be another child ignored is tough to deal with." He sighs. "Then I think about how Fallyn must feel. Considering she knows about me, I sometimes wonder if she hates that I haven't told them, that way their behavior is spread between the two of us and not just her." He shakes his head. "I don't know. I'll have to tell them eventually, because I want what everyone else gets to experience. Date nights. Falling in love. Happily ever afters."

"That's the romantic in you," I say with a smile.

"I've never been able to experience it. Not really."

I get up and lie on my side, facing him. With my head propped up in my hand, I say, "We can go on a date. Everyone will just think it's a friendly outing."

His smile is lopsided, but there's a tinge of sadness in it. He reaches out and brushes a lock of hair off my forehead. "I'd like to be able to touch you. Hold your hand. Or even kiss you."

I swallow. "Yeah, and the way you're looking at me right now would definitely give it away."

Jacoby chuckles. "I know how to put on an act when I have to."

I chew on my bottom lip. "But you don't want to have to."

"The career aspect of it is a big part of not wanting to come out too. I know there's plenty of queer actors out there that have good careers, but when it's you, you think the worst will happen, you know?"

I nod. "Yeah. I'm still really trying to make a name for myself. I don't want to risk anything, but the fact that it *could* be a risk is fucking annoying. I will still be the same actor whether I'm dating a guy or dating a girl."

He stares at me for a few long seconds, his lips twisting to the side. "And your sister?" he questions. "What does she know?"

I take in a deep breath and blow it out. "Nothing."

His eyebrows shoot up. "Oh."

"Yeah. I've only been with one guy. Well, two now, but up until you, just Emerson. With him, it didn't feel like anything, you know? I know that makes me sound terrible, but it was both of us just figuring things out. It felt like something fun to try, and while it was enjoyable, I wasn't too sure what it meant. We both went on to date girls after, and then if we were both single again and hanging out and drinking, we'd do a little touching but we never talked about what that meant. We both realized we were bisexual, but it's always been this secret between us. We know about each other, but we don't tell anyone else."

"He's not out either?"

I shake my head. "No. I guess I always felt like I was a poser. I was very straight-presenting to the world—always with a girl publicly, and then doing this secret thing behind closed doors. We didn't go out on dates, we didn't even talk about dating or feelings and emotions. I felt like I couldn't say I was fully into dudes, because I hadn't had a full-fledged relationship with one."

Jacoby's nodding along as I speak. "I understand that. I know you said you thought about coming out, so I'm assuming you'd tell her first. Have you thought about how she might react?"

"As far as coming out goes, while there is that fear that I'll ruin everything just as I'm taking off, I think I'd rather do it now than wait ten or fifteen years and have to lie and hide that whole time, you know? I have to trust that everything will work out. And as far as Chelsey goes, I don't think she's going to be negative at all about it. She'd only be surprised if I told her I was with you, because I may have done a little shit-talking prior to filming."

Jacoby chuckles. "Of course."

"But yeah, I think she'd be fine. My parents were always very easy-going about things, and they never taught us that homosexuality was a sin or anything like that. They were very chill about a lot of shit, so it wasn't a strict household by any means."

He nods. "That's good."

"They would've liked you," I say with a sad smile, avoiding his gaze. "My mom really liked *Never Forget Me*, even though she cried every single time she watched it."

I feel his hand on mine, but I don't look up. I can't.

Jacoby rubs his thumb over my knuckles. "My mom cries watching that one, too. Hell, I don't even want to watch that one."

I snort and look up at him, grateful that he didn't ask any questions or push for more information about my parents. It's the most I've said about them unprompted, but if I say any more, I'm afraid the dam will burst.

My stomach growls loudly, making us both laugh.

"Guess I should feed you," he says, sitting up.

"It's pretty late," I say, looking at the clock on his night-stand. "Should I go? I can grab something on the way home."

He thinks it over for a few seconds before meeting my gaze. "No. I'd like it if you stayed. If that's okay."

I bite back my gleeful grin. "Fine, you don't have to beg," I say, rolling my eyes playfully.

He gives me a look before pouncing on me, forcing me on my back. He barricades me between his arms as he leans down to kiss me.

"I think it was you who was begging me earlier this evening."

"Let's see what happens after we eat. I can turn the tables."

"Hmm. We'll see."

CHAPTER 35

IN THE LAST MONTH, I'VE ONLY SEEN ROMAN THREE TIMES. Two were work related because we had another photoshoot and a separate interview. We carved out as much time before and after those events to have some private moments. Once was simply us acting like teenagers in the back of my car before I had to rush off to the airport. The third time was better, because we were able to be back at my house, comfortable behind closed doors and with enough time to completely unravel each other with sensual touches and ravaging kisses.

Now, Roman's in Paris for fashion week, and I'm glued to my phone looking at every photo and video that comes out that features him. The video I'm watching now has him in a black, pink, and yellow suit, the colors splashed on there like graffiti art. The coat is a little loose and unbuttoned to the center of his chest, which is, of course, bare.

I definitely don't care much about fashion. My stylist keeps me in what works best for me, even if that's just plain colors and prints, but Roman's always been the opposite. This outfit wouldn't work on anyone but him. I'm actually convinced he could wear recycled garbage and still look good.

> Looking quite fashionable out there, Mr. Black.

Stalking me again?

> Maybe.

A photo comes through shortly after, and it's clear he's at some sort of party. His tongue is out, and he's holding up two fingers as he holds the phone up high and gets himself and several others around him. His shirt is black and completely see-through. And damn he looks good.

> Wow, you look awful. You should definitely go straight back to your room and lock the door.

Ha! Thank you!

With a smile on my face, I put my phone down and sit in the makeup chair. I have an interview on a late-night talk show to promote my most recently released movie and also the upcoming film with Roman.

Luckily, in two weeks, we'll both be at the People's Choice Awards, and hopefully get to spend some time together.

You know what I want to see you in?

Nothing.

Obviously. But also, green. I think your eyes would really shine in green.

Are you making a suggestion for the People's Choice Awards?

I'll be happy to see you in anything.

Black is classic. Everyone looks good in black. You should try it.

We don't show up to the award show together, but Roman does appear on the red carpet shortly after I do. The cameras flash, the screams get louder, and when I turn to look behind me, I try to keep from looking as giddy as I feel.

Roman's in all black, except his top is lace, giving everyone a peek at the exquisite body underneath.

I'm pushed along to the next interviewer along the carpet, but the woman is watching Roman. I get it.

When she meets my gaze, she smiles and her eyes widen. "Jacoby Hart, you look amazing. It's so nice to see you."

"Thank you so much. You're absolutely stunning in that dress."

She does a little shimmy, and the sequins sparkle against

her dark skin. "Well, thank you, sir. I tried my best. I see your co-star is coming up. Can I get you two together?"

"Of course," I say with a smile, looking back at Roman.

When his eyes find me, I see the briefest pause before he grins. I wave him over and he and his assistant make their way toward us.

"Jacoby," he says in his loud boisterous voice. "Good to see you, man." He drapes his arm around my shoulders as he smiles at the woman in front of us. "He looks good in green, right?"

She nods, her curls bouncing. "Oh yeah. His eyes really pop in that color."

His hand squeezes my shoulder before he releases me and puts some distance between us.

"And this outfit," the interviewer says, stepping back to look Roman up and down. "It is giving me life."

Roman spins in a circle, showing off. "Thank you. I heard black is classic, but you know I have to put a spin on it."

"I am loving it," the woman says. "So, you two are in *Another Life* together, and the hype around this one is real. I'm excited, everyone I know is excited, are you two excited?"

"Oh, most definitely," Roman answers. "I had such an amazing time working on this movie, and to work with Jacoby," he says, putting his hand on my shoulder, "was one of the best experiences. I'll never forget it."

I smile and glance over at him. "I agree. It's an incredible story, and I can't wait for it to come out. I hope everyone enjoys watching it as much as we enjoyed filming it."

"Good luck tonight, Jacoby," she says with a bright smile. "I know you're up for *Favorite Male Actor in a Drama* for *Seven Nights*."

"Thank you," I say with a dip of my head.

"I hope you two have an incredible night."

"You too," Roman replies before we walk away.

I turn my head to look at him, giving the cameras the back of my head as I pretend to scratch my nose to cover my mouth.

"You look so fucking incredible, I just want to throw you in a closet and have my way with you."

He chuckles, looking straight ahead. "A closet is an interesting choice."

Our names are called and cameras flash, so we take time to pose for some photos together. Roman's assistant tells him he's wanted for an interview, so he turns in an effort to keep from being seen by all the people opposite us.

"Seriously. Green is your color." His eyes travel the length of my body in a way that makes my stomach do a flip. "Busy tonight?"

"I hope so," I reply with a grin.

Once he disappears, I make my way into the building, feeling like I'm floating on a cloud.

It's not like I'm wearing a neon green suit or anything, but I did make sure to get a hunter green tuxedo jacket that has black lapels.

We're not seated together, though I do spot him a few rows behind my chair when I get on stage to accept my award. He ends up on stage later to present an award for favorite social media star, and I do my best to control my features. The joy I feel when I look at him is incredible and radiates through me.

When it's over, there's an afterparty that most everyone attends, but all I can think about is jumping in a car with Roman and doing despicable things to him in my bed.

An hour in, as I'm talking to Faye and her date for the

night—an R&B singer named Frankie X, I see Roman approach.

He changed into another outfit. This one is a little more casual with a white T-shirt, loose fitting dark denim and jacket to match. The jacket has the appearance of being bleached, with the bottom part and sleeves carrying splashes of white. It's definitely something Roman would wear.

"Hey, gang," he greets with a smile, holding a drink in his hand.

"Hey, Rome," Faye says, stepping in for a hug. "How are you?"

"I'm great. Living life and experiencing new things," he replies with a quick glance at me.

"Good. Have you met Frankie?" she asks, putting her hand on Frankie's shoulder.

Roman shakes his hand. "No, but I like your music. It's nice to meet you."

"You too," Frankie replies with a nod. "I'm gonna go get a drink. You want anything?" he asks Faye.

"I'm good. Thanks." Once he's gone, she turns her attention to Roman. "You look happy, Rome."

Roman gives her a bright smile. "I am."

"Dating anyone?"

He takes a sip of his drink. "Why? Would you be jealous?"

She scoffs. "Please. We went on three dates. I wasn't in love with you."

Roman clutches his chest. "Ouch."

Faye looks at me, shaking her head with a small grin on her lips. "How did you deal with him while filming?"

"It was hard sometimes," I reply, looking at him.

"How hard?" he asks, his smile still wide.

I give Faye a look that she reciprocates. "I can see that."

Roman barks out a laugh. "Come on. Jacoby loves me. I was a dream to work with, wasn't I?"

"A fever dream."

Faye snorts and a photographer comes over and snaps a few photos.

"The media's gonna go crazy over that one," Roman says. "Considering we're in a love triangle."

"Maybe now they'll stop with the story that you and I are fighting over Faye."

"If only they knew the truth," he says quietly, taking another sip.

"What truth?" Faye questions, her eyes finding mine.

She knits her brows as if asking me something, and Roman winces like he knows he said too much.

With a sigh, I say, "Roman knows that you and I weren't ever serious. We talked it out while filming because he thought I hated him for stealing you from me."

"Oh," she states simply, glancing between us. "So—"

Roman's eyes slide to mine as he once again takes another drink.

"He also knows I'm gay," I say as quietly as possible.

"Oh. Oh shit," she exclaims. "Wow, that's a big step for you, Jacoby. How did that come about?"

I shrug and Roman begins to look uncomfortable, peering around the room like he's looking for an exit.

"We can talk about it later," I say.

"Yeah. Of course."

Frankie comes back with a drink and he and Faye wander away to talk to some other people.

"Well, that was unexpected," Roman says. "I didn't mean to make her ask questions."

"It's fine. She knows everything."

"About us?"

"No," I answer quickly. "I wouldn't out you like that. I just mean she knows about me. I talk to her about everything that I can. Her knowing that you know doesn't change anything. She'll be curious why or how I told you, so I'll have to think of something."

Roman's quiet for a minute. "Tell her the truth."

"What?"

He shrugs. "I don't care. She's obviously trustworthy enough to keep your secret. I doubt she'd run off to the press with our story."

It takes several seconds before I respond. "Maybe. We'll see."

Some people several feet away vacate a couch and Roman says, "Wanna sit?"

We walk over and sit down and he finishes his drink before putting the glass on a table in front of us.

We're very aware of everyone walking around or lingering nearby and having conversations, but our eyes keep finding each other.

He grins, and I have to fight my smile from growing too wide.

"We haven't seen each other in a while," he says.

"I attempted to placate my addiction by keeping up with you on social media. That's how I got my fix."

His tongue wets his lips before his teeth gently sink into his bottom one. He doesn't look at me as he does it, but I can see the amusement in his eyes.

"You're addicted to me, huh?"

I let my eyes wander the room. "Oh, you have no idea."

"It's been sixteen long days since…" He lets it trail off, knowing I'll get what he's talking about.

"What have you done in those days?"

He looks at me. "At night? When I'm alone?"

I swallow, staring into his eyes before glancing away. "Yeah."

"Lots and lots of fantasizing. Reminiscing of previous times."

"Hmm."

"Counting down the days until they happen again."

"I wonder," I say, peeking over at him, "why we're still here."

Roman gives me a heart-stopping smile that makes me feel warm. "Are you needing a fix?" he asks, leaning back into the couch.

I inhale deeply through my nose, my eyes dropping to his lap, searching for something I can't even see through the baggy material.

"My craving is intense."

His teeth find his bottom lip again. He takes in a breath and looks away. "Yeah, we should get going."

I let my eyes move from him, and they land on Faye who is watching us curiously as her date speaks to another musician several feet away.

When she realizes I see her, she cocks her head slightly.

Standing up, I peer down at Roman. "My house is an hour from here."

"Mine is forty minutes."

"Text me your address."

I walk away and head toward Faye.

"Leaving?" she asks.

"Yeah. You know I don't really like these things."

She nods and her eyes move past me to where I assume Roman's still sitting. "You and Rome?"

"What do you mean?"

She smiles and leans in, giving me a kiss on the cheek. "We'll talk later. Enjoy your night."

JACOBY

CHAPTER 36

I ATTEMPT TO PUT WHAT FAYE ASKED OUT OF MY HEAD. Maybe she's suspicious. Perhaps after what I told her about the *mystery guy* and then seeing me with Roman, she pieced it together. I don't worry she'll say anything to anyone, so until we can talk about it, I'm not going to worry.

Pulling into Roman's brick-lined circular driveway, I take in the white Spanish style home with the clay tile roof. He told me to pull up past the front door and into the back where he'd leave the gate open. Once I'm parked, I close the gate for him and walk past the pool to get to the sliding glass doors.

After a couple knocks, he rounds the corner wearing a pair of pajama pants and nothing else. His hair is damp from a shower, and his light brown skin glistens like he just put lotion on.

"Took you forever," he says, pulling open the door.

"I ended up going home first. I wanted to clean up and change."

He yanks me in by my shirt, closing the door at the same time he pushes me against the wall. "You're so ridiculous."

265

I kiss him, wrapping my arms around him. "Why?"

"You could've showered here."

"Take me to your room," I tell him.

"You don't want the tour?"

"After. I knew as soon as I saw you I'd want you. I didn't want to wait for showers and niceties."

He groans. "Mm. In that case, let me show you where you can disrespect me."

With my hand in his, he rushes through the kitchen and living room, our feet pounding over the hardwood floor as we travel upstairs and down a hall until we're finally in his room. He spins around and begins undoing my pants as I remove my shirt. I kick out of my shoes right before he shoves the material down my legs.

He does the same thing to his own pants, leaving us both in our underwear before we clash together, our mouths connecting and our tongues tangling.

"We should never go three weeks again," I say against his lips before swiping my tongue against them.

"Technically, it was two weeks and two days."

"Stop being annoying." I shove him down onto the bed.

"I agree, though," he replies with a grin. "It was entirely too long."

With a rumble in my throat, I drop down and devour his mouth with my own. He wraps his limbs around me, and eventually we pull away long enough to remove our remaining clothing.

As I kiss my way around his chest and torso, I begin saying words I've never uttered before.

"You drive me crazy. I struggle to be around you now."

"How so?"

"I want you in a way I've never wanted anyone. With desperation and unfettered desire." I kiss down the middle of his stomach. "I don't know how I'll keep from giving myself away when you're around."

Roman moans and pulls me up. "I've been trying to play it cool, afraid I was feeling things you weren't, but my god, all I want is to be with you. Every minute of the day is littered with thoughts of you and hopes for us."

After those words leave his mouth, nothing sensible comes from either one of us for a while. We're diminished to moans and grunts as we explore each other's bodies, licking, kissing, and sucking every piece of skin possible.

I don't know how much time goes by before Roman manages to escape my barrage of physical attention, but when he does it's only to get some lube and condoms and throw them on the bed.

There's a brief moment when we look at each other as if we're each sizing up the situation. I want to be inside him on an animalistic level, but he very well could want the same thing.

My nostrils flare as my gaze travels down his naked body.

"Fuck me," he says, voice low but sure.

My eyes land on his. "Yeah?"

He nods, biting his bottom lip. "I'll get my turn later," he says, mouth curving into a wicked smile.

And with that, I take the lube and begin warming him up. My slick fingers slide inside him, eliciting the sexiest sounds I've ever heard. He moans and grunts, but it's the whimpers that begin to do me in. When he begs and pleads for more, my body shakes with unkempt passion. When his body moves uncontrollably, and his mouth drops open, I realize I'm teasing us both.

I allow him some reprieve while I cover my length in latex and coat myself with more lube. While I do this, he strokes his cock, his dark eyes assessing every move I make.

"Ready?"

He nods once.

I situate myself between his parted thighs and slowly push my way inside him.

"Yes, yes," he chants, eyes closed and neck exposed as he forces his head back.

I reach forward and brush my fingers over his Adam's apple before giving him a gentle squeeze.

Roman responds with a wanton moan as he hooks one leg behind me, and I thrust all the way in.

I take a moment to pause, allowing him to get used to the sensation while also giving myself time to relish how good it feels to be inside him again.

Leaning over him, I touch his lips with mine in a soft kiss. He kisses me back greedily, his tongue fighting past my teeth.

"Let me kiss you gently," I whisper against his mouth.

"Why?" he asks, his legs wrapping around me to bring me closer.

"Because it'll be the last gentle thing that happens between us right now."

"Ooh," he moans, planting a quick kiss on my lips. "Okay, then."

My tongue sweeps across his bottom lip before sliding into his mouth. I cradle the side of his face with one hand and enjoy our kiss. My hips rock on their own accord when his fingers slide into my hair. He gasps and moans into my mouth, and my thread of control snaps.

I back away and hook my forearms under his knees before my hips begin moving. I thrust deep and hard and am rewarded with blissful cries of pleasure as Roman grips the sheets below him in tight fists.

"I've missed this," I say through grunts. "I've missed you."

"Fuck. God, I've missed you, too. Oh yeah. So good."

"Stroke it," I tell him.

He immediately wraps his fingers around his shaft and starts moving his hand up and down. "God, it feels so good. You"—he sucks in a breath—"feel so fucking good."

"No, baby," I murmur. "You do."

His eyes fly open and lock onto mine. Time freezes and something passes between us in that brief moment.

Our bodies begin moving again, but it turns out I'm a liar, because our sex turns gentler. I rock in and out of him, but I press my stomach to his as I lean in and kiss along his neck. His fingers dig into my back as he breathes into my shoulder.

"Jacoby," he whispers huskily.

I angle my head and kiss the spot below his earlobe. "Hmm?"

He moans, his fingernails scraping my skin as I reach a deeper spot. "I never want this to end."

My heart clenches in my chest. I don't know if he means us or just this moment, but I don't want either to come to an end. And that realization is something I'm not sure I'm ready to delve too deep into right now.

"Me neither," I say.

"I want to get on top," he says, breathless.

I slip my arm around his waist and keep us pressed close together as we roll over. He sits up straight, his muscular body on full display as he begins rocking back and forth.

"Holy shit," I say, my fingers skating up his torso. "You're so fucking sexy."

He glances down at me, a small smile tugging at the side of his mouth before he drops his head back and drags his hands down my stomach.

Reaching out, I grab his erection and take it in my hand, stroking him from base to tip.

Roman sucks in a shaky breath, his gaze on my movements. "Yes. Oh, yes."

"You like my hands on you?"

"I like everything you do," he pants. "Please."

"Please what?" I ask, watching his handsome face contort with pleasure.

"I want to come."

I lick my palm and go back to stroking as he grinds against me.

"That's it," I say as his movements quicken. "Take it. Make a mess."

"Oh shit," he curses, his eyes squeezing shut. "So deep."

"So tight."

"So good," we both say at the same time.

"Come on, baby," I tell him. "Let me see how much you missed my—"

"Oh, fuck!" he roars, cutting me off.

He reaches for his shaft so I let go and watch as he strokes, and soon, warm liquid hits me on my chest, neck, and stomach. It's a beautiful mess and one that I welcome.

"Oh my god," he says through shaky breaths, his body quivering.

I grab his hips and plant my feet on the mattress as I thrust upwards over and over again. It doesn't take long before my muscles are clenching and I'm crying out into the room.

"Fuck!"

"Yes," he whispers.

"I'm...I'm com—"

"I feel it, baby," he says in a sexy tone. "Oh, god."

I come undone, my entire body tightening and flexing as I give him everything I have. Every drop. And then I turn into gelatin almost immediately after. He continues to slowly rock above me, moaning appreciatively.

Roman carefully gets up but quickly falls to his back next to me. We're both a mess, but too out of breath to do anything about it just yet.

"Holy shit," he says.

"Yeah."

"I've gone entirely too long without that."

I snort. "Two weeks and two days is definitely too long."

He's silent for several seconds and then his head turns to face me. He looks completely serious. "I mean without you. Without this," he says, gesturing between us. "I've never experienced something like this before."

My heart throbs in my chest, and I reach out to slide my fingers between his. "Me neither."

CHAPTER 37

I WAKE UP TO THE SOUND OF SOMETHING CLATTERING TO MY left followed quickly by the delicious aroma of freshly cooked bacon.

"Hmm," I murmur, cracking open my eyes to find Jacoby backing away from my nightstand.

"Good morning."

I sit up, my body moving slowly as I take in the scene. "You brought me breakfast in bed?"

He cracks a smile. "It's not that special. I used your food, so you'll need more eggs and bacon."

My eyes roam up his tall frame, noticing he's dressed in different clothes from last night. "Did you leave?"

"I brought a bag in my car last night. I woke up early, took a shower and got ready, then made breakfast."

I look at the clock next to the dishes and see that it's nine forty-six.

"Well, thank you," I say, pushing the covers off of me and standing up.

Jacoby's eyes travel down my naked body before I crash

into him and playfully nibble on his neck before giving him a kiss.

His hand curves around my hip and cups my ass. "I need you to get dressed before I have you for breakfast and the food goes to waste."

I wrap my arms around him. "Mm. That doesn't sound so bad."

He spanks me. "Go get some clothes. Let's eat, and then…" He steps away and ogles me. "We'll see."

"Fine," I say with a smirk before I make my way to the bathroom.

When I'm at the sink, I see Jacoby's toothbrush, toothpaste, lotion, hair gel, and deodorant lined up neatly on one side. When I smile, I know I'm in trouble, because seeing his stuff along with mine makes me feel a type of happiness I've never even thought about.

I had one girlfriend a couple years ago who tried escalating our relationship really quickly. She stayed over a lot, even without prior discussion. She brought over her things and set them up just as Jacoby did. But with her, I didn't feel the same type of joy. I was confused and annoyed. Why was she acting like we lived together when we didn't?

Waking up to Jacoby bringing me breakfast and learning he had already showered and got ready in my bathroom makes my chest feel warm. It feels normal, and I'm only annoyed that we haven't had more of these moments.

I enter the bedroom and find Jacoby sitting on the side of the bed with his own plate of food. He finishes chewing and looks me up and down.

"I thought you were getting dressed."

With a snap of the waistband of my boxer-briefs, I say, "I'm not naked."

He makes a growly noise in the back of his throat and I

make my way over to him and run my fingers through his hair as I give him a kiss.

Jacoby makes a surprised noise before it melts into a moan when I slide my tongue across his.

I pull away and grin. "Thanks again, for breakfast."

"Well, I probably taste like bacon, but you're welcome."

I go to my side and sit down, reaching for my plate. "I like bacon."

He shakes his head, a small grin on his lips. "So, you're free today?"

"Yep. I'm all yours."

I swivel my head and find him already locked onto me. We have a moment where we just watch each other, something passing between us in just a gaze alone. The same thing happened last night when he uttered the word *baby* and made my heart nearly burst.

We're not just fuck buddies. Something is growing between us and it's exciting, but there's also a fear there. Based on the hint of sadness in his eyes, I think he's more afraid than I am, or at least fearful for a different reason.

"Good," he finally says. "I like it like that."

My cheeks get warm when I smile. "Me too."

We skirt past any conversation that we probably should have regarding what the hell we're doing and how we're feeling, and instead enjoy each other's company.

We watch TV, or at least try to, but we end up talking over everything we put on, which is fine. I much prefer to listen to Jacoby.

He gets a text from his sister and smiles at the phone. "I told you my sister does special effects makeup, right?"

"Yeah."

He turns his phone toward me and shows me a picture of

a really ugly looking zombie. Her text says, *This is what I'm doing. What about you?*

"She's good," I say. "That's fucked-up looking."

"Yeah, she's the best."

He takes a picture of me with a smile on his face.

"What're you doing?"

"Telling her what I'm doing."

"By sending her a picture of me?"

He glances up and winks at me, and butterflies take flight in my stomach. "So, telling your sister about me, huh? You must like me a little."

"I could be telling her I'm being forced to hang out with this annoying guy all day. You don't know."

I laugh, but Jacoby keeps typing, and now I need to know what he's saying.

"What are you typing?" I ask, sitting up.

"Nothing," he replies with a grin.

I scoot over but he turns his back to hide his phone. "Go away."

"No. Let me see. I'll tell her what's really going on."

"Which is?"

I reach for the phone, our bodies touching as he attempts to hide it from me. "That you're being mean."

He barks out a surprised laugh and turns to face me, wrapping one arm around my waist and bringing me to his lap.

"I'm not being mean." He kisses my chin.

"You are."

Jacoby kisses the corner of my mouth. "Nope. I don't have anything mean to say about you."

He backs up and brings up the phone, showing me the screen.

It's the quick photo he took of me with a message that

says, *That's really good, Fal. I'm hanging out with this guy. He's better looking than who you're with.*

My lips curl into a smile before I mash them against his smirking mouth. "God, you're so obsessed with me."

"Am I?" he asks, dropping the phone and running both hands up my back.

"Maybe I'm projecting."

"Hmm." His eyebrow arches. "I want to make dinner for you tonight."

"Yeah?" I ask, slowly rocking my hips. "You want to wine and dine me?"

He dips his chin. "I do."

"Okay, but you're spoiling me a lot today. I should do something for you."

"Like what?"

I shimmy down his legs until my knees hit the ground near his feet. "I'll think of something, but for now…"

Jacoby puts his hands behind his head and spreads his legs. "By all means."

ROMAN

CHAPTER 38

"MY ASSISTANT SENT ME PHOTOS FROM LAST NIGHT."

"Oh, yeah? Let's look," Jacoby says, leaning into my side on the couch.

I flip through the photos, the first five being of me when I first hit the red carpet.

"Fuck. You looked so good last night."

"So did you," I say, getting to the next set where there's photos of both of us. "Damn. We look good together."

Jacoby snorts and squeezes my thigh. "Of course we do."

I keep flipping through the photos and come across more taken from when I was on stage presenting, and then from the afterparty.

"This one's probably on the gossip sites right now," I say, showing him the one of me, him, and Faye.

"Definitely."

There are more candids that were obviously taken when I wasn't aware anyone was watching me, but the ones that really capture my attention are the ones of Jacoby and me. In one, I'm staring at him with this child-like glee on my face. In another, Jacoby is looking at me like he wants to devour me. I've seen that look many times, and now it's captured on film.

My eyes slide over to his face to see if he has a reaction to these. After a few long seconds, he speaks.

"Faye knows."

"What?"

"She questioned me that night, and if she saw me looking at you the way I am in that photo," he says, pointing to my screen, "I know why."

"What did she say?"

"She just said, 'You and Rome?' I played dumb, and she just smiled and said we'd talk later. I haven't had the opportunity to yet, but I'm guessing she saw us on the couch. I also went to her house a while back and talked about you without saying it was you. She probably put it together."

I chew on my bottom lip for a while. "What are you thinking?"

He sits back with a sigh. "I should probably talk to my parents soon."

My heart thumps. "Are you going to tell them?"

"I need to."

I nod. "I'm supposed to meet up with my sister next week. I should have a conversation with her as well."

"I don't want it to become a big thing," Jacoby says with a loud exhale. "I don't need to do fifty interviews about my sexuality. I don't want it to be the only thing people want to discuss. You know?"

I nod. "But you're you. Jacoby Hart. People *are* going to talk."

He sighs. "I get that, but *I* don't want to talk about it."

I shrug. "Then don't."

"I want to be able to simply exist and let people find out

who I'm dating the way everybody else does. I feel like it should be simple, but—"

"Hollywood. I get it."

"What about you?" he asks, shifting to face me. "How do you feel about everything?"

"Everything?" I muse, tilting my head side-to-side. "Well, when it comes to letting people know about my sexuality, I feel the same as you. It doesn't have to become a circus. I'm okay with putting out a statement of some sort, that way everything is answered and I don't have to worry about a million questions after they see me with you." My eyes flash to his. "Or whatever."

Jacoby chews on his bottom lip. "Would you want to tell people about us? If we came out? Or would it be best to just get one announcement out of the way first?"

I can't tell by the way he asks if he'd prefer we not tell everyone about us or not. I debate my answer for a few seconds, wondering if I should respond the way I think he'd want me to, or to be honest.

"Jacoby, if I came out, it would be for my own sense of freedom and not having to feel like I'm hiding some big secret, but also, because I'd love to be able to go out with you and not have to pretend we're just friends."

His eyes scan my face, but he doesn't smile. He looks nervous.

"I'm afraid…" He pauses and licks his lips. "I'm afraid I'm going to hurt you."

My eyebrows draw in as I cock my head to the side. "What do you mean?"

"I've done it once, because fear got to me. I want to come out and have that freedom you're talking about. I really do, Rome." He shifts. "But I can't promise I won't be scared again. I want to be with you publicly, too. The way I feel about you—" He stops himself, shaking his head. "I can't put it into words, but I'm afraid I won't be good enough for you."

"Are you kidding right now? Are you actually joking?" He gives me a slight shake of his head. "Jacoby, every moment I'm with you, I wonder how I got so lucky. I worry it's a fucking dream that I'm going to wake up from. When I'm with you, I almost feel like you're doing me a favor. Why you would ever be interested in me is something I still question."

He reaches out for my hand and holds it between his. "Please don't do that. I don't deserve a pedestal, but I understand that last thought, because it's one I've had myself. I don't know what you see in me. We're very different."

I place my other hand on top of his. "Different doesn't mean not compatible."

His lips twitch, nearly forming a smile. "I really like you, Rome."

My smile can't be contained, stretching wide across my face. "I really like you, Jacoby."

CHAPTER 39

"I'M SO GLAD YOU COULD MAKE IT," I SAY, SQUEEZING MY sister, Chelsey, in my arms. "Sorry I couldn't be there to get you. I just got in from doing this photoshoot and interview with a magazine."

"No worries. I'm so happy to see you," she replies, squeezing me back. "I feel like it's been so long."

"Well, you're a busy woman. How was New York?"

"Oh my god, it was incredible!" she says, kicking off her shoes and heading for the couch. "I learned so much from Viktoria La'Shae. She's a fucking rockstar. She's so smart, and very no-nonsense, but also kind."

"So not like Miranda Priestly?" I ask with a grin as I sit down.

"Definitely not, but not quite the same job as her, so maybe that's why," she says with a laugh. "She's the art director for *Booked* magazine, but she used to do modeling in her twenties. She's always worked within the fashion industry, so she knows a lot. She even helped me with my portfolio."

"That's awesome. I'm glad you got that opportunity."

"I'm so grateful for Toni. He's been a great boss and I'm thrilled he hooked me up with that experience. I'm updating my website soon, so if you wanna be a model for your big sis, that would be great."

"Hey, I'm all about fashion. Count me in."

"I love you."

"I love *you*. I'm so glad you're doing what makes you happy."

"I've always loved clothes, you know that," she says.

"Well, you're gonna be the best stylist there is soon enough. I believe in you."

"Thank you," she says, tilting her head. "Now, tell me what you've been up to. I've been seeing a lot more of you on the internet lately."

"Well, the second trailer for the movie came out and everyone's excited about it."

"Yes, I saw it! It looks so good, Rome."

"Thank you," I say with a grin. "I had a really good time on set. It's a great story."

"Yes, I read the book."

"Really?"

"Uh, duh. Of course. My brother's gonna star in the movie it's based on. How was it working with Jacoby? You only texted me about him a few times."

"Well, he's Jacoby, you know? He's an amazing actor, so it was great seeing him in action. He really pushed me to be better, and not really by doing anything, but you want to measure up, you know? We've hung out a few times and—"

I instantly notice my sister's face change as I'm talking and I wonder if I said something I shouldn't have.

"Wow. That's quite the change from *he's an entitled little shit*."

"Did I say that?" I ask, scratching the back of my head.

"Uhh yes. And a lot more."

"Well, you know, we talked about a few things and got some stuff sorted. He's not that bad."

"Interesting," she says, making sure to pronounce each consonant and vowel, drawing the word out.

"What?"

"I don't know," she says, holding her hands up. "I'm glad you guys worked out the issues. I saw the picture with Faye. Everyone was buzzing about that one. I think I heard the rumor that you three were a throuple."

"Oh lord," I reply, dropping my head to the cushion. "I haven't seen that one yet."

"Are they back together again?"

"No," I answer quickly. "Just friends. Everyone is friends." I get up, suddenly nervous. "Drink?"

"No, I'm good. Getting hungry though. Do we have dinner plans?"

"Uh, yeah. I made plans, but I want to talk to you about something first."

I grab a bottle of Gatorade and bring it back to the couch with me. "I'm not really sure how to even go about this conversation, but…"

She gasps loudly. "You're engaged!"

"What?"

Chelsey flaps her hands in the air. "You're nominated for something!"

"For what?"

Her eyes are wide and she claps her hands together like we're playing a game of Charades. "Ooh. You hooked up with Jacoby!"

My fingers clench around the bottle in my hands. "What?"

She eases back, her excitement gone. "What? I thought I

287

could guess."

"You just said three completely different things, and I don't even know where to begin."

Chelsey shrugs. "Okay, so probably not engaged."

"That's the first to go?" I question, sitting down.

"I know you'd never get engaged without me having met the person. That's not you."

"Right," I say with a nod, wondering why the third choice seems more plausible to her.

"So, what is it?" she asks, crossing her legs on the couch.

I look down to avoid her gaze. "Well, I'm bisexual."

She's quiet. Silence stretches between us and I glance up from the bottle in my hands to see if she's looking at me, and she is. I can't read the expression on her face though.

Her mouth opens but there's a few seconds that go by before words come out. "Okay," she says with a small dip of her chin. "Is this—"

"New? Not really."

"No, no," she starts, giving me a strange look. "I mean…I think I always kind of knew. Or at least thought."

My shoulders drop and I feel like I sink further into the couch. "What?"

"Yeah. I was gonna ask if this was supposed to be a secret."

I choke out a laugh. "Wait. What are you saying? You always thought I was bisexual?"

"Not always, but maybe around the time you were seventeen or eighteen."

"Why didn't you ever say anything?"

She shrugs. "What was there to say?"

"That was around the time I was hanging out with Emerson."

"Yeah!" she says, pointing at me. "Emerson. You guys

had this way about you. Like it was obvious you were trying to keep a secret but you were terrible."

"Excuse me?" I say with another laugh. "I'm a good secret keeper."

"Right. Like when you let Mom and Dad know I had opened up our Christmas presents early and re-taped them."

"They were gonna get mad at me for it!" I screech.

Chelsey laughs. "Anyway. I didn't bring it up just like I wouldn't bring it up if you were secretly hooking up with some girl. You'd tell me if you felt like it was something I needed to know. Plus, you always said things like, 'That guy has nice arms.' And when I'd point out a guy, you'd either agree or disagree on their attractiveness." Her voice goes higher. "Or that one time when you said you had a crush on Brad Pitt."

"Oh okay, who didn't have a crush on Brad Pitt in *Troy*? Hello, leather skirt." I pause. "But I thought it was like an innocent sort of appreciation of beauty."

"Appreciation of beauty?" she mimics.

"Yeah."

"Sure, but you were so open and carefree about it that I figured you felt you didn't need to have a whole conversation about your sexuality. I thought maybe it was a special thing between you and I, because I didn't hear you say similar things around Mom and Dad, so I kept it to myself."

"Well, that's because they were Mom and Dad. You know you and I would talk about a lot more together than we did to them, simply because they were our parents. I've always been my most comfortable around you though, because you never judged me or did the typical older sister thing where you felt you had to parent me as well. You gave me parts of your personal life, so it was natural."

She reaches out and grabs my hand. "You're my best

friend, you know that." I smile, feeling emotion well in my eyes, and I squeeze her hand. "Are you saying you just had this bisexual revelation?"

"No," I say with a laugh. "Emerson was my first experience with a guy when I was eighteen. We fumbled around quite a bit for a while, just figuring things out. Since then, we've messed around on and off when we're around each other, but since I moved away from Sacramento, the near six hour drive keeps us from getting together very often."

"You said first. There are others?"

I bite my lip but can't keep the smile from my face. "Well…"

"Oh my god, it's current!" She pokes me in the ribs. "Who is it? Are you in love? Oh my god!" She grips my arm and shakes me.

"There's been another guy," I say. "Just one, and yes it's current."

"Tell me everything! What does he do? How did you meet him? What's he look like?"

I recall the conversation I had with Jacoby last week. We had spent all day together and finally discussed the possibility of coming out to our families and then going from there. When I told him my sister was visiting for a few days, and that I'd take the opportunity to come out to her, I asked how he'd feel about including him in the conversation. He said he didn't mind if I told her about him and about us, but it still feels weird to out someone else, even to my sister.

"Well, he's very handsome. Very, very. He's sexy but in this super elegant, put together way. He's the complete opposite of me. I wear bright colors and kind of push boundaries with fashion. And he's always in a classic suit. Black or gray. Blue if he's feeling spicy," I say with a laugh. "He's controlled, but he can be sarcastic and funny, too. And he's just so…" I sigh, gazing above Chelsey's head through my living room. "He's great," I finally say with a nod.

"Wow. You are smitten."

I roll my eyes but don't bother denying it. "I want you to meet him."

Her eyes bulge. "Really? When?"

"Tonight. For dinner."

"Oh my god, you're introducing him to family?" she squeals, launching herself at me to wrap her arms around my neck. "Oh, I'm so happy you're happy. What's his name? What should I wear? Is this casual or—"

"Okay, calm down," I say, detangling us as I laugh at her antics. "It's casual. I'm having food delivered here so we can all talk and, you know, not cause a scene."

She backs away, her brows drawn in as she studies me. "Cause a scene?"

"You'll see. Look, I think you're gonna like him. I hope you do. And we'll discuss more once he's here." My phone rings from the kitchen and I stand up to go get it. "That's probably him."

"Oh my god, I need to shower. I look like a mess."

"Yeah, you do. Smell pretty bad, too."

"Fuck off," she says, heading toward her suitcase.

I laugh as she wheels the luggage toward the stairs, then I answer the phone.

"Hey."

"You sound happy," Jacoby says on the other end.

"I am."

"I'm guessing everything went well."

"Apparently I'm not as good at hiding as I thought."

"She knew?"

"Yeah, I guess I told her I had a crush on Brad Pitt before."

"*Troy?*"

I bark out a laugh. "Yes."

"Did you tell her about us?"

"Kind of. I kept your name out of it. So she'll be surprised when you walk in."

"I told you I didn't mind if you told her."

"I know, and I was going to, but before the words could come out, I started feeling weird talking about your sexuality."

He's quiet for a few seconds. "I don't know why I was ever afraid you'd open your mouth and spill everything."

"Cause you're a dick."

"Ah. That's right."

I laugh. "I'm kidding. But yeah, she's getting ready now. Be here in like an hour and a half?"

"I'll be there."

"Okay. I can't wait to see you."

"I can't wait either. We said we couldn't go a week without seeing each other, and now look at us. I may have to abduct you and bring you back to my house for a couple hours."

My smile is so wide it hurts my cheeks. "Why couldn't we stay here?"

Jacoby's voice drops lower. "I wouldn't want your sister to think I'm hurting you when you can't stop screaming out for God."

"Oh, god," I say with a whimper.

"Exactly, but much louder."

I press my palm to my cheek and feel the heat. "Okay, well, yeah. I look forward to that, sir."

He chuckles. "I'll see you soon."

"Yes. See you."

I end the call with a smile still on my face.

CHAPTER 40

I HANG UP THE PHONE AND GET OUT OF MY CAR TO WALK UP to Faye's door. I figure if Roman's telling his sister, I should tell someone, too. When I have the conversation with my parents, it'll be face-to-face, and with my sister by my side. Hopefully that'll happen as soon as our schedules work together.

"It's about time," Faye says as she pulls open the door. "I was wondering if you were going to back out and drive away."

"Please. I was on the phone."

"Mmhmm," she says, stepping back to let me in. "With who?"

"Can we sit first? What kind of hostess are you?"

"Oh, whatever. Take off your shoes."

"I know, I know," I say, already toeing them off. "We gotta make this quick, because I have somewhere to be in precisely ninety minutes."

Faye scoffs. "What kind of friend are you, putting a time limit on a gossip sesh?"

"You'll forgive me in a minute."

293

She plops down on her couch, her black and gold patterned silk robe floating around her. "Spill. Even though I already know," she says, narrowing her eyes.

I purse my lips. "Okay, maybe I'm kind of seeing someone."

She rolls her eyes. "Why are we pretending I don't know that it's Roman Black?"

With a sigh, I say, "Okay, but I just got off the phone with him and he's not even telling his sister about me because he felt weird discussing my sexuality with her even though she's going to find out tonight, and now here I am talking about his with you."

Faye's eyes widen. "Sister? You're meeting his sister? Tonight?"

My smile is uncontainable. "Yes. Which is why this conversation can't go on too long."

"Well, I guess I can understand," she says, pulling the sides of her robe together as she settles into the cushion. "And you don't have to say much. I'll talk to Rome myself. Or we should all get together and talk," she says, the wheels spinning in her head. "I'll host. You two can come over and I'll have some snacks and things."

"That sounds perfect."

"But y'all are obviously together," she says with a shrug, her eyes once again rolling upward. "It was pretty clear at the afterparty."

"Well, that's sort of frightening considering neither one of us is out."

"Yeah, well, you better be careful. You were basically eye-fucking him all night. And y'all were so smiley together."

"Smiley?"

She gives me a look. "Puppy love."

"There's been no use of the L word."

"You know what I mean. But how the hell did that happen? You guys were hardly friends. All the internet drama and rumors about you two, hell, about us three. And y'all are secretly hooking up?"

My lips quirk up. "Well, it only started halfway into filming, so it's not like we've been together for a long time. Plus, we went a while without speaking even after filming, because I was dumb and said something I shouldn't have."

"The NDA?" she exclaims. "That was him?"

I wave a hand in the air. "Never mind that. But yes, we can all talk sometime soon and you can get more of, but not all of, the juicy details."

"Fine, fine," she says, standing up and shooing me. "Go, get out of here. Go meet your future sister-in-law."

"Stop," I say with a chuckle, wrapping my arms around her when I get up. "I'm glad I have you as a friend. You know that?"

"I know. I'm glad you two have each other. I truly hope everything works out." She backs up but continues to hold me by the biceps. "But if you're serious about this—him and everything that comes with being with him—then it's better to come out sooner rather than later. Whatever coming out is to you. It doesn't have to be a fucking primetime interview, but sooner or later someone will get a photo and it will be thrust upon you without a warning. Be careful."

I nod and kiss her cheek. "I will."

"Love you."

"Love you more," I reply, making my way to the door.

My heart feels like it might break through my skin by the time I get to Roman's door. I know his sister will be fine. She loves her brother and apparently has been privy to information Roman thought he was keeping secret from her. I don't think for a second she'd go to the press with our secret romance, but meeting his sister has definitely brought on the nerves. I suppose I just hope she likes me for him.

When Rome opens the door, his smile is wide and his eyes are filled with joy. I step inside, and as soon as the door closes behind me, he clasps both hands on my face and plants a kiss on my lips.

I bring my right hand up to his neck and slide it up into his hair as my other hand grabs his hip and keeps him close.

"Missed you," I whisper against his lips.

"Missed you more. Hope your kidnapper skills are up to par, because Chels may try to keep us both hostage once she finds out who you are."

I chuckle and take a step back. "Where is she?"

"Still upstairs," he says, rolling his eyes. "You'd think she's getting ready for her own date." He tugs on his indigo blue, long-sleeved Henley shirt. "She also said I had to dress up even though I told her it was casual."

"This is dressed up?" I tease.

"Hey, I was in a tank top and basketball shorts. Now I'm in jeans and this," he says, pushing up the sleeves of his shirt like they're offending him. "You look good." His eyes drink me in lasciviously as he wets his lips.

"Behave," I reply, arching a brow at him. "But I figured you can't go wrong with chinos and a Polo."

"I am behaving. It's not like your pants are around your ankles."

I snort and follow him into the living room where we sit side-by-side and hand-in-hand.

"I talked to Faye before I got here. Basically confirmed what she already knew, but had to promise the three of us would get together to discuss more details."

He laughs. "Okay, that sounds good."

"Okay, okay, I think I'm finally ready. Do you think this is okay?" a woman's voice says from somewhere behind us.

Roman smirks at me and stares past my head at the opening to the kitchen. "We're in here, Chels. Both of us."

"Oh."

I stand up and turn around, finding a beautiful woman standing just inside the kitchen wearing a beige and black sundress. It cinches at the waist to accentuate her curves and falls loosely to her knees. Her brown hair is half pinned back and falls just past her shoulders, and her eyes are almost exactly the same shape and color as Roman's.

I give her a smile and start walking toward her, but her jaw drops and she watches me like she's afraid. I hear Roman chuckle behind me and watch as Chelsey's eyes move from me to him and then back to me.

"Shut the fuck up."

I turn to look at Roman but he just shakes his head. "Nice first words, Chels."

When I face her again, I extend my hand. "Hi, it's nice to meet you. I'm Jacoby."

Chelsey is frozen in place, her mouth still open and her eyes studying my face. Sweat starts forming along my hairline as the seconds begin to feel like hours.

Her bottom lip meets her top one, and she slowly begins to nod her head. "Yeah. Yes, I know who you are." Her hand finally slides into mine. "I'm just...I don't..." She laughs, her eyes wide and confused. "I'm not sure what to say here."

Roman comes to my side and I release Chelsey's hand.

"So, this is why I didn't want to go out in public, and why I didn't want to tell you who it was beforehand."

"Right," she says, eyes bouncing between us. "So, you two."

Roman nods. "Yeah."

"What and how and what?" she questions.

"Let's go sit down," Rome offers, putting his hand on my back as we turn and head for the couch.

Chelsey sits in the center of the loveseat across from us, eyes still unbelieving.

"I'm sorry," she says. "It's not because of anything bad," she says, her hand going to her chest. "I'm just so shocked. You're Jacoby Hart."

Roman snorts. "The first and last name thing."

"What?" she squeals, turning to Roman. "He's Jacoby Hart."

"Yes, Chels. I know."

"You hated him."

She presses her fingers to her lips, eyes bulging.

"Thanks for that," Rome deadpans.

I laugh and run my palms over my thighs. "Well, I guess I sort of hated him, too. It's fine."

"My mind is blown," she says, shaking her head. "This was not what I was expecting." She takes in a deep breath and pushes her shoulders back. "Okay. You're Jacoby Hart, and you're gay, and secretly dating my brother."

Roman rubs his hand across his forehead as he exhales. "Wow, Chelsey."

I reach out and touch his leg. "It's fine. It's the truth," I say, nodding at his sister.

"And this started while you guys were filming?"

I nod while Roman says, "Yep."

"And now you're just like…together. But hiding it."

"Right," we both say at the same time.

"Okay. But the way you were talking about him earlier. You're really…"

I glance over at Roman who's widening his eyes at his sister.

"What did you say earlier?" I ask with a smile.

"Nothing."

I meet Chelsey's gaze, but she flattens her lips together as she grins. "And you like my brother."

"I do," I say with a nod. "Surprisingly a lot."

Her smile grows wide just as Roman scoffs. "Surprisingly."

"He can be a pain," I say.

"Oh, I know," she replies, nodding her head.

"But he's also very genuine and funny," I say, looking at Roman. "And talented." I turn back to Chelsey. "And I'm the truest version of myself when I'm with him, while also wanting to be better. I admire the way he carries himself, and I—" I cut myself off, realizing she has unshed tears in her eyes. "I'm probably saying way too much."

"No, no," she says, waving her hand. "That's very sweet. It was nice to hear." Her eyes flicker to Roman. "I know he's funny and carefree, but I only ever saw those things when it was just him and I. Growing up, when we were around others, he was fairly quiet, shy, and a little nervous. Kind of sensitive."

"Oh god," Rome groans.

Chelsey smiles. "In the spotlight, he's different, you know?"

I nod. "I do."

"The bravado is for the public. That's not the Rome I grew up with. Once you know him," she says, poking at her heart, "the real him, it's impossible to hate him."

I grab his hand and squeeze, and she looks over at him with an expression that lets me know she's about to get deep.

"You know about our parents?"

"Chels." Roman says her name like a warning.

"I know what happened," I reply.

She nods, her eyes assessing Roman. "It changed him, and we're both still finding our way through the grief, but I know without a doubt I wouldn't have survived if I didn't have him. He's the best person to have at your side through anything, even if he's directly affected as well. If you two decide to come out as a couple, regardless of what happens, you'll be lucky to have him at your side."

The emotion is thick in the room. Rome sniffles next to me and Chelsey stops a tear before it can fall down her face.

Words struggle to make their way past a lump in my throat, and I tighten my grip on his hand as I nod. "I am lucky, and I'm going to try to be the best person I can be for him."

"Good," she says with a nod, slapping her hands on her knees. "So, does anybody in your family know?"

I feel Rome shift next to me.

"My sister knows I'm gay. I sent her a photo of Roman the other day but haven't really had the time to fully explain everything. She's working and I just got back into town late last night, but we've had some text exchanges where she's been able to deduce that we're together in some capacity. I'm meeting up with her tomorrow, actually."

"Oh, good," she says with a nod. "Your parents?"

"They don't know. That'll be a tougher conversation, but one I'm hoping isn't too hard. My sister is a lesbian, but based on their reaction to that fact is why I'm unsure how this will go."

"I see." Her eyes dart to Roman and I can see the concern in them.

The doorbell rings and Rome quickly stands. "Oh, that's the food."

After he walks away, Chelsey smiles at me and whispers, "Can I give you a hug?"

"Yes, of course," I reply, standing up to meet her in the center of the rug.

She holds me tight, her head resting on my chest. "He really likes you."

I smile. "I really like him."

Pulling away, she holds onto my forearms as she peers up into my eyes. "He hasn't dealt with his grief. He spent his time being strong for me and I don't think he's processed it the way he needs to. If things go bad when you two come out, he will focus on you first, because that's just who he is, but he can't keep stockpiling trauma. He's going to need—" Her voice cracks.

I rub her shoulders. "I will be there for him. I promise."

She nods, swallowing down her emotions.

"Dinner's here!" Roman calls out.

Chelsey wraps her arm around my waist, and we walk toward Rome together.

CHAPTER 41

DINNER GOES JUST AS GOOD AS YOU'D WANT WHEN MEETING the family of the person you're dating. There were no uncomfortable moments or awkward silent lulls. Watching Rome and his sister interact just gave me a new side to him that I've never seen. You can tell he loves and looks up to his older sister, but is also very protective of her.

I got a handful of fun stories from them about their childhood and teenage years, and a couple that Rome found embarrassing but that Chelsey had too much fun discussing.

One was about how he had a crush on a teacher in the eighth grade, except that the teacher was well into her fifties, according to Chelsey. Rome argued that she was definitely younger, but Chelsey pointed out the thick bifocals and *Golden Girls* hairstyle.

I was also told about the time he was in a talent show but forgot the words and kept singing the chorus over and over again.

We all ended up bowled over in laughter, but mostly because of the way they tease each other.

After cleaning up, the three of us end up out back,

lounging in the chairs next to the pool with our drinks of choice in hand.

"So, the movie comes out in a couple months, right?" Chelsey asks.

"Yep," Rome answers.

"Nervous?"

"I don't think I'm nervous, but I'm just hoping it's successful. I want the readers of the book to be happy with our interpretation," I say.

"I want them to think I'm the better actor of us two," Rome jokes.

Chelsey rolls her eyes but Roman winks at me when I look at him.

"Have you both seen the posts about you two?" she questions.

"Some," Rome replies. "The ship name is hilarious."

"Wait, what?" I question, not having heard that one.

"They're referring to us as Racoby."

My brows draw together. "That sounds like something you'd name a raccoon that kept showing up on your porch."

Roman barks out a laugh. "That's specific."

"There's gotta be something better."

"Manoby? Jacman?" Roman muses.

"I hate those."

"I'd just say Blackhart," Chelsey chimes in. "Works better. Anyway, people have already put together these little edits just from the trailers. People are obsessed with you both. I think it's gonna be a huge hit."

I glance over at Roman and smile. His eyes rake over me, making me feel things I shouldn't be feeling with his sister next to us. I mouth *stop* at him, but he just grins.

Chelsey yawns and looks at the time on her phone. "I think I'm gonna have to call it a night," she says, stretching her arms above her head. "I flew straight in from New York, and it's starting to catch up to me."

I stand up with her and extend my hand for a shake, but she bypasses it and gives me a hug. "It was so nice meeting you, Jacoby."

"It was nice meeting you, too."

"You'll be around the next few days?"

I nod. "Yes. I'll be here."

"Good. I hope to see you again before I leave."

"Definitely."

She walks over and wraps her arms around Roman's neck. "Love you. See you tomorrow."

"Love you." Rome's eyes flicker to me. "Uhh. We might leave for a little bit, but I'll be back tonight."

Chelsey snorts. "Okay."

Once she's inside, I force my way onto the same chaise lounge, straddling him and forcing him to lie back. "Way to play it cool. We could've left and she wouldn't have known. Now she knows what we're up to."

He runs his hands up my sides and wraps them around my back. "I just didn't want her to wake up and be alone and confused."

I kiss his forehead, nose, and then mouth. "You're sweet."

Roman groans. "Not *that* sweet."

My lips brush across his cheekbone and down his jaw until my tongue finds his neck. "Mm. Very sweet."

He thrusts his hips into me. "Keep going lower and we won't make it to your house."

"Not sure I want to wait that long anyway." I pull his shirt up, my fingers touching his skin. "You have a shed back here."

"It's a nice one, too," he replies, his hands on my ass as he pushes me into him.

"Got lube?" I question, scooting down and kissing his stomach.

"Yes," he breathes. "In the house. No condom, though."

"Hmm," I murmur as my tongue licks a path under the waistband of his boxers. "How do you feel about that?"

"You're the only one I've been with since the first time," he says through a breathy voice, his hips undulating.

"You're the only one I want to be with," I tell him, kissing his erection through his jeans as I peer up at him. "I can't even think about anyone else but you."

Roman stares at me for several seconds before sitting up quickly. "Okay, I'm getting the lube. Meet me in the shed."

He rushes into the house and I make my way across the grass, heading for the shed that sits on top of a large square of pavers. There's a window next to the door, and when I step inside, I notice how organized and clean it is.

The lights from the backyard shine through the window, allowing us to not be in pitch blackness. I undress, waiting to see Roman scurry across the grass. When he flies into the shed, I watch his head swivel around until he finds me.

"Oh fuck yes," he breathes, immediately coming to a stop in front of me and dropping to his knees.

The first touch of his wet tongue on my cock has me groaning in pleasure as I thread my fingers in his hair. "Yes, baby."

Roman moans around me, taking me into the warmth of his mouth and edging me with his tongue and hands until I can't take it anymore.

"I need you," I say between deep breaths. "Come here."

Roman stands and removes his clothes before he steps closer. My fingers wrap around his erection before I give a languid pull.

"God, your touch is like the strongest drug," he breathes, exposing his neck to me.

I angle my head and gently bite his skin while I continue to move my fist up and down his shaft.

"How so?"

"I forget everything else. I'm absolutely captivated by you and whatever you want to do to me. It consumes my every thought."

The strength of the feelings that are threatening to come out in the form of words I'm not sure I should say yet have me choking on a response. I don't even know if I trust myself to know that they're true. I've never been in love. Is there a set amount of time you have to be with someone to know for sure?

Instead of dwelling on it right now, I simply say, "Let me consume you." And I lower myself to my knees so I can taste him.

My tongue flickers and swirls, and my fingers close around him to stroke, guiding him to the back of my throat.

"Baby," he breathes, his body shivering. "Fuck. I need you."

I ease away and wipe my hand across my mouth as I stand. "Take me."

His eyes assess my face for several seconds before lust takes over completely. He bends over to grab the discarded lube bottle and begins pouring it into his palm.

"There's a little table over here," he says, walking to the other side.

I make my way over and rest my palms on the wood as he strokes himself with the slick liquid. His fingers then slide between my cheeks, and while he readies me, he stands at my side, kissing my shoulder and upper arm while huskily telling me everything he loves about my body and how he can't wait to be inside me.

"Give it to me," I whisper, driven to desperation by his touch. "Now."

"So bossy," he teases, easing away from me.

"I think the word is *horny*."

Roman grabs the lube again and steps behind me. My need for him makes the wait feel like hours. I bend at the waist even more, dying for his touch.

His fingers tease me in a featherlight touch.

"Rome," I growl.

His legs brush against mine as he begins the gentle push in. "Oh fuck," he moans.

"Yes," I hiss, drawing out the word.

He begins slowly, his hands caressing me reverently as he carefully moves his hips. It doesn't take long before I'm greedily rocking back, demanding more. My soft moans turn into desperate pleas, and soon enough, Roman takes pity on me.

His grip tightens on my hips and his thrusts go deeper.

"God, you feel incredible," he says. "I can't get enough."

Our moans collide together, rising higher and higher until we fill the backyard with a chorus of our pleasure. My cock aches, needing to be touched, but I keep my hands on the table. When I come, it's going to be by his hand.

Roman begins slinging words together that don't make sense. He curses and he praises. He grunts like an animal and then sucks in quivering breaths. He brings my knee up to the table that precariously rocks on uneven ground, and he attempts to fuck me through it.

I can tell he's getting close by the way his fingertips dig into me and the change in his breathing.

"Oh, god. Jacoby. Fuck, baby. You're so good. I—oh, god, I'm about to fucking come!"

"Yes, yes," I chant, loving the way he shatters, his words shouted into the night as his body trembles behind me.

After a minute of sucking in oxygen like he was just under water, he carefully pulls out. I place my other foot on the ground and turn around to find him lowering himself to his knees.

His long fingers wrap around my shaft and his lips part to take me into his mouth. With his dark eyes on my face, his tongue twirls around my tip.

"You taste so fucking good."

I groan, dropping my head back as my eyes close. "Please," I beg, my voice cracking.

Roman makes an appreciative noise in the back of his throat. He loves getting me this way.

His fingers tighten and his hand moves up and down my shaft, only stopping when his fist touches his own lips.

My shuddering breaths and small grunts are all that can be heard as I stare down at him, trying to stave off the orgasm simply to be able to keep this view for even longer.

"Baby," I moan. "Oh god."

Roman makes a noise around me and moves faster, ready to taste more.

I don't even get to warn him. I let out a cry just as my release hits his tongue.

"Oh god. Oh fuck. Oh…" I suck in a breath, "yes."

When he finally pulls away, he just sits back and rests on his haunches, looking up at me with dark eyes surrounded by long lashes, and swollen, wet lips.

I've always known that Roman's attractive. I've been attracted to him for years, but that word doesn't fully encapsulate his allure. He's charming, sexy, funny, and seductive.

He's shy and sensitive, but brave and honest. He's incredible, and I don't know what good deeds I did to have this sort of karma.

"Holy fuck, I think I'm obsessed with you," I say.

His mouth forms a smirk as he gets up. He steps forward and brings our naked and sweat-slicked bodies together. "Obviously." Planting a kiss against my lips, he then whispers, "The feeling is mutual, babe."

CHAPTER 42

Due to some miscommunication, I thought my sister was showing up at three in the afternoon, but it turns out it was three in the morning, and we happen to show up to my house within minutes of each other.

"Oh my god, am I witnessing the walk of shame right now?" she asks as I open the gate for her to be able to drive in.

"I would have to be ashamed for that to be possible, and I am far from that."

"Oooh."

"Why are you here right now?"

"Can I park first?"

I shuffle toward the front door as she parks, the gate closing automatically behind her. As I'm typing in the security code, she pops up behind me with way too much energy for the time of day.

"I told you I was coming at three."

"Normal people would assume that means three p.m."

"When did you ever think I was normal?" she says with a laugh as we step inside.

"True."

"I got off work at one, went home and packed this bag," she states, dropping the duffle bag to the floor, "then I picked up some fast food and drove over."

"How's West Hollywood these days?"

"I'm literally only thirty minutes away and you're acting like it's a whole new state." She plops down on one of my barstools at the breakfast bar. "But you know, still amazing. Trendy as fuck and super queer. My kinda place."

I go to the fridge and grab two water bottles. "I love you and I'm happy to see you, but I'm in desperate need of a shower," I say, sliding one to her.

She catches it in her hand, a smirk on her lips. "You definitely reek of dirty, nasty, secret sex."

I purse my lips at her. "Anyway. I'll see you in the morning." I round the bar and drape my arms around her neck, playfully nuzzling my head into hers.

"Gross. Get your sex aura away from me."

I chuckle. "Sex aura?"

She shoves me off of her. "Go shower. See you later. I'll expect details about how the hell you two are doing."

"Yeah, yeah."

In the morning, I make my way downstairs and run into Fallyn at the foot of them as she takes off her tennis shoes.

"You went for a run already?" I ask, looking at my watch. "It's not even nine. I had to drag myself out of bed."

"Yeah, well, I'm used to not getting much sleep, and a run in the morning really wakes me up."

"I don't understand you kind of people. Psychopaths, really."

She laughs. "Shut up."

"You remembered the code to the gate?"

"No, I hopped it," she says sarcastically, standing up. "Got some photographers out there."

"They've amped up recently. They gotta be bored."

"Nah, your neighbor two houses down is a singer. They're watching her, too. You're not that important."

I roll my eyes. "Thanks."

"I was gonna make breakfast."

"That's what I'm doing," I tell her. "I thought I was getting a head start, but apparently you're an overachiever."

"Let me cook," she says, pushing past me as I make my way to the kitchen.

"Why?"

"My kitchen isn't this big or this nice. Let me live out my master chef dreams."

I chuckle. "You're such a weirdo, but please, feel free. Want to make me some coffee too?"

She shoots me a scowl. "Uh, no. You can do that yourself."

My bare feet pad across the floor to the coffee maker while she starts pulling out food from the fridge.

She washes her hands at the sink and says, "So, you and Roman. How's that?"

My smile takes over my face before I even turn around. "It's really good."

Fallyn's grinning at me when I face her. "Gah! Tell me everything. You've been giving me the runaround over text. Are y'all official? In love? Moving in and adopting babies? Or are we like, low-down fucking and just having fun?"

"Well, we are still very much in the closet, so there's that. And while it's fun, it's not *just fun.* I really, really like him."

She shakes her head, a smile on her lips. "This was *nothing* at Christmas."

"Things change," I reply, turning back around when the coffee maker goes off.

"So, he's bi or gay?"

"Bi."

"And you're not worried he'll tell anyone anything?"

"No. I was, and I did bring up the NDA thing but it really blew up in my face and we didn't talk for a while. I know now that Roman would never do anything like that."

"What are your plans going forward?"

I spin around and put a cup of coffee near her while she peels some potatoes. "I have to talk to Mom and Dad."

Her brows shoot up. "When?"

"Soon. I want you there."

She grumbles, the noise deep in her throat. "For you, I will be. But you know it's been several months since we've spoken."

"We need to figure out our relationship with them. They'll either have to accept us for who we are, or we're going to have to cut ourselves off from them permanently. You shouldn't be expected to put up with their disrespect just because they're our parents. If they decide to act like that toward me once they know, then at least we have each other."

She gives me a little smile. "I'll always be grateful they gave me you. A built-in best friend."

"I love you." I kiss her forehead. "Gross, you're sweaty."

Fal laughs. "Sorry."

"But yeah, I think once I tell Mom and Dad, I'll feel a little better. Coming out publicly is still a little scary. I know there's lots of queer celebrities who are out now, but it feels different when it's you. The media frenzy is something I'm not looking forward to. I just wish it didn't have to be a big deal."

"Yeah." She's quiet for a while as she chops the potatoes. "Well, I think you should do whatever makes you happy. Love is beautiful. It shouldn't be a secret."

"Nobody said the L word."

She gives me a knowing look. "Right. What did you do yesterday?"

I sip my coffee before speaking. "You know, just hung out with Roman for a little while."

"Uh-huh, didn't you tell me you were meeting someone?"

"I met his sister, so what?"

She smiles. "Do I get to meet him?"

I set my mug down and my lips stretch wide across my face. "I was gonna ask if you wanted to later," I say excitedly.

Fallyn playfully rolls her eyes. "Duh."

"Okay. I'll let him know."

"Good."

My heart is full, and my smile never leaves my face.

ROMAN

CHAPTER 43

"Oh my god, I'm so nervous."

Jacoby laughs. "Why?"

He shakes his shoulders back and forth like he's trying to get the extra energy out. "I don't know. Were you this nervous?"

"I was a little nervous, but not shaky, can't stop fidgeting nervous."

"Well, I've never met anyone's family before."

"Ever?" he questions with surprise.

"No. If she hates me, are you gonna break up with me?"

He barks out a laugh. "You're insane. She's not going to hate you."

"You didn't say you wouldn't break up with me."

Jacoby draws me in by tugging on the bottom of my shirt. Against my lips, he says, "I'm not going to break up with you."

I put my hand on his lower back and kiss him. "Okay. Let's do this."

"Is your sister on standby?"

"Yeah, I told her not to go anywhere," I say as he leads me into his house.

Inside, I take another deep breath, and Jacoby reaches for my hand. "It's fine."

I give him a slight nod and tighten my grip as he takes me toward the living room. A woman is standing near the entertainment stand, her back to us. Her hair falls well past her shoulders and is coiled into tight, shiny curls. Though she's wearing baggy jeans, the plain white tank top showcases her slim frame.

Jacoby clears his throat and she spins around. Her skin is slightly darker than Jacoby's, but they have the same exact eyes. Her lips form a friendly smile, and then she puts down something on the shelf before walking over.

"Hey, Roman." She greets me like she's always known me. "You've turned my brother into a mushy, lovesick puppy."

"Oh," I say, a little surprised, but a lot relieved. My eyes flicker to Jacoby.

He's shaking his head. "This is Fallyn. She likes to embarrass me."

Fallyn extends her hand and I shake it. "I have a feeling you two are complete opposites."

She laughs. "I'm definitely more fun."

Jacoby scoffs.

"Well, it's nice to meet you."

She dips her chin. "So, do you want to hear all the things my brother had to say about you before he decided to fall for you?"

My head swivels toward Jacoby who's rubbing his head. "Absolutely."

Fallyn jerks her head toward the couch and I follow her.

"Don't believe anything she says," Jacoby calls out, close on our tail.

She rolls her eyes and it looks exactly like Jacoby's famous frustrated eye-roll. "Anyway, this guy really did like you. Until he didn't. He called you some names, but don't worry, it's like when kids do it to mask how they really feel or because they're upset. I knew they never came from the heart. He was just trying to protect himself."

Jacoby's still shaking his head in the seat across from us and it makes me grin. "Well, he wasn't alone in his name-calling."

"Definitely not. He called me pompous to my face."

Fallyn cackles. "Pompous?"

"He was acting very…" I let the sentence trail off and straighten my back and lift my head. "You know, snobby."

Fallyn laughs even more. "Yeah, he can come off that way."

"This was a really great idea, guys," Jacoby deadpans.

"I don't think that now," I say, smiling at him.

He rests his chin in his palm and grins.

"Ugh. You two are so cute it makes me sick," Fallyn says. "How the hell are you guys gonna hide this from everyone if you look at each other that way?"

"We're actors," Jacoby says.

Fallyn's shaking her head. "I don't think that's gonna help."

"Anyway," Jacoby states. "I'm talking to my parents in a few days. Fal and I are gonna drop by for a visit."

"Yay," Fallyn says with zero joy.

"Oh yeah?"

Jacoby nods. "After that, we'll see what happens. Maybe we won't have to worry about hiding for long."

My chest warms and my heart gallops in my chest.

"Are you okay with going public, Roman?" Fallyn asks.

Staring at Jacoby for a few more seconds, I reply, "Yes."

For two hours, we all sit in the living room and talk. Fallyn has the type of presence that makes you instantly feel comfortable. After just a few minutes, it's like I wasn't talking to a stranger at all.

When it was approaching five thirty, Jacoby told me to run back home and grab my sister so we could have dinner together.

Now we're outside his house, and as I'm pushing in the code on his gate, Chelsey is attempting to fix her hair as she stares at herself in the small mirror of the sun visor.

"Ugh. I wish you would've called me when you were on your way. I would've had thirty extra minutes to get ready."

"I'm sorry. You look fine anyway."

She shoves the visor up. "I look like a mess, but okay."

The gate opens and I pull up and park in front of one of the garages before getting out and waiting for Chels to round the car.

"This is so cute," she squeaks. "Older sisters and their two baby brothers who fell in love."

"No more embarrassing stories."

She ignores me. "What's his sister's name again?"

"Fallyn."

"Fallyn. Okay."

Jacoby opens the door and hugs my sister first. "Wow. I see how it is."

He chuckles and wraps me in his arms, planting several quick kisses on my cheek. "There. Happy?"

I shove him away. "Pity kisses? No."

"Oh, stop being a baby," Chelsey quips.

"Whatever. Let's go inside and eat. I'm starving."

"Fal ordered some Mexican food. Like, catering style though. Pans of enchiladas and tacos and huge bowls of beans and rice."

We walk inside and hear Fallyn shout out, "And chips and salsa!"

"Chelsey, this is my sister, Fallyn, with salsa on her chin."

Fallyn wipes at her face and then grabs a napkin. "Sorry," she says mid-chew. "Hi, it's nice to meet you."

Chelsey shakes her hand. "It's nice to meet you. Thanks for getting all this food," she says, gesturing to the entire breakfast bar that's been taken over with food containers.

"I feel bad for not asking what anyone else wanted, but I've been craving Mexican food for so long."

"She doesn't feel that bad," Jacoby says.

"Oh shush. It's good."

"We were supposed to get Mexican food recently," I say, giving Jacoby a look.

"Hmm. That's right."

"Umm," Fallyn muses. "Anyway. So, Chelsey, what do you do?"

"I'm in fashion. The hope is to be a designer one day, but I'd love to work as a stylist until then."

"Oh, awesome," Fallyn says, grabbing another chip. "I'm in makeup. Special effects mostly, but I work on movies and TV shows."

"Really?" Chelsey squeals. "Oh my god, that's so cool. What've you worked on?"

The girls end up piling food on plates and take their conversation to a small table off the side of the kitchen.

"Seems like they'll get along," I say, watching them with a smile on my face.

"Yeah. That's good."

Jacoby kisses my temple and we make our own plates and sit at the breakfast bar.

Everything is perfect. I've never felt so happy and at ease. Since losing my parents, I lost the sense of family. Chelsey is amazing and our bond is top tier, but sometimes, though there's two of us, it can still feel lonely. Quiet. And now we're here with Jacoby and his sister, and the house is filled with laughter and chatter. We're sharing meals together and watching movies, and it feels like I have a family again.

My phone vibrates with a text, and when I pull it out, I read the message on the screen.

> Hey! I'm going to be in town in a couple days. I can't wait to see you! ;)

CHAPTER 44

I<small>T'S BEEN A DAY AND A HALF SINCE</small> I <small>GOT THE TEXT FROM</small> Emerson alerting me of his visit. I didn't tell Jacoby right away, since we had our sisters around us, but the next day I told him about the message.

He asked if it was fair to assume that Emerson would expect something to happen between us, which I answered honestly. Yes. Probably. He then asked what I planned on telling him.

I told Jacoby I'd definitely not be doing anything with him and that I'd explain I was in a relationship. In this instance, Jacoby doesn't think it's the best idea to tell Emerson that it's him I'm in a relationship with. Which I agree with.

If Emmy gets mad or jealous, he could spread this information around before we're ready for it.

So, as Jacoby is gearing up to drive to his parents' house to tell them that he's gay, I'm awaiting Emerson's arrival and hoping like hell this goes well.

Initially, I didn't want to invite him to my home. Nobody else is here, it's private, and Emmy may assume we'd do what we'd usually do since we always hooked up in secret. However, going out and meeting him in public didn't feel right either, because not only would the paparazzi be out and taking photos, but I don't really want to have this conversation where other people could overhear. Plus, he's in town for a few days. I'm sure I wouldn't be able to avoid him coming over at least once.

The bell rings, and I take a second before making my way to the door. When I open it, he's standing there with a huge smile on his face, his green eyes sparkling in the sun, and a backpack slung over his rounded shoulder.

Emerson immediately steps forward and gives me a hug. "God, it's so good to see you. It's been so long."

I return the gesture, patting him on the back twice before I step away and let him in. "Yeah, it has been a while."

"You went and got all *movie star* on me," he says with a chuckle, dropping his bag next to the door.

"Please. I've always been a movie star. Want a drink or anything?"

"I'm good for now."

I make my way to the living room and choose to sit in the single armchair. He gets comfortable on the loveseat next to me, but his eyes remain focused on my face, and his smile lasts forever.

Emerson is an attractive guy. He's got bleach blond hair that he really pulls off well, bright green eyes, an angular face, and pouty lips. He's wearing a plain white T-shirt that fits snug around his toned arms, and a pair of jeans that hug his thighs as he sits. He's really not hard to look at, but he's no Jacoby Hart.

"You could've been a movie star with me, you know," I say with a grin.

He waves his hand in the air. "I don't know how you

survived the child actor curse. Or honesty, how you wanted to continue. That shit was mentally grueling. All the auditions, and the casting directors telling you that you didn't have the right look or you needed to lose weight, or change your appearance in some way. No thanks."

I nod. "Yeah, it was definitely tough sometimes."

I met Emerson through auditions when we were teens. We always ended up at a lot of the same ones and struck up a friendship. At eighteen, he decided he didn't want to do it anymore and ended up doing a little modeling before quitting that, too.

"I'm doing a little photography now," he says with a proud smile. "Mostly up and coming models. People who want headshots or nice pics for their Instagram feeds." He shrugs. "It's something."

"That's good. As long as you're happy."

"I am," he says with a nod. "God, I still can't believe how big you're getting. I've been seeing you all over social media. The girls and gays are going crazy over you."

I chuckle. "It's been pretty great. I'm so excited about the upcoming movie."

"Yes!" He sits up, his eyes wide. "Jacoby Hart! Holy shit. He's big time. How was it working with him?"

I try to keep my stupid giddy smile off my face, simply nodding. "Yeah, it was really good. He's very talented."

"And hot."

I twist my lips in an attempt to keep from smiling. It's not like I have to lie to him about thinking he's hot. Emmy knows I'm bisexual, but I'm afraid I'll give too much away. "Yeah, he's all right."

Emerson barks out a laugh. "Oh, don't be jealous. I still think you're hot, too."

Great. Not where I wanted this conversation to go.

I just give him a small smile. "But yeah, I'm hoping the movie does well. My manager has an audition lined up for me for another movie. Supposed to be another starring role."

"That's good, man."

I nod, wondering if I should tell him now, or just let the day progress and wait to see if I have to say anything at all. He may not expect us to do anything. That's sort of presumptuous thinking on my part. He could be dating someone, or just not interested.

"So, did you have any plans while you were out here?"

"Yeah, I have a shoot tomorrow. Besides that, I was just hoping we'd have some time together."

I swallow, nodding. "Yeah, we can go get something to eat or maybe catch a movie. There might be paps though."

"We could just stay in," he says, and the tone leaves nothing to be questioned. I know what he means.

"Well," I start, "I should probably tell you I've been seeing someone."

His brows shoot up a bit. "Oh?"

"Yeah."

He takes a second. "Is it Faye Crespo?" he questions with a little laugh.

"Oh god, no. You've seen the stories, I take it."

"Who hasn't?"

"Nah, we're not together."

"So, who is it?"

I rub my palms over my knees. "It's complicated. We're kind of secretly dating."

He angles his head slightly. "Hm. Why secretly?"

"It's…a guy."

Now his eyebrows nearly touch his hairline. "Oh wow."

"Yeah."

"Is he famous?"

I hesitate. "He's not out either."

He doesn't let it slide. "Who is it?"

I shake my head. "I can't say. He's not out, and it's not right for me to tell anyone."

Emerson seems to understand because he begins to nod, but then he says, "I won't tell anyone."

I let out a chuckle that he might take as nervousness, but I'm starting to get frustrated and trying not to let it show. "Soon," I say, getting up to walk to the kitchen.

Footsteps follow behind me. When I open the fridge to grab something to drink, Emerson speaks.

"I came out."

I pause for a couple seconds before spinning around, forgetting about getting a drink. "What?"

He nods, his fingers dancing along the countertop. "Yep. About two months ago. Put it on social media and everything. No going back."

"Wow. How do you feel? How did it go?"

Emmy grins. "Good. I feel better than ever. I didn't realize how much I was hiding or how often I was lying until I didn't have to anymore. My parents are fine. Based on their reaction, I'm thinking they already were aware or at least, questioning. It wasn't a huge bomb drop or anything. The few close friends I have seemed cool with it, and it made me feel like I was scared for nothing."

"Not everyone has accepting people in their life though," I say, thinking of Jacoby's parents.

"Yeah, I know," he says with a nod. "I understand there's still reasons to be afraid. There are still homophobic assholes in the world, but…" He sighs, a smile on his lips. "It's been good."

"I'm so happy for you, man," I tell him, a genuine smile on my face. "It's been a long time coming, huh?"

He chuckles, looking down. "Yeah." After a few seconds, he says, "So, are you pretty serious with this guy?"

I shift on my feet. "Umm, yeah. I'd say so. Our dates have been private, obviously, but our time together is significant."

"Have you thought about coming out at all?"

"Yeah. A lot more recently. You never know how the public will react or the articles or tweets you might see about yourself, but..." I shrug. "It has to happen, right? I can't keep hiding and lying, like you said."

He nods. "If you do it for yourself, you won't regret it. You'll know when it's time."

I smile at him. "Wanna get something to eat?"

"Definitely."

Emerson and I spend the rest of the day together, and it feels like we're teenagers again. We laugh and joke, go through a drive thru for greasy fries and messy burgers, talk about old friends, and dodge paparazzi. Well, we didn't used to do that as teenagers, but everything is mostly the same.

We stop by a shopping center where he buys some new camera equipment and a couple new shirts. After that, we drive around, just checking out some scenic areas where Emerson snaps a few photos.

He doesn't question me about the identity of my secret boyfriend, and I'm happy to have this time with an old friend.

Before we head back to my house, the sun is already setting and we're hungry again, so we pick up some pizza and drive home.

We eat, drink, and continue having a good time until it's almost three in the morning and he's sober enough to drive to his hotel.

Before leaving, he grabs his backpack and unzips it. "Oh, I wanted to give you this."

I take the photo album from his hand. "What's this?"

"Memories," he says with a small grin. "I'm really happy for you, Rome. I'm extremely grateful for your friendship. For our history. Thank you for being so kind."

My brows dip a little, sort of confused by the fact that he sounds a little sad. "Of course. You're the oldest friend I have. I had such a good time today."

He grins and steps forward, wrapping his arms around me in a hug. I return the gesture and feel him give me a final squeeze before he steps away.

"See you."

"You're in town for a couple more days, right?"

"Yeah."

"Okay. I'll text you."

He nods again before making his way to the car.

I take the album to the couch where I drop into the soft seat and open it up.

CHAPTER 45

"So, what's been going on with you?" my mother asks from the sofa opposite the one where Fallyn and I sit.

"Well, I've been promoting two different movies the last few months. One is already out, and the other one will premiere next month."

She nods her head before taking a sip of her coffee. "That's right. You're so busy. That's amazing, honey, I'm so proud of you. Your dad and I both are."

"Yep." Dad's voice booms from the kitchen before he appears through the doorway. "You're doing really well for yourself, son."

"Thanks, Dad."

He sits next to my mom and pats her knee twice before settling into the couch.

"And you," Mom says, aiming her hazel eyes at Fallyn. "What's new with you?"

"Well, I just got done working on a zombie movie. I did the makeup for them."

Mom nods like she's waiting for Fallyn to say more, and

Dad watches her with stoic attention, his fingers stroking his graying beard.

"Great," Mom finally says. "That's great. I'm sure you did that well."

Fallyn scoffs quietly.

"Fallyn's actually one of the best special effects makeup artists in Hollywood. She's quite sought after."

"It's okay," she whispers to me.

"Well, that's amazing," Dad says with a nod. "Really. I guess I don't think about the work that goes on behind the scenes. I just watch the actors doing their jobs," he says with a gesture in my direction. "But yeah. You two are doing great."

"Now, what's this new movie about, Jacoby?" Mom asks, a slight scowl already on her face. "You know I don't go on the internet a whole lot, but I did see a little teaser on TV the other day. I was a little confused about what it's about."

Fallyn and I both shift a little in our seats. I didn't go into detail about this movie's storyline when I told them I'd be filming. They don't ask for too many details anyway, but now that it's about to be out, it makes sense they'd have heard a little more about it.

"It's a romance," I tell them. "Lots of emotion and some drama, but a romance at its core."

"It's based off of a really popular book," Fallyn adds. "Everybody is excited about it."

"Hmm," Dad murmurs, giving me a single nod. "And it's between you and…a guy?"

I nod. "Yep. It's a film I'm very excited about."

Silence.

"Well. Okay." Dad claps his hands and sits up. "Should we eat?"

"Actually," I start, sweat already beginning to bead along

my hairline. "I had something else I wanted to talk to you guys about."

"Oh?" Mom questions, concern on her face.

Dad settles back into the cushion. "What's going on?"

"Well." I look at Fallyn who gives me a small smile and nod. "This has been a long time coming. It's not a new development, and yes, I'm absolutely sure." I pause, taking in their expressions one last time before I say it. "I'm gay."

More silence.

Uncomfortable silence.

Fallyn reaches over and grabs my hand, squeezing it in hers.

"You're…gay," Mom states.

"Yes."

"And you have been since…" Dad says, trailing off to let me finish it for him.

"Since forever. Since attraction began."

"You couldn't possibly know at such a young age," Mom says.

"I was a pre-teen, Mom. I wasn't two. When did you first realize you were attracted to boys?" I turn my attention to Dad. "When did you first realize you were attracted to girls? In school, right? It's the same for me."

"Yeah, but—" Dad begins.

"No. There's no exception. You knew you were attracted to girls and that was that. There was no big decision day where you had to decide you were going to be straight. You just were. And I'm gay. It's really as simple as that."

"Why have you been lying to us?" Mom asks, her anger turning up a notch. "Why did you tell us about girlfriends?"

"Can you blame him?" Fallyn chimes in. "After seeing how you reacted to me, it's understandable."

"What do you mean how we reacted to you? We've been supportive."

Fallyn lets out a humorless laugh. "Okay, sure. I'm not trying to have this fight again."

"Fallyn, we haven't mistreated you," Dad says.

"No, you just act like I don't exist. You don't want to hear about my girlfriends or who I'm dating. I'm basically an acquaintance at this point."

"We just don't understand," Mom cries. "It's not a lifestyle we know."

Fallyn shakes her head, crossing her arms over her chest as she mockingly murmurs, *"lifestyle."*

"We're still people. Still your kids. You don't have to understand, but it's something you should try to accept and respect," I say. "And yes, I was afraid to tell you because as a kid, being gay wasn't something I knew was okay. I only saw straight couples. I saw you and Dad. I saw men and women on dates. I saw straight people in movies and TV shows. I don't remember the first time I saw a gay person in the media that wasn't just a stereotype made simply for laughs. Then when you found out about Fallyn, and I saw how your relationship with her ended up, I was afraid of that happening to us.

"On top of that, I'm an actor in Hollywood. Of course I was afraid. I still am. I don't want to be a talking point, simply because I'm attracted to men. I don't want to be the target of homophobic asshole's tirades on the internet. I really don't want my sexuality to be a big deal. I want to continue to work and get jobs based on my abilities and I want to be able to fall in love."

"Well, it is. It's going to be a frenzy," Mom says, her voice getting high and squeaky. "It's all everyone will talk about for a while."

"Then it's a good thing you don't watch TV or get on the internet, huh?" Fallyn adds, her arms still crossed.

"Are you saying you are going to go public with this?" Dad asks, the lines in his light brown face deepening with a furrowed brow.

"Yes, at some point. I don't know how or when, but I will, and I wanted to tell you guys first." I take a breath. "Because the truth of the matter is, I've met someone, and I really like him."

Mom rubs a finger across her eyebrow as she exhales.

"Your kids are gay. You're going to have to deal with it," Fallyn exclaims, her arms uncrossing and flying out in front of her. "And if you can't, then we're prepared to be done with both of you. You've made me feel like shit for too long, and if you choose to treat Jacoby the same way, then you'll be losing both kids in one fell swoop. You're supposed to love us unconditionally. We are your *children.* Just because we're grown doesn't mean we don't still want love and support from our parents, and just because we are your kids doesn't mean you get to disrespect us and we have to take it." She gets to her feet and turns toward me. "I'm sorry." Fallyn storms out of the room.

After several seconds, I speak up again. "I guess we'll be leaving. I hope to hear from you both soon, but if not, then…" I shrug. "Well, that's your decision."

"Jacoby," Mom says, curling a brown lock of hair behind her ear. "We really want the best for you. Both of you. You have to understand we're afraid. The world is cruel."

"Yes, but *you* don't have to be."

I stand and they both follow suit. Dad gives me a couple pats on the shoulder.

"We love you."

Mom still looks panic-stricken, but there's some unshed

tears in her eyes when she nods. "We do. If you're happy, then I'm happy. Please tell Fallyn the same thing."

"Call her and tell her yourself. I think she'd appreciate it."

Mom nods. "We'll be in touch with you both soon."

I give them both quick hugs before I turn to leave.

"Good luck," Mom calls out. "With your announcement."

"Thank you."

CHAPTER 46

After Fallyn and I left our parents' house, we drove straight back to Pasadena, the trip from Malibu taking over an hour due to an accident on the highway.

Pulling up in front of my house, I put the car in park. "Would you hate me if I went to see Roman?"

She grins. "See? Lovesick."

"No," I reply with my own smile. "I just want to tell him how it went and see how his time with Emerson was."

"Of course I'll be fine," she says as she undoes her seatbelt. "I'll probably head home later today, but I'll wait until you come back. I'm gonna raid your fridge and watch trash TV."

I chuckle. "Sounds good."

"I love you. I'm proud of you for telling them."

"I love you," I tell her.

I feel a thousand pounds lighter as I drive toward Roman's place. I never knew how heavy the weight of this secret was until now. Telling my parents is just step one, so I can't imagine how I'll feel once the public knows. I worry it won't be as freeing. Will it bring about stress or anxiety?

Fallyn and I drove out to Malibu yesterday and spent the day relaxing on the beach before crashing in a hotel and visiting my parents today. I knew Emerson was coming to town, so in order to try to keep from worrying about his visit, a trip to the beach felt like the right call.

Thankfully, he gave me the code to the main gate of the community he lives in, so I drive in and park outside his house and send him a text, hoping like hell he's home. As I wait for him to respond, I get on social media and waste some time.

Immediately, I'm met with images of Roman and Emerson from yesterday. The paparazzi were out in full force and captured everything. Pictures of them laughing in his Benz with the windows down as they went to a fast food restaurant. More photos as they drive off down the road. It seems they also went shopping and then got pizza.

Most of the headlines are, *Roman Black seen out and about with a new friend.* Or *Roman Black has bro date.* One article questions, *Who is the cutie seen out with Roman Black?* It further details everything they found out about Emerson, which includes the fact that he's a photographer, ex-model, and openly bisexual.

People online leave comments questioning whether Roman is gay. Are they dating? Someone seems to know they are childhood friends and retweets an article saying so. Some users slam the press for instigating anything and question why people can't live their lives without everyone assuming something.

I'm definitely falling victim to clickbait as I feel the need to read everything posted. I'm not even sure why I'm doing this to myself. The photos are all innocent. I'm not even worried that Roman would cheat on me.

But something about the fact that people are simply

talking about him being with someone else bothers me. He's mine. I am his. I want that to be what people talk about if they have to talk about something.

A car horn blares, making me jump. I snap my head up and find Roman driving past me with a smile on his face. He opens his gate and drives in, so I follow suit.

As soon as I get out, he slams into me, giving me a tight hug.

"Why does it feel like it's been forever since I've seen you?" he questions, his lips against my neck.

"I feel the same way."

"Let's go inside."

I follow him to his back door, and as soon as we're inside, I grab his wrist and tug him into me, planting my mouth on him in a searing kiss.

He moans appreciatively as his hand cups the back of my head. It's a couple minutes before we manage to break away.

Roman gives me a crooked smile before pulling me toward his couch.

"Okay, tell me everything."

So, with his hand in mine, I do. I tell him that I told my parents I was gay and that I had met someone, though I didn't announce who he was. I tell him about how Fallyn told them we were prepared to distance ourselves from them if they felt like they couldn't respect us and love us regardless of our sexualities, and how at the end, I was given a tiny bit of hope that they'd reach out and be okay.

"You feel good about it?" he asks.

I nod. "Yes. It's definitely a weight off my shoulders. I want to hope they'll accept this and everything will be normal. They're fairly aloof people anyway. We don't get together regularly. I have a busy schedule, and they're living their best retired lives. Their only concern is filling their days with spa trips or yacht rides, or overseas vacations."

"Oh, so they have money," Rome says with a laugh.

"Yeah. My dad sold his tech company a few years back. Mom was a doctor. They've been well-off for years, but selling the company has them set for life now."

"Nice," he says with a nod.

"So, normal would be good. Normal is phone calls maybe three times a month. A visit every six if we're lucky. We've spent some holidays together, but it depends on our schedules. I don't expect them to be over here every week or anything like that, but I don't want all communication to die either. So, we'll see." I exhale. "Anyway, how about you? How did it go with Emerson?"

Roman takes a breath. "It was good. I was nervous at first, but after a little moment of him kind of mentioning he'd be okay with us staying in, I told him I was dating someone. He asked who it was and was surprised when I said a guy, but after insisting I wouldn't reveal the mystery guy's name, he moved on." He shrugs. "We had a good day. Got some food and drove around. Stayed up eating pizza and then he left."

"So he wasn't upset?"

Roman shakes his head. "Nah. I don't think so."

"I saw the—" I'm cut off by the sound of his phone ringing from the other room.

"Oh, sorry. I left my phone here to charge. I'll be back. I'm expecting a call from my manager."

He takes off through the living room and into the small dining room on the other side of the kitchen. I make my way to the fridge to get a drink and spot an open photo album on the counter.

As I take a sip from the bottle of water, I spot a teenaged Roman Black in the first photo, and my lips curl into a smile.

After a few flips, I realize there's another guy in a lot of these pictures. His hair is dark, but I'm pretty sure it's Emerson.

I come across a page where there's only a single photo and then the words, *Remember this??* The photo doesn't make sense to me. It's just a picture of a graffitied wall.

There are more pictures of the two of them, some of them with other people, and solo shots. More pages have writing scribbled on them—inside jokes perhaps.

I watch as they get older in the photos, and a few candids taken by someone other than one of them tells me that Emerson's liked Roman for a long time. It's obvious in the way he looks at him.

I stop when I get to a couple pages of pictures that have Roman and what has to be his parents. In a couple, they're in the background, but then they all get together and pose. He looks just like his dad, but he has his mom's nose.

"Sorry. It was my publicist," Roman says as he walks in. "I guess there's some photos of me out there today."

"Yeah. I saw them."

He goes to the fridge and sighs. "It's causing a stir on social media. Everyone wants to know more about Emerson and who he is to me."

I glance down at the album. "Looks like you guys have a lot of history."

Roman laughs. "Yeah, we were just kids. A lot of those were at auditions or at restaurants down the road from where auditions took place. I haven't looked at the whole thing yet. Anything embarrassing?" he asks as he takes a sip of his drink.

"Nothing embarrassing."

"What's wrong?"

I shake my head. "Nothing."

He steps closer, eyes flickering to the open book and then to me. "You don't have anything to be concerned about if that's what it is. Emerson brought that to me, for memories sake."

I turn the page away from the one of his parents and am greeted with another one of Roman and Emerson when they're clearly past their teen years. Looks like they're at a party, but again, it's a shot that shows just how enthralled Emerson was with Roman. Written next to it are the words, *I was afraid of letting you know how I felt, but it had to have been obvious to everyone.*

On the next page is another one. This time they're on a couch, sitting closely, but looking at each other mid-laugh. More writing surrounds it. *We had so many firsts. Here's to hoping we can have lasts.*

I look at Roman. "He's in love with you."

CHAPTER 47

"No, HE'S NOT."

"He is," Jacoby states, pushing the photo album toward me.

I look it over and feel a pain in my chest. Not for any reason other than I feel bad that I possibly hurt his feelings last night. I had no idea he had come with the intention of giving this to me. With this message.

"There's more. Photos of him looking at you the way I do. He's been in love with you for years. You have history. Are you sure—"

"Don't even finish that thought, Jacoby."

He puts his bottle on the table and slides his hands into the pockets of his chinos. "I want you to be sure."

"I like Emerson. I do. He's the only friend I have outside of Hollywood. I've known him for years, and yes, we have history, but I've never loved him. I've never daydreamt about our future together. I've never lost sleep thinking about him."

I watch him swallow, his eyes never leaving my face. "Are you saying—"

"Yes," I say definitively with a nod.

"You dream about our future?" he asks.

I start to feel nervous, like maybe it's too soon. "I mean, yeah." I avert my gaze. "I hope and—"

He steps forward, a finger under my chin to force me to look him in the eyes. "I can't imagine a future without you in it. I've tried. I've stayed up late in bed, wondering if it would even be possible to give you up. I've struggled, thinking you deserve better than me. Someone who wasn't so afraid. Because I am. I'm nervous about what my announcement could thrust me into. I'm probably not prepared for it. I've debated whether I should just remain single and in the closet, so at least nobody else has to be affected by my decisions, or lack thereof.

"But god do I want you," he says with a sigh. "The way I think about you might border on obsessive. All day, thoughts of you make my brain float off into the sky. When I'm not in the clouds, I'm cemented in concern that you'll change your mind about how you feel about me. I worry I'm falling too fast, and yet not moving quick enough to keep you." Jacoby shakes his head. "I've never experienced anything like this. My sister is right. I am absolutely lovesick. I hate not being with you, and all I can think about and countdown to is the moment you're in my arms again." He pauses, his eyes scanning my face. "I love you, Roman. I love you in a way I never thought possible. I'm afraid of coming out, but I'm afraid of a life without you more, and no matter the fallout, having you to come back to will make it better."

My insides are all out of place. My heart is in my throat and my stomach is twisted in knots. His words penetrate my brain, and I feel like it might be short circuiting. This man loves me? Me? I can't fathom it. Everything in me tries to make sense of what he just said, and it's not until he shifts slightly that I realize I've been quiet this whole time.

"You love me?" I finally say, not sure those are the best words to come out first.

He smiles slightly. "Yes."

I slam into him, my arms wrapping around his neck as my lips taste his. "Oh my god." I ease away to study his face again before planting another kiss on his mouth. "I love you, too."

His exhale of relief is audible and the release of tension in his body is visible. "Yeah?"

"Of course."

He cradles my cheek as he kisses me again and eventually we sag into the stools nearby, our hands remaining entwined and the smiles on our faces etched into placc.

"Where do we go from here?" I ask.

His thumb rubs the back of my hand. "We figure out when and how we want to come out. Do we make separate statements at different times? Do we start with our sexuality before we mention that we're dating?"

"I guess we should talk to our teams first."

Jacoby nods. "They'll need to be prepared for the questions."

"After that, I don't know."

"We'll figure it out," he says.

I glance over at the photo album. "I can get rid of that."

Jacoby shakes his head. "No. There's some photos in there you might want."

My brows draw in as I think. "Oh. My parents?" He nods, and I reach out and turn the pages until I find them. I touch their faces with my finger. "They'll never know."

"Never know what?" he asks softly.

"Anything. They won't know their sacrifices paid off. They saw me act before they died, but they didn't see the movies that thrust me into the spotlight. They'll never know that I got a starring role. They'll never know that I'm bisexual. They'll never know you. They won't see what I accomplish or—" I choke on my words, swallowing them down. "I have so much life left, and they won't see any of it." I look at Jacoby. "And you'll never know them, and I hate that. It's not fair. They should still be here and I should have parents to go home to and tell things to."

A tear slips past my eyelashes and falls down my cheek. I swipe at it angrily, but another one replaces it.

Jacoby doesn't try to placate me. He doesn't tell me it's okay and that they *can* see all these things. He seems to know that saying so won't offer me comfort. I'm mad. I'm devastated. And I'm allowed to feel those things.

"It is unfair," he offers. "You were born to two amazing people who created two amazing kids, and they should be here to watch you both grow and live."

I shake my head. "It's so dumb. They went on vacation. They wanted to see snow and it killed them. Icy roads and low visibility in the middle of December in fucking Maine, and now they're dead."

His thumb continues to stroke my hand, and all the years of pent up anger and sadness are released. I crumble, but he's there to hold me. He stands and wraps me in his arms as I rest my head against his stomach and sob.

I don't remember the last time I cried. I know I shed tears when I first found out. I cried alone in my room the night their bodies were flown into town. But then my sister started breaking down. She wasn't taking care of herself and I put my feelings aside to make sure she was okay. I insisted she eat when she didn't feel like it. I held her as she wailed into the room. I was strong for her. I protected her. Because I know that's what my parents would've wanted me to do.

When she came out of her depression, I was already used

to faking it. Faking like I was fine. Pretending I wasn't shattered inside. I didn't want to talk about what happened. I acted as if nothing did. It worked for me, or at least I thought so.

Now I'm curled into Jacoby, crying like it just happened, and ruining the ecstatic moment we just had. What a fucking mess I am.

"I'm sorry," I say through sniffles, trying to pull away.

"Don't be," he says, tugging me closer and running a hand through my hair.

I cry some more and mutter my frustrations into his shirt. I get out every feeling I ever suppressed until I have no more tears to cry and no more anger to lobby into the universe.

Jacoby pulls me up and holds me close as he walks us to my bedroom. Getting me seated, he pulls off my sneakers before toeing off his own.

"Lay with me," he says, climbing on top of the covers.

I scoot in close to him and rest my head on his shoulder as he wraps his arm around me.

"You can tell me about them whenever you want. You can be vulnerable, angry, or sad. I can know them through you and your memories, and I'll be sure to keep them safe," he says, tapping on his chest. "Or you can keep them to yourself. That's fine, too. I'm here for you. Always. In any way you need."

I squeeze him around his middle, feeling the tears well up again. This time, for a different reason.

"I love you," I say quietly.

"I love *you*, baby."

CHAPTER 48

WHEN I WAKE UP FROM A NAP, JACOBY IS STILL AT MY SIDE, his phone in his free hand typing away.

"Welcome back," he says.

I ease away and stretch my arms. "Were you awake the whole time?"

"Yeah. I've sent emails to everyone on my team: management, PR, and my agent. I even texted my assistant. Everyone I work with on a regular basis now knows."

"That you're gay or that you're gay and with me?"

"Both." He puts his phone down. "That's okay, right?"

I sit up and rest against the headboard. "Of course. Yeah!" My smile takes over my face. "Let me send emails too. They'll probably be calling both of us and scheduling meetings soon."

"I've sent calls to voicemail already," he says with a chuckle. "Followed by a message letting them know we'll get together soon."

I reach over for my laptop on the nightstand and open it up. After a few clicks, I'm in my inbox and typing out emails to everyone who needs to know. I close it and look at Jacoby with a smile.

"Now we just have to figure out the how and when of it all."

He grabs my hand. "Yeah, and we will, but for now," he says, climbing into my lap and straddling my thighs, "I want to show you how much I love you." He leans in and kisses my neck. "Or at least how much I love your body. I hope to show you how much I love you in the years to come."

"Well that sounds good to me."

I remove my shirt while Jacoby steps off the bed to undress. I scoot down until I'm on my back and start pushing down the pair of basketball shorts I'm wearing.

When he returns, he begins kissing and licking me from my neck, across my collarbone, down my chest, and slowly and teasingly lower and lower on my torso.

I wriggle and writhe, gripping his hair in my fingers as I try to force him to one particular spot, but he's stubborn. He kisses the tops of my thighs before dragging his tongue across the inner parts of them. When he does show attention to my erection, it's only with brief kisses on my shaft.

"Flip over," he whispers.

I quickly oblige. "You're gonna tease me to death, aren't you?"

"I'm worshiping you. Now shut up and let me."

With a playful grumble, I wiggle my ass and endure his languid and deliciously torturous touches. He gently massages my shoulders before nibbling at the flesh on my neck. He kneads my lats as his tongue dances down my spine. And then he cups each of my ass cheeks, spreading and lifting so his tongue can travel easily down the crease.

"Holy mother of god," I blurt out, my fists squeezing the pillow. "Holy. Yes. God. Oh."

He pulls away to say, "I didn't know you were so religious."

"Shut up. Keep going."

For several minutes, Jacoby makes up for all the teasing as he devours me. I push my hips into the air, resting on my spread knees in the hopes that he'll never stop. His hand reaches under me, tugging and teasing my throbbing erection. Jacoby's thumb brushes over the wetness on the tip and slides it down my shaft as he moans into my ass.

"Fucking Christ," I curse. "Oh my god, it's so good. You're so good. Yes."

I feel the loss of him when he moves back, and I whimper and whine until he smacks me on the ass.

"Be patient."

Before I know it, he's back, and cool liquid covers the wetness his tongue left behind. His fingers slide up and down before he slowly begins to push them in.

For another several minutes, Jacoby ensures I'm ready for him as he edges me to the brink of bliss. When he's done, he flips me over to my back and nestles between my legs. Holding one of my thighs up, he positions his lubed up cock where it needs to be and starts sliding in.

My own erection feels heavy on my stomach, desperate for attention.

Jacoby's hips move slowly at first. When I begin to beg and plead, and wrap my arms around his waist to pull him closer, he knows I'm ready for more.

Leaning over me, his lips find mine. I wrap one leg around one of his while I clutch the back of his head with my hand, keeping him in place so I can suck his tongue into my mouth. He continues to rock back and forth, drawing out moans and grunts.

"I love you," I whisper against his mouth.

"I love you."

Jacoby moves back, his thrusts going deeper, his movements a little faster. He reaches for my erection and strokes.

"Oh, yeah," I say, stretching each word with a moan.

"You feel so good, baby," he murmurs, looking down at me with lust and affection. "I can't believe you're mine."

"Yes, yours," I pant, sounding more wanton and desperate than anything. "All yours. God, please."

Jacoby fills me deeply and thoroughly, making fireworks go off behind my eyelids while his hand simultaneously brings me the friction I need. I don't know how he can work his hips and hand in different rhythms so perfectly, but I'm not complaining.

"Jacoby." I cry out his name, the sound deep and guttural. "I'm gonna come."

He moans. "Good. Let me see it."

"Oh, god. Baby, yes!"

My muscles tighten, and I thrust my head deeper into the pillow as my orgasm hits. I yell into the room, the noise cutting my vocal cords on its way out. Warmth spills down my shaft, and I open my eyes to look at Jacoby.

He's enraptured. His teeth bite into his bottom lip as he continues to stroke me. My body quivers with aftershocks and my chest heaves with deep breaths, but I can't stop looking at him. He's completely undone. Sweat drips from his forehead, his skin is a little flushed around his neck, and his breaths come in deep pants. He's blissed out completely and so fucking sexy.

Jacoby lets go of my cock, the mess still between his fingers when he grips the underside of my thigh and starts fucking me harder. My body slides up with his movements, my head hitting the headboard with each thrust.

His grunts grow a little more animalistic. His muscles

flex, his lips part, and his fingers dig deep into my skin when his orgasm overtakes him.

"Oh, fuck," he cries just before letting go of my legs and catching himself on either side of me.

He continues to thrust, his rhythm changing slightly as his body jerks with every pump of his release. His sweat-slicked forehead rests on my chest as he sucks in breaths and releases cuss words with each exhale.

Jacoby kisses along my jaw before he pulls away. He flops onto his side with a long satiated sigh. "Give me a second and I'll grab a cloth."

I chuckle, still a little winded myself. "I'm not in a rush to move. It's fine."

We give ourselves several minutes to catch our breath, but Jacoby gets up first. He washes up and uses the bathroom, bringing with him a warm, wet washcloth when he returns to the bed.

I wipe up the mess on my skin before dabbing at a spot on the covers. "Ah, well. I have spares."

After I'm done in the bathroom, I climb back into bed with Jacoby even though it's still the middle of the afternoon.

"Your phone's been buzzing quite a lot."

He sighs, his eyes closed. "Yeah. They can wait."

I smile and wrap an arm around his waist.

Our respective teams *do* wait. But not for long.

CHAPTER 49

OVER THE COURSE OF A WEEK, BOTH JACOBY AND I HAVE meetings with our publicists, managers, and agents. The publicists have more to do in this particular case, but it's best to get everyone on board. After individual meetings, Jacoby and I, along with our publicists, have a meeting to tackle the information about our relationship and what information we will and will not be providing to the public.

As of now, nobody in the public knows anything, but at least we're prepared for when it does come out. Jacoby and I have talked a little about how we want to go about it, but mainly we're focused on each other and soaking up all the private moments we can because as soon as the news breaks, we know the paparazzi will not leave us alone for a second.

In the weeks after our meetings, we've both had talk show slots to fill, and the two-day press junket just ended, so we were at a hotel together, doing an insane amount of interviews.

It's been exhausting and exciting. Our sisters have sent us multiple clips they've found on social media; they always include the screenshots of the comment sections because people are going crazy over our banter and friendship. People are commenting on the way Jacoby looks at me or how my hand might've lingered too long on his shoulder. There's definitely quite a lot of people hoping we fall in love, even without knowing the truth of our sexualities. I understand that people get wrapped up in characters and love them so much they want that chemistry to become love. Obviously, that's not always the case. Almost never. Jacoby and I know now how big of a deal it will be when we do come out as a couple. And now the time has finally come. Our movie premieres tonight.

We're getting ready separately with our own stylists, and we'll be arriving at the red carpet around the same time.

Choosing to match the theme for the book cover—a sea of red tulips against a clear blue sky, I'm wearing a bright blue designer suit with a red trench coat draped over my shoulders.

My hair is slicked back and my facial hair is trimmed short, and with a couple spritzes of cologne, my look is complete.

I pose for a few photos in the suite of the hotel before I'm ushered downstairs and into a waiting car. The theater isn't too far away, but the traffic is intense and slow moving.

My phone buzzes.

Jacoby: I can't wait to see you.
Me: Miss me or something?
Jacoby: Only a little.
Me: I can't wait to see you either.

I smile at my phone until my publicist, Alisha, clears her throat, getting my attention. "Jacoby will get there first. We're probably two cars behind. Once both of you are on the carpet, they'll likely try to get photographs of you two together. The rest of the cast will be there, but I'm not sure on their arrival timeline."

"Okay."

"Is there anything I need to know?"

"What do you mean?"

Her eyes flash to the driver. "Just anything I need to be prepared for?"

"I don't think so."

She nods once and we ride in silence the rest of the way.

When we pull up, someone opens the door, and I step out. There's a ton of people, lots of noise, and the endless sound of camera shutters.

Some of the crowd notices me before I officially start walking the carpet, and I make sure to wave and smile. They have their phones pointed at me and happily jump up and down while screaming my name.

"Okay, we're up," Alisha says, gesturing for me to walk forward.

I enjoy this part. I love being in front of cameras, and I like talking to people about my work, so this is always fun.

My eyes scan the carpet ahead, searching for Jacoby. Unfortunately, there's a lot of black suits, so it's not like he'll be easy to spot.

Alisha runs ahead as I step up to talk to an entertainment news channel.

"Roman, it's so good to see you. You look amazing."

The interviewer is a household name, having been a red carpet reporter for this station for at least ten years.

"Hey, Nessa. Thank you. It's good to be here."

Motion at my right steals my attention, and then the person doing the moving steals my breath. Jacoby rushes toward me, wearing all white. It's not a bold color by any means, but it's strikingly different than anything he usually wears on red carpets, and damn, he wears it well. The suit is crisp and fits him like a glove. My eyes trace his body before I realize I shouldn't be looking at him like this.

"Hey, I just had to come say hi," he says with a friendly smile, draping his arm around my shoulders like any friend would do. "Sorry to interrupt," he says, directing the words at Nessa.

She's wearing a bright grin on her face. "No, no. Please interrupt. Let me ask you two: How was it working on this movie together?"

Jacoby removes his arm from around my shoulders and we stand shoulder to shoulder in front of the statuesque reporter.

"It was…" I pause, wondering how to finish the sentence. "It was the best decision I ever made. I made incredible friends, had the best experiences, and came out of it a better person, I think."

Jacoby nods along. "It was the perfect story to tell, and we're so happy to have been chosen to bring these characters to life."

After a couple more questions, we move on and get asked to stop and pose for photos from dozens of photographers lining the other side of the gate. We take them both together and separately. We laugh and smile along the way, stopping for a few more quick interviews, and finally we're inside the theater.

After speaking with other actors and celebrities inside, we get settled into our seats and watch the movie.

Everyone laughs when they should, which is good. People let loose a few *awws* at cute moments, and then Jacoby and I shift when we know the first sex scene is coming.

"Try not to get turned on," I whisper into his ear.

He leans back over. "You were the one calling out my real name during the scene."

My cheeks heat up, and I have nothing to say back right now.

I spot a few people dabbing at their eyes during the emotional scenes—when William and Andrew are fighting because they want to be together, but William is unable to give Andrew what he wants at the time.

The camera zooms in on Jacoby's handsome face as tears brim in his eyes. "Andrew, I want this. I want us. You have to know that. I've never had anything like this before in my life, and I never want anything else. I only want you and me for eternity." He pauses, shaking his head. "But I can't. Maybe in another life. If it wasn't this one where I have parents who would disown me. If I could be myself with you in public. If I could love you the way you deserve to be loved." His voice cracks. "You have to know how much this is killing me." He grabs my hands in his as we stand in his dorm room. "But I don't think I can do this."

The camera pans to me, and I have tears falling down my face. "We only have this life, William. We deserve to live it. We deserve to find love in it. We deserve happiness."

Jacoby knocks his knee into mine. A subtle touch to let me know the words mean something to him, not just the characters we played.

When the movie ends, the theater erupts into applause and cheers, and my heart feels full. Jacoby pulls me into a hug. Nothing intimate. Just a congratulatory hug between co-stars.

"I love you."

I smile and pull away, but before I can reply, we're surrounded by people wanting to congratulate us.

I long to reach for his hand and hold it in mine.

CHAPTER 50

THE AFTERPARTY STRETCHES INTO THE WEE HOURS OF THE morning. Normally, that would be fine, but I just watched a movie I'm extremely proud of with the man I'm now in love with, and I want nothing more than to hug him and hold him and kiss him. I want to tell him how grateful I am for his presence in my life. I want to whisper *I love you* over and over. I want *us*. I don't want to spend the night apart, talking to everyone separately because I'm afraid I'll slip and touch him in a way I shouldn't.

I'm tired of acting like I'm not attracted to him, like I don't want him or love him.

Faye sidles up to me. "It's killing you, isn't it?"

"Yes."

"The movie is incredible."

I finally tear my gaze away from where Roman stands amongst a group of three. Facing her, I smile. "Thank you."

"The message is important, too."

"Some of it hits pretty close."

She nods and glances away. "I'm still waiting to host dinner."

"We'll be there."

"Good. Here comes your man."

I turn, too excited to see Roman making his way toward us. My smile grows and I feel light as I watch him. He grins and ducks his head in the shy way he only experiences when he's around me.

"Hey."

"Hey," I reply, my fingers twitching, wanting to touch his.

"I don't really want to stay away from you anymore."

"Good."

"He's been staring at you this whole time," Faye adds. "And don't let him forget about dinner."

"I won't," Roman says with a smile.

"Want to sit and have a drink?" I ask.

"Of course," he says, grinning ear-to-ear.

We find our way to a table along the edge of the room and scoot into the small booth. We leave enough space between us, but considering it's darker back here, I'm able to reach over and touch his thigh.

After only a few minutes, a couple other people from the cast join us, forcing us closer together. We do a lot of knee taps and quick hand holding under the safety of the table, but it doesn't feel like enough.

When Eric and Marco leave, neither of us scoot farther away. I angle my head and study his handsome face, my smile never leaving my lips.

"I'm so happy we did this movie together. Regardless of how it started, I think it ended just the way it was supposed to. Or at least the way I *wanted* it to—even if I never thought it would."

"I couldn't have dreamed this up," he replies with a grin. "I never thought it was a possibility, and every day I feel so lucky and extremely happy that it's my reality. I love you."

We automatically begin to lean in, our bodies doing what we're so used to. We want to be close. We want to show each other affection. We want to live.

The both of us pause. Waiting, wondering, and questioning.

Roman's eyes scan the room behind me. I don't ease back.

"My publicist specifically asked if she needed to know anything about tonight."

I grin. "I guess she's gonna be mad at you."

His smile stretches across his face. "Guess so."

We lean in and kiss. It doesn't last long. It's not like we make out and lick each other's faces for sixty seconds. It's a quick brush of the lips. And then one more.

We hold hands under the table and look out into the room. A few people seemed to have been watching. Most don't know anything happened. More importantly, the world does not come to an end.

JACOBY

CHAPTER 51

WE DON'T SPEND THE REST OF THE NIGHT SHOWCASING PDA, but if my hand lingers on his back, then so be it. If he leans into me when he laughs about something, I don't pull away. If I want to smile at him while he excitedly tells someone a story that makes him light up, I do so, and I don't care if it gives away how much I adore him.

Faye notices first.

"Going public at the afterparty, huh?" she muses, nudging my arm.

I shrug. "Our publicists and management know already. I've sent them a message to alert them that it'll likely be out there tomorrow."

She scoffs. "More like in the next two hours."

"I love him, Faye," I say, watching Roman dance with some of our co-stars. "And I don't want to act like I don't."

She slips her arm around my waist and rests her head on my shoulder. "I'm happy for you."

Roman turns around and spots us. His mischievous gaze lets me know what he's about to do.

"Oh, no."

Faye chuckles. "He's gonna get you out there."

He slowly approaches, dancing his way over with a grin on his lips.

"He could probably get me to do anything."

"Yep. You're in love all right."

"Come on, handsome," Roman says, reaching for my hand. "Let's dance."

I feign reluctance, but I'd go anywhere with him willingly and with excitement.

At first, nobody seems to notice anything. We're a group of people dancing together and having a good time. During a song change, Roman steps close and wraps his arm around my waist while whispering in my ear.

"I'm so happy with you."

My fingers encircle his wrist as I smile at him. "You've made me the happiest I've ever been."

Music rises and he slowly pulls away to continue to dance. I feel someone at my side and turn to find Jessica.

She looks shocked. "So," she starts, looking between us, "a few things are beginning to make sense."

"It's a long story."

"I bet. I knew he liked you, though. He was sort of obvious, but I didn't think for a second that it would be reciprocated. At least not until that night at the wrap party."

"I've probably liked him longer than he's liked me. We had some issues that kept us from realizing the truth sooner, but none of that matters now." I turn to face her. "I'm sorry if I hurt your feelings or—"

She holds a hand up. "Don't. It's okay. It wasn't my business to know. I've lied about things a lot less important or personal."

"Thank you."

She smiles. "The fans are gonna go crazy. You know that, right?"

I don't have a response. We're not together for the fans, but if people end up loving our relationship, I'd consider it a good thing. There will be some that won't like it, so I'll take all the support I can get.

Roman walks over and grabs both of us, dragging us back to the dance floor. We dance for another hour before we decide it's time to go.

When we walk out, we do so hand-in-hand.

In the morning, we're all over every magazine and the headline of every news article on the internet.

We give the go ahead for our publicists to release our personal statements, and a joint statement from our agents, and then we shut off our phones and spend the whole day in bed.

I've been gay my entire life, and in order to keep that part of me hidden, I've lied and snuck around and kept myself from living authentically. I've been afraid for many reasons, but I've finally reached a point in my life where I no longer want to hide and no longer want to be afraid. Love shouldn't be hidden. People shouldn't be hidden. Going forward, I'm living my truth and hoping for a world where nobody has to "come out" because we should be able to love who we love without needing a public announcement.

-Jacoby Hart

. . .

I've never felt like I was lying. I've felt like I was figuring things out on my own, and I'm aware that, as a public figure, people think they are owed personal details of my life. The truth is, I'm bisexual, and that changes nothing about me. I'm only saying this now because as you know, I live out loud. I want to love out loud as well.

    -Roman Black

Our clients, Roman Black and Jacoby Hart, are in a committed and loving relationship. They fell in love on the set of *Another Life*, a movie about two queer men who struggled with their relationship due to fear of rejection and other outside factors. Roman and Jacoby don't want to mirror their characters' struggles, but understand it's a common occurrence in the world. They both believe people should be able to love who they want and that everyone is deserving of acceptance, respect, and love regardless of sexuality or sexual orientation. They don't expect absolute privacy on this matter, as they're both public figures, but they do ask for respect. They ask that if you find yourself having negative thoughts about queer love, think about your kids, family members, or friends who could be in the closet right now, listening to your opinions. Make sure you are someone that others could go to and know they are safe. Don't be the reason anyone is afraid to come out. Be the reason they feel supported.

CHAPTER 52

As expected, the internet blew up over the news. If we thought there were a lot of video edits before, they've at least tripled now. We're constantly being sent clips from our friends who come across them online. People have gone through every public interaction Roman and I have had and discussed the way they should've seen it—how it was so obvious.

The movie is doing exceptionally well. I'm sure the news of our relationship helped push people to the theaters, but the critics reviews are positive, so we definitely have a hit on our hands.

In the last week, we've laid fairly low, talking only to friends and family. Our sisters both came over to hang out a few days ago, and we all had dinner and drinks together. My dad called to say he and my mom love me and hope to see Fallyn and I soon. I imagine he got wind of the news, but he didn't specifically say he knew anything about the announcement. Based on the timing, I'd assume they know it's out there. The phone call and invite tells me they're trying, and that's all I want.

We have about a weeks' worth of primetime interviews and daytime talk shows to further promote the movie, and then soon, both of us will be starting new projects. Since our schedules will become a little more hectic, tonight I'm taking Roman out for our first, official, public date.

He's wearing a dark green, short sleeved button up with a pair of black pants, and a gold watch around his wrist that matches a thin chain that hangs around his neck. And I'm wearing navy blue chinos with a light blue button up, and a black-banded watch.

We look like opposites, but we're perfect for each other.

"Ready?" I ask as he slips his phone in his pocket.

"Oh yeah," he replies with a grin.

I step toward him and kiss his lips before we hop into my car and make our way to Nobu in Malibu.

Paparazzi find us almost immediately, snapping photos and following us as we drive along the highway. When we park, we try to get out quickly before they can swarm, but it doesn't matter. I don't know how they all seem to know where to go or how to be readily available at any time, but there are several guys already surrounding us, taking photos, and asking questions.

We do our best to politely nod and smile as we try to get to the building, but the flashes are blinding, even if the sun is still low on the horizon.

I take Roman's hand in mine and rush us along.

"Hey guys. How long have you been together?"

"Is this your first date?"

"Look here. Jacoby, please. Roman, I like the shirt."

"When did you first realize you were attracted to each other?"

"Have a nice night, guys."

The questions are hurled at us, but they go unanswered.

When we finally get inside, we get taken to a table in the corner.

"Well, we survived," Roman says with a chuckle.

"Might need to call security out here before we leave. I imagine there will be more people outside once word gets out."

"Yeah, probably."

"In the meantime," I say, reaching for his hand across the table, "Let's enjoy our date."

He smiles and squeezes my hand. "I can't believe you get to shoot in Vegas."

"Well, when you get some time, come out and visit."

"Oh, I will."

I laugh. "It's only a month there, then I'll be back in LA."

"Then New York."

"Only for a few weeks."

He rolls his eyes. "All my locations are here in California."

"Once we're done, we can take a vacation to wherever you want."

Roman grins. "Okay, fine."

The waiter comes over to drop off some glasses of water and get our drink and appetizer order. Once he's gone, I ask, "Did you talk to Emerson?"

"Yeah. He took some time to process once he found out, but then we talked. Mainly, he was just shocked. Then he said he understood why I was so secretive about it when he was here and how he'd want to keep you to himself too."

I snort. "Well, I'm glad you two are still okay."

"Yeah. We'll be fine."

The waiter comes back to take our order, and we end up spending over two hours in the restaurant. We eat, talk and laugh, order drinks, eat some more, and then call our security team out to meet us at the entrance before we leave.

"So, this is probably the best date I've ever had," Roman says, sitting back in his seat.

"Probably?" I question.

"Depends on how it ends," he teases, wiggling his brows.

I roll my eyes and shake my head. "Safe to say we're both getting lucky."

He chuckles. "I am very, very, lucky." He draws the words out, his eyes exploring every visible part of me.

"Behave, or I'll have to pull over during our hour ride home and make you pay for those sinful looks."

Warmth fills his cheeks, painting them pink. "Fine."

After we pay, we stand up and I give him a kiss before taking his hand. "I love you. Thanks for coming on this date with me."

He smiles and presses his lips to mine once more. "I love you *more*."

"Don't be annoying."

Roman laughs and we exit the building where our security waits along with a large and roaring crowd of onlookers.

Everyone is happy to see us together, taking photos and recording videos with their phones as they yell our names.

We look at each other and smile, and everything feels right in the world.

EPILOGUE

ROMAN

-

Seven months later

"Look at us getting ready for the Golden Globes together," I say, checking the fit of my blazer in the mirror. "Wanna match?"

Standing in front of another mirror to my left, he says, "You gonna wear a classic black tux?"

"Pfft. I was thinking you could wear like…bright red."

"No."

I scoff. "Suzie, tell him he would look great in red," I say to my stylist as she's grabbing a pair of slacks from a rack.

"He would," she says. "Just as good as he looks in black."

"Thank you, Suzie," Jacoby replies, making a face at me.

"Well, I think what we're doing works. You'll be in your black on black, and I'll be in my white on white. Opposites, but the colors still complement each other."

He smiles at me through the reflection. "I agree."

I walk over wearing only my underwear, undershirt, and

blazer, and spin him around to kiss him. "You look so fucking good," I whisper.

His eyes dance over my face, before following the strands of my hair. "I love how long your hair has gotten," he says, reaching up to tug on the ends. "I want to—"

"Don't mess up the hair," my hairstylist says from the vanity.

Jacoby drops his hand with a sigh. "Later, I guess."

"Hey," I say, grabbing his hand. "I have a surprise for you. After the show, I'm kidnapping you and holding you hostage for a few days."

"Ooh. Sounds kinky."

I laugh. "We didn't get to spend Christmas the way I wanted to because of our schedules, so we're having Christmas in January."

"Do I need to get packed?"

I shake my head. "We're gonna be naked the entire time."

"Oh, right. Of course."

I smack him on the ass before I go back to my stylist to finish getting ready. "I got everything packed and taken care of. Don't worry."

We go down the red carpet together, sometimes holding hands, sometimes needing to split up for different interviews. We take photographs together and separately, and then we're inside where we wait to see if we win anything.

Jacoby is nominated for best actor in a leading role for his portrayal of William in *Another Life,* and I've been nominated for my role as Andrew in the supporting actor category.

My category comes up first, and to my utter surprise, I win. I lean over and plant a kiss on Jacoby's mouth before hugging the director who sits at the table with us.

On stage, I take the trophy and get up to the microphone.

"Wow. Wow, you guys. This is so unexpected." I inspect the trophy in my hand before looking out into the crowd. "This role was a dream come true. It was exactly what I needed, and I'm so thankful to Mike Campo for giving me a chance. Thank you, Mike. To everyone I worked with every day, you all are amazing and talented, and I feel so lucky to have been a part of this. To the fans." I lift the trophy and shake my head. "This movie came with such a rabid fan base and you all accepted Jacoby and I as the characters you had already fell in love with in print, and we're so thankful. Your support and love has meant the world to me. And of course, I can't get off this stage without mentioning a special someone." I lock eyes with Jacoby whose smile is stretched wide across his face. "Working with Jacoby was one of the best experiences of my life. He's beyond talented, and just working with him made me a better actor. Thank you, for everything," I say, looking into his eyes. "I love you so much and I'm so glad this movie brought us together." I look up at everyone else. "Thank you. Thank you so much."

When I get back to the table, he squeezes my thigh under the table and leans over to kiss me. "I'm so happy for you. Congratulations, baby."

"Thank you," I say, returning his kiss.

Later, when it's time for his category, I'm not at all surprised when he wins. I stand up with him and hold him tight.

On stage, he holds the trophy in his hand and looks calm and collected. Once the applause dies down, he clears his throat and begins.

"I played a character who was hiding who he was. He was afraid to love. Afraid of who would find out and what the outcome would be. He found the perfect person for him and made heartbreaking decisions for the sake of others, not thinking about himself or his partner. He loved him from the beginning and yet hurt him because the world made him feel like he was wrong or bad for being exactly who he was born to be. I'm not only talking about William, but I'm talking about myself. This movie helped me in more ways than I'll explain here on stage," he says with a slight grin, "but I'll be forever grateful for the experience. To my love," he says, looking at me, "you're the best thing to happen to me. Thank you for accepting me for who I am and loving me despite my faults." He looks up and holds the trophy up a little. "Thank you, guys. Truly. I'm honored to win any award, but winning for this role really touches my heart. Thank you."

After posing for a few dozen pictures with our trophies and talking to another dozen people, Jacoby and I sneak away and jump into our waiting limo.

"What a fucking night," I say with a smile on my face.

His hand lands on my upper thigh. "And I imagine it's only gonna get better."

"Oh, you have no idea."

The driver already has instructions on where to go, and our bags have already traveled ahead of us.

Jacoby and I act like horny teenagers on the drive to the airport, making out and touching and rubbing on each other like we'll die if we separate. By the time we park, our ties are undone, blazers discarded, and shirts rumpled. My hair is thoroughly disheveled and Jacoby has whisker burn on his face.

We step into the evening air and Jacoby looks around at

the small airport. "Where are we going?" he asks with a laugh.

"You'll see. Come on."

The flight is only an hour and a half, and we both decide to take a power nap so we can be energized when we arrive.

Once we land, a car takes us from the airport to a cabin at Black Bear Lodge, where there's currently snow on the ground.

As we walk to the door, I take his hand in mine. "I remember when you said there was something about being in a cabin with snow outside and a fire lit. I've had everything arranged so we can have the perfect, albeit late, Christmas out here. We have a fireplace, candles that smell of cinnamon, plenty of apple cider and hot cocoa, and I even got your favorite movie—*Romeo and Juliet*."

He stops just outside the door, mouth agape as he stares at me. "You really did all this for me?"

I shake my head. "Nope. For us." I open the door and spot our luggage set up behind the couch.

Jacoby grabs my arm, yanking me back before pushing me against the door. "I'm gonna fucking marry you, Roman."

I suck in a breath right before he rips my shirt open, buttons be damned. "Oh?" I manage to get out before his mouth is on mine.

He pulls away and nods, undoing my pants and shoving them down my legs. "If that's okay with you."

My teeth bite into my lip as I dip my chin, still shocked by his words. "Yeah. Just let me know when."

Jacoby cracks a grin. "Will do." Then he drops to his knees and steals the rest of the breath from my lungs.

ABOUT THE AUTHOR

Isabel Lucero is a bestselling author, finding joy in giving readers books for every mood.

Born in a small town in New Mexico, Isabel was lucky enough to escape and travel the world thanks to her husband's career in the Air Force. She and her husband have three kids and two dogs together, and currently reside in Delaware. When Isabel isn't on mommy duty or writing her next book, she can be found reading, or in the nearest Target buying things she doesn't need. Isabel loves connecting with her readers and fans of books in general. Keep in touch!

Sign up for my newsletter.

Join my reading group.

ALSO BY

Think Again
Darkness Within
Dysfunctional
The Prince of Darkness
Splintered

Kingston Brothers Series
On the Rocks
Truth or Dare
Against the Rules
Risking it All

South River University Series

Stealing Ronan
Tasting Innocence
Breaking Free
Tempting Him

ACKNOWLEDGMENTS

Thank you for reading! I truly hope you enjoyed reading about these two as much as I enjoyed writing them. Their story was a lot of fun to write. I've been witness to a lot of the same type of comments that actors get when playing lovers in a movie. Us romance readers just want them to be in love in real life too! So in this story, I allowed us to get the outcome we've wanted with other actors. Haha!

I want to thank my husband for all of his support and help during the writing process. I'm so glad I have you in this writing journey as well as this journey called life. Love you so much!

Huge thanks to all of my beta readers for their help and opinions. You make the story better.

To every ARC reader, influencer, and reviewer—I'm grateful for your time and dedication to reading, reviewing, and posting.

To Robin Harper, my designer, I'm beyond grateful for your time and work.

To my editor, Tori, thank you so much for getting this done so quick after our little mishap. You're the real MVP.

To Laurie, thank you for the promotional graphics.

I can't thank the ladies at The Author Agency enough. I'm so glad I found you two, and incredibly grateful for everything you do!!

Thanks to Jasmine, my PA, who does everything I'm not good at doing. Haha. I appreciate you.

And another thanks to you for reading this. I appreciate you!

Made in the USA
Columbia, SC
31 March 2024